THE EXTRAORDINARY COLOURS OF AUDEN DARE

Zillah Bethell

Piccadilly
PRESS

First published in Great Britain in 2017 by
PICCADILLY PRESS
80–81 Wimpole St, London W1G 9RE
www.piccadillypress.co.uk

A CIP catalogue record for this book is available from the British Library.

ISBN: 978-1-8481-2608-4
also available as an ebook

1

This book is typeset using Atomik ePublisher
Printed and bound by Clays Ltd, St Ives Plc

Piccadilly Press is an imprint of Bonnier Zaffre Ltd,
a Bonnier Publishing company
www.bonnierpublishing.com

To my father

I asked the little boy who cannot see,
'And what is colour like?'
'Why, green,' said he,
'Is like the rustle when the wind blows through
The forest; running water, that is blue;
And red is like a trumpet sound; and pink
Is like the smell of roses; and I think
That purple must be like a thunderstorm;
And yellow is like something soft and warm;
And white is a pleasant stillness when you lie
And dream.'

ANON.

PART ONE
GREEN

1

A Difficult Word
to Pronounce

Sometimes after school I stand and watch the traffic lights. I wait for the red to turn to amber and then the amber to turn to green. Not that I understand what is meant by red, amber or green. They are just words to me. Words to describe things, to tell one thing from another. To pick things apart. Only that's something I just can't do. The top light is red, the middle one is amber, the bottom light is green. I know that much. Like a fact from history that means nothing nowadays. Like the names of Egyptian kings and queens, or the ancient tribes of Great Britain. But if somebody had got up early one morning and turned the lights upside down – switched them around – I never would have known. They all look exactly the same to me. They all look the same sort of gooey grey.

Green, blue, red, pink, purple, yellow: I don't understand any of them.

I have a condition, you see. It's got a funny name – a long name – that I can barely pronounce or spell. It sounds impressive, I know. But having a condition with a long name that you can barely pronounce or spell isn't much of a comfort when you can't even tell which side you're on when you play football at school. (The number of times I've given the ball away to the opposing team . . . !)

Not that I notice my condition most of the time. I suppose everyone gets used to everything about themselves. I'm used to seeing everything look black and white and a washed-out grey. Everything.

I mean, it's not even like I was once OK. I've always been this way. Right from my very first breath. It would be worse, I'm sure, if once upon a time I had been able to see colour. Then I would know precisely what it was I had lost.

But the truth is I didn't lose anything.

I am how I've always been.

My name has always been Auden Dare.

I am eleven years old.

2

The Bot Job

Over the years my mother developed lots of ways to avoid using colour to describe things to me – she would try to use other means to single things out. She counts – 'the second one along' sort of thing. She compares sizes – 'the third smallest'. She does both at the same time – 'the fourth smallest in the fifth row'. She even uses the alphabet to describe different shades of a colour (where A is the very lightest and, theoretically, Z would be the darkest. However, she only ever really gets up to a D or an E as her feel for shades is a little too crude for an entire twenty-six letters). When I was really young, she drew symbols to help me understand the colours of certain things. For green she would draw an apple. For blue she would draw two wavy lines. She would scribble them on stickers and go around putting the stickers on everything so that I got to understand which things were which colour. I don't think she did it for my benefit though. I mean, it didn't actually bother me to know if a particular jumper was red or yellow. But I think she did it so that I wouldn't struggle around other people and stand out too much from the crowd. She did it so that I wouldn't look too much of a freak.

However . . . having said all that . . . even though my mother had come up with some inventive ways of avoiding making reference to colour, sometimes – just sometimes – it would slip her busy mind.

Like it did the day she bought the Bot Job.

'I've bought a car,' she said, pulling her coat off and slamming the front door behind her.

'You've bought a car?' I echoed. 'Why?'

She hooked the coat over the hanger on the back of the door and ignored my question.

'Don't you want to know what sort of car it is?'

I put the pencil and the magnifying glass I always wear down on the pad of paper. I'd barely started the sketch of Sandwich curled up and purring on her cushion, her eyes squashed shut, contentedly dreaming of baby birds and tiny mice. All I'd drawn so far were her ears.

'OK then. What sort of a car is it?'

'Not sure. I don't know much about cars. All I know is it's a big one.'

I sighed. 'A big one?'

Mum nodded. 'Have a look for yourself. I've parked it out front.'

'How much did you pay for it?' I pulled the curtains aside and peered down to the road, ten flights below. A number of cars – all of them old – were lined up along the sides of the road, each of them waiting for their owners to return to spark them back to life.

'How much? Only a quarter of a million pounds.'

'A quarter of a million?' I couldn't believe it. You couldn't get any car for a quarter of million nowadays. It must've been a real bot job. Perhaps it only had three wheels or something. Perhaps the passengers had to hold their legs up because of the holes in the floor. 'That's cheap.' I turned back to look at my mother, who was now kneeling in front of the chest of drawers and pulling out lots of pieces of paper. 'I bet it doesn't even go,' I added, hardly able to hide my suspicions, 'if that's all it cost.'

Mum did her scowl face at me. 'Of course it goes. Drives very well. It got me back here all the way from Romford, didn't it?' She took the large pile of paper and shoved it roughly into a plastic bag, before opening up another drawer and doing exactly the same. 'Honestly, Auden. You should have more faith.'

I looked back down at the segmented snake of cars below. 'Which one is it?'

And that was when she did it.

'The green one. The long green one.'

Green!

'Mum!'

'Oh.' She shoved the large bag aside, stood up and came over to the window. 'Sorry, Auden. I didn't mean

7

to do it.' She snapped the elastic band she kept around her wrist for such occasions against her thin skin. A tiny punishment for a tiny crime. 'You know what I'm like. Too much on my mind.' She looked out of the window and stabbed her finger downwards. 'That one there. This side. One, two, three along.'

I could see it. It had a long bonnet and a long roof and looked as if some giant creature had picked it up at both ends and stretched it.

'It *is* big.'

We stood there in silence for a while, watching the people down below coming and going like dust on the breeze. Behind us on the sofa, Sandwich gave a short squeak and clawed the corner of her little fluff-covered cushion. She scratched it hard, pulling out threads.

'I don't understand why you've bought a car,' I said. 'We don't need one.'

'You know why,' she answered, not even bothering to turn to look at me. 'We talked about this last week.'

It was true. We had talked about it last week. Or should I say *she* talked about it while *I* tried my best not to listen.

'Yeah, but what about Dad?'

'What about him?'

'Well, when he comes back home, he's not going to know where we are.'

She reached along the windowsill and tried her best

to give my hand a gentle squeeze. 'It'll be all right. I'll write him a letter.'

A letter? What good was a letter?

'But he's fighting. You can't just send him a letter. He won't get it. It'll just get lost or something. It'll get trampled into the mud in Paris or Rome or wherever he is. Then, when the war's over and he comes back here, he won't find us.'

She leaned in close, trying to hug me and kiss me on the head. But I wasn't having any of it. I *am* eleven years old after all.

'Silly,' she said. 'He'll know where we are. Don't worry.'

Out of the window a Scoot drone – one of the ones with reflectors for eyes and extended antennae – hovered its way along the street, its tiny camera head swinging left to right to left to right to left as it went. The sound of the buzzing wings dropped a semitone as it passed by, watching out for trouble on the streets below. Eventually it disappeared from view.

'So . . .' It was no good fighting it. It was all going to go ahead anyway, regardless of what I said. She obviously thought it was for the best. 'When do we go?'

'I've given two days' notice on this place. I've notified the Water Allocation Board and the War Authority, so we'll have to pack up and be gone by Thursday.'

It wasn't like there was a great deal to pack up anyway. We didn't own much stuff. A load of clothes, a stick or two of furniture, a handful of books, some documents and papers; Sandwich. That was about it. Two days was more than enough in which to pack all that away. We could probably do it three times over in that amount of time.

'When we get there,' Mum added quickly, keen to stop me from changing my mind again, 'we'll find a nice school for you. A good school this time. Somewhere you can make friends. Yes?'

I wandered over to where Sandwich was yawning and stroked her until she began to dribble.

It might well have been a bot job (the way the doors rattled every time you opened them seemed to suggest that it had never been exposed to a single human being during its construction, only robots) but the car was massive. Absolutely massive. It had more than enough room to fit all of our belongings, and by the time we had finished filling it, there was still space for a few more suitcases and crates. I propped Sandwich – who was in her wicker basket – on top of a box of books just behind my seat and, after we had said our goodbyes to the empty flat and the neighbours who couldn't have cared less about us anyway, we strapped ourselves into the car and headed off.

At the garage, Mum filled the Bot Job full of the cheap petrol – price at an all-time low apparently – and then, reluctantly, added some of the much, *much* more expensive water to the water reservoir.

'It's a long trip, I'm afraid,' she said, climbing back into the driver's seat. 'It'll take us a few hours. Make yourself comfortable.'

The car rumbled unconvincingly along beneath us as my mother steered and braked and crunched gears in spectacular fashion, speeding up through the narrow, twisting streets of east London. There seemed to be very little traffic on the road. A couple of other cars. A few food lorries. Some war-effort supply vans. A heavily protected water tanker. One or two refugees with heavy packs on their backs or pushing handcarts full of possessions. That was about it.

As we drove on – the Bot Job giving out the occasional backfiring bang – the buildings became smaller and fewer, and the roads longer and straighter. Eventually the city faded into the countryside. There weren't many trees, not since the rains slowed and water got scarce. Field after field of ornamental cactuses lined the roads while small towns and villages swept by.

'Let's play I-Spy!' Mum suddenly sounded weirdly enthusiastic. If only Dad was here, I thought, so they could jabber on together while I sat in the back listening to music.

'I'm not four years old!'

'Go on. You go first.'

I sighed. 'Erm . . . I-Spy with my little eye something beginning with . . . er . . . *R*.'

'Road!' she shouted triumphantly.

'You got it.'

'That was too easy. Do another one.'

'OK then. I-Spy with my little eye something beginning with . . . *T*.'

'Tree?'

'No.'

'Truck?'

'No. No trucks here anyway.'

'Er . . .' Her eyes scanned around, trying to find something. 'Telegraph pole?'

'Nope.'

'I give up. What is it?'

'Tarmac.'

'Tarmac?'

'Yep.'

'So you've had "road" and you've had "tarmac". Hmm. I think I see a pattern emerging.'

'It's pretty much all I've seen for the last two hours.'

'Well, not to worry.' Mum smiled. 'We're nearly there.'

Having consulted my QWERTY ten minutes earlier, I knew this already. Cambridge was five miles away and at the speed we were travelling (fifty miles an hour which, for my mother, is speedy, let me tell you) we would be there in six minutes. I also knew that the chance of precipitation was nil (as always) though breeze was fair to moderate, that Cambridge was the epicentre of good taste and vending machines and that the vintage cinema on Collier Road was screening a black-and-white movie for the Old & Mouldies, even distributing free popcorn to those who still possessed a set of their own teeth.

I eyed my mother sideways, wondering whether to try the joke out on her but decided against it. She looked tired and strained and her hands were gripping the steering wheel like she was going a heck of a lot faster than fifty miles an hour.

'Yippedee-do-dey!' I said, trying to reach behind my seat to stroke Sandwich through the bars of her basket.

3

Unicorn Cottage

You might imagine that a house called Unicorn Cottage would be a magical, enchanted place possibly made out of sweets, like in that story about Hansel and Gretel. You know the one. The one with the two irritating kids who nearly get eaten by a witch and only escape due to her poor eyesight and a thin stick. Yeah, really believable! For a start, a stick doesn't even feel like someone's finger. It's all cold and stiff. A finger, on the other hand (Ha! On the other hand! Geddit?) is warm and a bit squashier. Also, why would anyone build a house out of sweets? You couldn't possibly live in a house made of sweets. In the summer it would get all sticky and bits of it would probably start to melt. After a while it would also start to rot. What a load of ridiculous, childish rubbish. I'm glad I'm not such a kid any more. All the stupid stories you get told when you're a child . . . I mean, *reeeeeally!*

Anyway. As I was saying. You might imagine that a place called Unicorn Cottage would be hidden away deep in a wood, surrounded by trees that whispered to each other, next to a rickety wishing well with a little roof and a shiny bucket dangling down. With uneven walls that seemed to bulge in and out, and a roof made of wiry thatch. Perhaps a neat, fenced-off rose garden overlooked by shuttered windows and a creaky wooden door with a small heart cut out of its centre.

That's what you might imagine.

Instead, the Unicorn Cottage that my mother pulled up outside looked as though it might once have been a public lavatory. Or an electricity sub-station. Something dull and practical with no charm or beauty whatsoever. As if the men who put it together couldn't be bothered coming back the following day to finish it off.

It sat on a lane on the very edge of the town, backing onto a low flat field that stretched into the distance. There were no houses either side of it – not for a good few hundred metres anyhow – and only a small crop of tall trees across the lane in front of it.

If this house was a person, I realised, it would have been a very sad and lonely one. A trail of damp underneath one of the two wide windows even made it look as if it had recently been crying.

Actually, to call it a house was wrong. It was one of those little bungalow thingies which had been converted so that it had an upstairs. A dormer bungalow, I think they're called. Weird things. *A contradiction in terms* – that's how my mother puts it. *A contradiction in terms*. A bungalow, by its very definition, is a single-storey construction. If a bungalow has an 'upstairs', surely it's not a bungalow any more? Surely it becomes a house? Yes? No? Yes? Don't worry about it. I'm always going off on a tangent like that. Sorry. You'll get used to it.

Anyway, Mum parked the Bot Job on the gravelly hard standing to the side of the house and we both got out.

'Why did Uncle Jonah call it Unicorn Cottage?' I asked, shifting my seat forward so I could pull Sandwich out more easily.

Mum shrugged awkwardly and fished about for the keys. 'I don't know.'

'I think . . .' I said, looking upwards and shading my eyes from the sun. 'I think it must have been because the chimney looks like a horn. Do you see? It looks a bit like a horn coming out from a unicorn's head.'

She looked up too and squinted, trying to focus. 'Not really.'

I smiled. 'No. It doesn't really, does it?'

'No.' She gave the keys a shake and they tinkled against each other. 'Shall we take a look at our new home, Auden?'

It was in a terrible state.

After Mum had managed to shove the front door open, pushing the weeks' and months' worth of old letters and political flyers out of the way, the first thing we both noticed was the smell. The cold, stale smell of damp. Like somebody had given a particularly fat and pungent fungus a kick, sending spores flying all over the place.

It was obvious from that smell that no one had lived here in a long time.

The second thing we noticed was the mess.

All across the hallway were strewn papers and folders. Books bent back hard on their spines, with buckled pages and half-ripped corners. A side table had been toppled, the contents of a small drawer spilling out and trailing like a tongue towards the floor.

'Oh dear.' Mum trod carefully across the debris, the occasional worrying scrunch under her feet, and pushed open a door into a different room. I followed.

The curtains were still drawn in what, I assumed, was the sitting room. What little light there was struggled to reveal anything. Now, one of the few good things about my condition – my inability to see colour – is that I can actually see pretty well in the dark. Everything is much clearer to me than to other people, so they reckon. The outlines of shapes are better defined. The detail more obvious. Call it a lucky side effect, if you like. So to me the mess in the sitting room was easy to see. However, my mother was finding it difficult, so I grabbed the nearest curtain and pulled it hard.

If there was a carpet, you would never have known. The floor had more papers and folders and bits and bobs thrown all over it. An armchair had been rolled onto its side, and the cushions on a nearby sofa were all pulled out of place. On a table near another door sat a number of dirty plates and bowls, a small cloud of flies buzzing over them. A picture of a ship on the wall was hung at a very dodgy angle and it was clear nothing here had been dusted for a long, long time.

'There's been a robbery,' I said. 'Somebody's broken in and turned the place over.'

Mum smiled and shook her head. 'No. I doubt it.'

'What do you mean?'

'Well, your uncle Jonah was a brilliant man. Absolutely brilliant. The cleverest person I ever knew. He could come up with the most incredible ideas, and find their solutions, like that.' She clicked her fingers in front of my face. 'He was a genius. No question.' She looked about at the scruffy sitting room. 'However, one of the things he always had difficulty with was taking good care of himself and his things. Sometimes, when he was in the middle of a brilliant idea, he would forget all about food – he ended up in hospital once due to not eating. Or he would neglect his appearance – his hair and beard would grow far too long and his clothes would start to look dirty. The other thing he didn't do very well was to clean up after himself. Remember, I grew up with him, and even as a child he never tidied his room. In fact –' she gave a wink – 'he was rather a lot like you.'

'Ugh!' I moaned. 'I couldn't live in a place like this. Just look at it.'

'Well, this is your home now, Auden,' she said, scraping a finger along a very dust-lined shelf and inspecting it, 'so you need to get used to it. Come on. Let's grab some bamboo sacks and start filling them.'

4

Trinity

You see, the house had once belonged to my uncle Jonah. Jonah Bloom. *Doctor* Jonah Bloom. A brilliant physicist and mathematician at the University of Cambridge. *Jonah Bloom MA (Oxon), PhD (Cantab)*, to use his full and correct academic title. My mother's brother. Six years older than her. He had spent years working in the areas of Artificial Intelligence and Synchronicity. Apparently. Not that I had any sort of clue as to what that meant. We haven't done much of that in school!

He was only thirty-eight when he was discovered dead in a field close to Unicorn Cottage.

Heart attack, they said.

Stress from overwork, they said.

Unable to cope, they said.

When he died, he left all of his worldly possessions to his only living relative: Christabel Dare (née Bloom). Wife of Leo Dare. Mother of Auden.

My mum.

All his worldly possessions. And that included Unicorn Cottage.

The room that was quickly to become my bedroom overlooked the garden and the lifeless beech tree. A large metal bed took up most of the space and I think I'd once slept in it when we visited Uncle Jonah a few years before. Before the war started. Before my dad went off to fight.

I tried to make the room mine. I hung all my clothes in the flimsy wardrobe. I put some of my sketches up on the wall – even the really bad one of my dad chowing down on an ice cream. I kept my pencils and my pads on the tiny desk squished up next to the door. I put Sandwich's bed on the floor alongside my own.

Sandwich had made herself at home as soon as we had arrived. She slunk out first thing in the morning, popping back for food and the occasional tickle and sleep. In the evening, she would slink out again before bringing something dead into the kitchen and dropping it on the floor like a gift for us. Sometimes, though, it wasn't dead. If it was a mouse it would skitter off under the tables and dressers until Mum would manage to drop a metal colander over it, slide a large piece of card underneath – petrified squeaks as she did so (from the mouse, not my mother) – and carry the poor thing out to the bottom of the garden, freeing it near the ramshackle collection of

21

sheds that Uncle Jonah had acquired and filled full of utter junk.

When not trying to catch mice, Mum spent those first few days making the place nice and arranging our water rations. She went off into the town and filled the cupboards with food from the shops and markets.

One day I went with her. We both got into the Bot Job and, on the fourth or fifth attempt, the engine started and we trundled on our way. We drove up the long road to the roundabout with the big hospital and then further on into town. The houses were large with big wrought-iron gates and everything looked clean and neat. Civilised.

Eventually we got to the shopping area and Mum parked the car, which seemed to shudder itself to death when she turned off the ignition.

Most of the shops were open. Only a handful had boarded-up windows and 'To Rent' signs sticking out at right angles to the walls. Which surprised me, as most of the shops in Forest Gate had long been abandoned. In Forest Gate, we had had to walk or catch the bus all the way to Stratford to get to anywhere we could buy stuff. There was nothing in Forest Gate. Not even a sweet shop.

Here, people – mostly women and old men, of course – were working their way along the shopping precinct, nipping in and out of the hardware shops and newsagents and clothing stores, stumping about with their carrier bags.

We slipped into one of the electrical shops and Mum bought a new toaster which was on offer. Fifty per cent off. Only fifteen thousand pounds. A bargain. She pushed it down into the bottom of her little hemp sack and we carried on.

At the end of the pedestrianised area we turned the corner towards the food markets. And the world seemed to change.

The buildings suddenly seemed to leap back in time.

The pedestrianised area had been lined on each side by incredibly shiny and modern-looking buildings. Brand spanking new (or new-ish) and sterile and dull.

But these buildings . . .

Huge and impressive, with wide arched doorways and slim-cut windows. Spires and battlements and straight-out-of-the-ground columns. Flat, even lawns lay stretched in front of the buildings, some of which looked like churches, some like castles. Even the roads had changed from spacious level tarmac to narrow cobblestones.

'What are these?' I asked my mother, my head swivelling from one side of the road to the other as we walked.

'Colleges. The Cambridge colleges. Part of the University.'

Trapped in between the walls of the old buildings, however – sitting in the centre of the old road – was a massive slice of modern life. The rectangular, shiny food-vending machine – perhaps a quarter of a mile long – looked completely out of place here. Row upon row and column upon column of metallic drawers, each with a small scrolling screen on the front revealing what was inside and the price.

King Edward Potatoes, flashed on some of the drawers. *£5,000 a bag.*

Carrots . . . Fresh Today . . . £1,000.

Beef steak . . . £80,000.

Naturally, very few people were buying any of the meat – hardly anyone could afford it, after all. So the chilled drawers of beef and chicken and lamb and pork mostly remained untouched.

The shoppers' chattering voices all blurred into each other and bounced off the stone walls in this strangely cramped street while a couple of the squat, rather funny-looking Dodo drones were busy cleaning and refilling the empty drawers from a supplies trolley, their short, shuffling feet making them waddle from side to side.

'The university? Where Uncle Jonah worked?' I asked eventually.

She nodded. 'Yes. He was a Fellow of Trinity College.'

'A Fellow?'

Mum shrugged. 'I don't really know what it means.' She fed a thick handful of notes into the slot next to one of the drawers. The door lowered, there was a happy sort of bleep and a small paper bag of potatoes was gently pushed out into her waiting hands. 'But I think it means he was very high up. Very clever.' She took the potatoes and shoved them into the hemp sack alongside the toaster.

'Where's Trinity College?' I asked. 'Which one is it?'

'I don't know.'

'Can we go and find it?'

'What? Now?'

'Why not?'

Mum sighed. 'But there are things at the house that I need to do, Auden. Things that can't wait.'

I put on one of my *puhlease* faces – she can never resist one of my *puhlease* faces – and she shook her head, giving herself up to the idea.

She asked one of the shoppers and he pointed us in the right direction. We made our way along the street and turned off down an even narrower and much quieter cobbled road.

A couple of signposts later and we were standing outside the main entrance to Trinity College. Set back slightly from the main lane, it was one of the ones that looked like a castle, with towers either side of the main door, each with a funny stunted turret.

To the right of the main, portcullis-style doorway was a smaller entrance, and we watched as two young men – clearly not conscripted – both dressed like that old comic-book hero Batman, with capes and funny hats, slipped in through this second door.

'Shall we have a look?' I asked.

'I don't think we're allowed, are we?'

'We could try. See what happens.'

'Well . . .'

'Come on.'

We both walked in through the small door, Mum a few steps behind me.

The room we entered felt a little bit like a tunnel. To the rear of us was the door through which we had just come, and ahead of us was a larger open door leading out onto a grassy square. But the room itself was dark.

Along one of the walls I could make out row upon row of boxes, each of them with tiny names written on them.

'What is it?' Mum couldn't see as clearly as I could in this half-light.

'Boxes. Pigeonholes. For mail.'

The boxes were in alphabetical order, and in some of them envelopes and sheets of paper curved or slumped to one side.

I went in closer and ran my fingers over the names. When I got to Jonah Bloom, I froze. The pigeonhole was empty; that was to be expected. But the fact that the university authorities hadn't removed his name, even though it had been a good six or seven months since he had died, gave me a chill. Perhaps it was just because if they removed Uncle Jonah's name then – because it was all alphabetical – they would have to move the names of everybody whose surname came after Bloom too. Shift them all along one place. Perhaps they just didn't want to have to bother with all that. That's what I thought. My little idea about it. I don't know.

Mum came alongside me, saw the name and ran her fingers over the lettering.

'You all right, Mum?' I asked.

'Yes,' she said unconvincingly. 'I'm OK.'

We walked out through the second door, and found ourselves in the brightness of the morning once again. Some of the young students flapping about in their weird costumes gave us a quick glance, but otherwise nobody paid us any attention. The square into which we had stepped was unlike anything I'd ever seen before. Surrounded on all four sides by tall windowed walls, it felt a little like a really old prison – although there were loads of doors leading off to other places. The grass was neatly trimmed but dull, and a weird domed fountain thing sat oddly off centre, looking like it needed a good shove to put it into its correct position – like an accident nobody ever sorted.

Mum and I stared up at all the windows, neither of us saying – but both of us wondering – which one belonged to Uncle Jonah. Our feet tapped lightly on the flagstones as we worked our way around the square, which Mum said was called a 'quad'.

In the far corner, we found ourselves drifting through

another small door into a passageway with cold stone steps – like those from a dungeon, but leading upwards. Suddenly a young girl with dark hair, about my age, came running down the steps and looked at us without saying anything before rushing out into the courtyard.

'Shall we go up?' I asked, pointing to the stairs.

'No,' Mum answered quickly. 'No. Let's not. I don't think I want to get further into this place. It's cold. Let's get out of here. Knowing he used to work here . . . I don't think I like it.'

'OK, Mum.'

Instead of taking the stairs, we found another door coming out onto a small pebbly path to the side of the college. We followed the path around a corner until the skyline opened up a bit and the remnants of a river flickered in the sun.

'Sorry. It was silly of me to make you go into the college. I just thought that . . . I thought that perhaps that was one of the reasons for moving to Cambridge in the first place. To . . . sort of . . . find him.'

Mum tried that squeezing-the-shoulder thing with me again, and this time I thought I'd better allow her to have it.

'There're a load of reasons for moving here, Auden. Loads. That might be one of them, I suppose. But it's not one of the main ones.' She smiled. 'We were paying a lot of rent in London. With Dad away, it was crippling me.

28

We were really starting to struggle. And then poor Jonah passed away, leaving us with a tiny bit of money but also his house. A house we can live in free of rent. And what with the situation in London – it's not really a place for a young boy to grow up in, you know – I just thought we could live a better life here. Start again. Wipe the window clean and start from the beginning.'

'Yeah.' I nodded, not saying anything else.

'We'll make a go of it, yes?'

5

Snowflake 843A

Uncle Jonah's death had come as a shock to everyone – particularly Mum. She took it hard.

Now, I suppose that's the thing with having older brothers or sisters – they start off bigger and braver than you, so you imagine they'll *always* be bigger and braver than you. You imagine them going on and on and that they'll be there forever. (Not that I've any experience of that myself. Being a single child means I've missed out on that particular perspective of existence – yet another gap to add to the list!)

Of course, older brothers and sisters *don't* go on forever, and they aren't *always* bigger and braver than you. Only most people have an entire lifetime to realise that. But Mum had to discover it a little too early.

What with Dad being away and the whole war thing going on, I suppose it was inevitable that, as soon as the keys to Unicorn Cottage had been handed over by the solicitor, Mum was going to want to try to get closer to her late brother. There was nothing really holding either of us in London any more, so why not? Why not move into Uncle Jonah's old house? The whole 'moving' thing was, in a way, a sort of therapy for her. Perhaps, over time, when this stupid war had run itself into the earth and Dad had returned, she would come to terms with her own brother's death and life would just move on as it should.

But for now . . .

For now she was surrounding herself with Uncle Jonah's things, seeing sights that Uncle Jonah would see every day. It was a sort of grieving process, I guess.

Of course she wasn't the only one who was sad about Jonah Bloom's death. I'd lost an uncle – a bonkers, fluttering genius of an uncle who would send me pictures of the phases of the moon and ancient unsolvable cryptic crosswords and yellowing books on European amphibians. A man who once told me that everything in life goes around in a circle – the planets, the universe, the days, evolution, molecules, blood . . . even water. All of it on a long-winded journey back to where it all began. I've no idea what he meant, but it sounded impressive. Most things he said sounded impressive.

Once he had visited us in London and had taken me out for a walk. We made our way to where the old canal had once flowed – me with my coat pulled tight across my shoulders, him with his wild, flailing arms pointing and drawing figures in the sky. Always talking. Always explaining.

Broken houseboats, sucked down by the mud, lolled unevenly in the wide groove that had once been filled to the top with water.

Uncle Jonah gesticulated all around us.

'Tell me, Auden . . . Tell me, what do you see?'

I twisted this way and that. 'Er . . . some buildings. An old bin. A couple of smashed-up boats. A bit of rope. A man over there with a limp.'

Jonah smiled.

'Why?' I asked. 'What do *you* see?'

'Well . . .' He straightened up and looked around. 'Obviously I see everything that you see – you missed that half a ripped-up bench over there, by the way.' He pointed and I nodded. 'But the thing you must always remember is that what you see – whatever images pass across the retinas of your eyes – is not what will *always* be.'

'Eh?' He sometimes did that. Talked as if what he was saying was obvious even though it wasn't.

'What I mean is, that image –' he swept his arm out towards the canal – 'is not the end of the story. It is not fixed. It is not how it will be for the rest of time. For example, those smashed-up boats, as you put it, may, one day soon, be stripped and taken apart and the wood reclaimed for another purpose. Something useful. They may be rebuilt, or even simply disintegrate, rotting into the mud. We can't assume that the broken boats are broken boats and that is that. Broken boats forever. Everything

32

evolves in some way or another – either with or without our help. The old bin may be put right and serve its purpose once more. The limping man may simply have a blister on his foot and will recover in a day or two. On the other hand it may be the onset of bone cancer, and he will die soon.'

'Nice,' I groaned. 'Cheery.'

Jonah ignored me. 'In fact, who knows, the whole canal may one day be filled with water again. You see, things evolve – they turn themselves completely around and upside down – and all you can really say about anything is that that is how it is *right now*. In a year or two's time . . . in a minute or two even . . . who knows?'

I watched the man on the opposite bank hobbling up the steps and hoped for his sake it was just that his boots didn't fit him properly, or that one of his socks had a big hole in.

'What about colour?' I asked after the man had stumbled away completely. 'Colour is fixed. Red is always red and blue is always blue and I can never see any of them. What about colour?'

'Colour itself is unimportant.' Uncle Jonah wrinkled up his forehead as if to squeeze some extra thoughts out of his brain. 'Colour is just a label. A way of comparing things.' I quickly thought back to the way my mother always tried to skirt around the concept of colour. 'Admittedly it is true that colour *does* occur in nature . . . but the colour itself is often unimportant. It is what the colour *represents* that matters.'

I didn't have a clue what he was on about.

We stood there in silence for a while, listening to the buzz of the city up above us.

'Uncle Jonah?' I eventually asked. 'You're a scientist. Do you think you might be able to invent something that could help me to see colour?'

He stared into the distance as if the other side of the canal was about a mile away. Then he smiled. 'Maybe, Auden. One day. When my current work is complete, I shall give it some thought. Yes?'

When the solicitor brought the keys over to our flat in Forest Gate, he brought a few other things too. Most of them were boring legal things: the deeds to Unicorn Cottage; Uncle Jonah's bank details; his Water Allocation Board Usage Record. Stuff like that.

But there was also a little cardboard box.

With my name on it.

'Your uncle left this. For you,' the small, sweating solicitor had whined as he handed it over to me. I gave him fifteen years tops. If you're a sweater you're a goner – on the way to being extinct. Losing all that fluid puts too much of a strain on the kidneys, you see.

Inside the box was a rock. Well, half a rock. It was egg-shaped – or had been egg-shaped once upon a time, before whatever had caused it to break had occurred – and was smooth along its curved surface, but all jaggedy and rough in the middle. I picked it out and held it up to the light. It wasn't particularly beautiful or exciting and I twisted it around to see if there were any secret diamonds hiding inside it.

'There's a letter too.' The solicitor held an envelope out to me before wiping his brow with his handkerchief.

I took it off him and ripped it open. Unfolding the paper, I could see line after line of Uncle Jonah's spidery handwriting, slightly curling down as it made its way across the page from left to right.

I read what it said to myself.

Auden, [it said] *If you are reading this then I suppose I am no longer alive. Which is a bit of a shame as I rather enjoyed our friendly chats on the Etherweb and occasional walks around London. Hopefully you got a degree of enjoyment out of them too. Perhaps a little knowledge even.*

Anyway, I have left all of my possessions to your mother – I'm sure you know this by now – but there is a small something that I have deliberately kept aside for you.

In the box that accompanies this letter is what appears to be half a small rock. A funny

thing to be left by your uncle, you may think.
Only this rock is a rather special one. In fact,
it is not a rock at all. It is a meteorite. Its
official name is Snowflake 843A, given after it
fell just outside the small town of Snowflake
(yes, there is such a place) in Arizona in 1957.
An appropriate name, I'm sure you will agree.
Its estimated time of arrival: 8.43 Mountain
Standard Time.

Imagine. For millions of years this ball of
chondrite was hurtling around the deepest
parts of space, minding its own business, before
eventually straying into our tiny insignificant
little galaxy and finding itself pulled into the
Earth's atmosphere where it finally slammed
into the soft sands of Arizona and split in two.

Now, given the practically immeasurable,
infinite nature of space, the chances of any
one meteor getting close enough to crash
into this speck of a planet are undoubtedly
somewhere in the region of a trillion to the
power of a trillion to one, I am certain. The
probability of its coming into contact with us
is – essentially – negligible.

So do not be put off by the fact that it looks
like any other lump of stone or rock that
you can find on any hillside or in any quarry

or even in the garden at the rear of Unicorn
Cottage.
What it appears to be is irrelevant.
What it is, is something of a miracle.

I picked up the chunk of meteorite and turned it around
in my hand.

By the way [I continued reading], *its sister –*
Snowflake 843B – I have left to someone I know
at Trinity College – my dear friend Six Six. Six
Six is one of the brightest, cleverest, kindest
people I've ever met in my life and, if you should
ever find yourself needing to . . . I don't know,
say, find out about space, stars, constellations
etc., then do pay a visit to Six Six.

Six Six? I thought. What sort of a name is Six Six?

Anyway, Auden . . . Look after yourself and
your dear mother, and remember that your
condition may sometimes actually be a strength
and not a weakness.
Dig deep, my boy. Dig deep.
Always remember to dig deep.
Yours,
Jonah

Nowadays Snowflake 843A resides in the right-hand pocket of my jacket, so that whenever I am outside and I find my condition getting me down, I can reach inside and run my fingers over it, scratching the tips across the sharp, jagged ridges in the middle, or even give it a little squeeze to try to remind myself of Uncle Jonah's words.

Sometimes it helps, I find.

But sometimes, I'm afraid, it doesn't.

A few weeks after moving in, I found myself standing in the tiny attic at Unicorn Cottage. Uncle Jonah had put a sort of retractable ladder thing into the hatch and, after lowering it, you could easily climb up into the damp-smelling loft.

It was dark up there, but my eyes could cope easily with such dinginess. Nevertheless I used the torch function on my QWERTY to see as far as I could into the furthest corners and crannies.

Spider webs filled the spaces between the buckled rafters, and tiny specks of dust floated aimlessly in the beam of the torch. I waved them away with my hand and looked around.

A number of packing boxes – big wooden crates without lids – were dumped randomly across the uneven floor. I peered into one, only to find a ton of old clothes neatly folded into ten or twelve seagrass bags. I pulled something out of one bag and held it up. It was probably the busiest and most horrible waistcoat I'd ever seen in my life. I dropped it back into the crate before fishing out a long tie with a zigzaggy pattern that seemed even more nasty and headache-inducing than the waistcoat, and for once I was actually quite glad that I couldn't see colour. Uncle Jonah might well have been a genius, but he had no taste in clothing.

I looked into another of the packing cases. It was filled with books. Dull, pictureless scientific books mostly. The damp had somehow managed to ease its way inside and the pages of most of them looked curled and soggy and almost unreadable.

The other crates were just as dull. Nothing to bother yourself with. Just piles and piles of junk that Uncle Jonah had probably intended to get rid of at some point, but in the end never got round to. It was like a sort of waiting room for garbage.

I turned to go back down the ladder but, as I did so, something caught my eye and I stopped. In a small stony alcove – probably nothing more than an imperfection in the brickwork – sat a fat manila envelope. I came around one of the packing cases and picked it up, blowing thick lumps of dust from its glossy surface. It had not been sealed, so I lifted up its end and let the contents slide out into my other hand.

Photographs.

Lots of photographs.

Mostly pictures of a young family. A mother, a father, a son and a daughter. There were photos taken in a wide, tree-filled garden. Some showed the family washing an old-fashioned car – yes, actually using water to wash a car! A dog . . . no, a *number* of different dogs jumping up and licking the faces of the boy and the girl. One picture of the boy standing proudly next to what looked to me like a homemade rocket. A picture of the girl standing on a chair in a kitchen, making cookies with the mother. Both children leaping around in the pouring rain.

Photographs. Dozens and dozens of them.

I recognised them all of course. The girl was my mother. The boy, Uncle Jonah. The mother and the father, my long-dead grandparents.

I straightened the photos in my hand and was about to just throw the envelope down onto the floor when I realised there was something else inside. Something a bit heavier than some photos. I gave the envelope a quick shake and a short, fat lump of metal landed on top of the pictures.

It was a key.

Looped around it with short lengths of string were two labels. The first – a newish-looking label – had the words 'OFFICE SPARE' scrawled in the unmistakably bulbous capitals that Uncle Jonah liked to use when he thought something was important. The second – smaller and much older than the other – had neat, tiny handwriting that certainly didn't belong to Jonah Bloom. 'Property of Trinity College, Cambridge', it said like it was ever so slightly ashamed of the fact.

I slipped the key into my pocket and took the photographs downstairs, where Mum proceeded to spend the next two hours laughing and crying over the images in about equal amounts.

I didn't tell my mum about the key. You see, I don't think I really wanted her to know. The fact that it was me that found it hidden away in the attic made it – sort of – my property in a way. I gave her the photos – they belonged to her. But the key was mine.

Anyway, I wanted to do some investigating of my own. You see, I was starting to have doubts about Uncle Jonah's death.

He was very young to just die. Heart attack or no heart attack. And I started to fear the worst. What if there was more to his death than just a bad heart? What if something had triggered his previously undiscovered heart condition? I might just be scrabbling up the wrong tree, but I wasn't completely sure.

I wanted to check.

Thinking back, it was weird the way Unicorn Cottage had been all messed up when we arrived. I mean, I know Uncle Jonah was not the tidiest of men, but there was something about it that made me worry. It was too . . .

all over the place. Mum didn't question it at first, so I went along with her. After all, she knew him better than anyone.

But after a while I found myself wondering. What if the mess wasn't made by him? What if it was made by someone else?

It didn't make sense to me at all. It was just an idea. A nagging, if you like.

But I was determined to find out.

Late one afternoon, I hopped on the bus into town. I'd told Mum that I was going for a walk to get some fresh air – after all, the stink of cleaning products in the cottage was getting a bit overwhelming. She smiled and nodded before going back to polishing Uncle Jonah's framed degree certificates on the wall.

I got off the bus as near to Trinity College as I could and walked the rest of the way. Perhaps it was just my suspicious mind, but there seemed to be a surprising number of Water Allocation Board men patrolling the city centre that afternoon. Armed with their machine guns and equipped with bulletproof vests and helmets – every single one of them with ice for eyes – they cast a fear across your chest which made you feel automatically guilty. In a way, I suppose they were there to protect us all, but you couldn't help feeling that it was *you* they were watching. Of course the people who had most to fear were the black-marketeers – the men and women who tried to sell on contaminated or corrupted water. Cat's Pee as everyone referred to it. Thirst and dirt and desperation drove many people to extremes, and for a couple of thousand pounds they could buy a litre of water. A *reeeeeaaally* stupid thing to do, trust me. It wasn't fit for consumption. I'd heard stories of entire families going mad after drinking just a cupful of the stuff. Old-&-Mouldies would curl up and die in their beds just hours after supping it. And the teeth of toddlers would just drop out if they were washed in the terrible radioactive liquid. That's what people said anyway, and even if some of the stories badly exaggerated or weren't true, Cat's Pee was definitely best avoided.

I kept my head down and hurried past a pair of particularly vicious-looking WAB agents.

A couple of corners later and I found myself standing outside the entrance to Trinity College once again. I stopped to look up and admire the wide open arch and the turrets on each side. It really did look as if it had come from another planet or at least another time. There was nothing in east London that I could compare it to.

Suddenly feeling nervous, I tugged up the collar on my coat and walked in.

In the dark alcove the rows of pigeonholes clung to the wall, some of them stuffed with envelopes and packages. Making sure there was nobody around, I reached up and pushed my hand into the slot marked 'Dr Jonah Bloom'.

I swept it around, left and right, and reached to the very back of the pigeonhole, but there was still nothing inside.

I stood back a little and looked at all the names. Was there a Six Six? My eyes read along to the 'S' level . . . but, no. There was no Six Six. Not that I was expecting one. Six Six was not exactly your average common-or-garden surname, after all. No. Six Six must be a nickname for somebody. Or a codename even!

I carried on through the second arch and stepped out into the large open space surrounded on all four sides by the old, crumbling walls of the college. The windows stared down like a ring of ancient professors closely observing the comings and goings, and that strange, domed fountain thingy was still sitting in what seemed to me like quite the wrong place.

A couple of students with their daft-looking cloaks were lounging on the dull lawn to the right of me, so I quickly turned left and headed towards another wide arch, my feet scrunching over the gravel. I went inside and made my way up some stone stairs, not knowing where I was going.

As the stairs turned and curled back on themselves I came out onto a corridor. Along the corridor were doors, each of them with a name displayed in ornate carvings. The doors were all heavy and wooden and even though I put my ear to some of them and tried to quieten my breathing, I couldn't hear a single sound coming from inside. Were there people in there? Were they so clever and obsessed with their work that they were all sitting silently at their desks, scribbling their genius little ideas into notebooks? Perhaps some of them were even away fighting. After all, I suppose not all professors are old and crumpled-looking. Some might be quite young.

I pushed on around the corner and up another, smaller flight of stairs. More doors lined the long, chilly corridor. Suddenly the passageway opened up into a wide room where a number of fat, comfy-looking armchairs and coffee tables sat in front of a growling fire burning away in a huge granite hearth. As I wandered through the room towards the doorway opposite I realised that a pair of the chairs contained, snuggled into them, two wispy-haired old men reading newspapers. They were so engrossed in the news stories that they appeared to be ignoring each other and hadn't even spotted me coming into the room. I sped up and passed lightly through into the next corridor.

The place was enormous, and after about twenty minutes of getting myself lost in the maze that was Trinity College, I was about to give up.

It was then that I found it.

Tucked down a tiny dead end with an almost microscopic window looking out over the rooftops was the door I'd been looking for.

Dr Jonah Bloom (Dept. of Physics)

My hand dug about in my jacket pocket. Nudging Snowflake 843A aside, my fingers picked out the short, stumpy metal key that I'd found in the attic of Unicorn Cottage. Looking around to make sure no one was watching, I slipped it into the keyhole and tried turning it.

It wouldn't budge.

I grabbed it with both hands and twisted hard, but still the lock wouldn't turn.

Frustrated, I gave the door a kick. The loud thud echoed down the long corridor and I swore at myself for being so stupid.

Desperate, I pulled the large ring handle with all my strength and tried the key once more. It was hard to move it but . . .

Click.

It unlocked.

I smiled.

The door was warped. That had been the problem. It curved ever so slightly inwards and the mechanism had been grinding against the part of the lock inside the frame.

I looked more closely at the door near the lock. Was that damage? Chunks of the wood were missing and a couple of small splinters were sticking right out. I brushed them onto the floor before pushing open the heavy oak door.

Inside was a huge wooden desk in front of an ornately designed fireplace. A shiny leather chair – one of those ones you could lie down on if you wanted to – was against the wall under the window, and on the opposite wall were row upon row of shelves.

They were all empty.

There was nothing on them – nothing at all.

Because all the files and books that had once been stored on them were now tossed and crumpled all over the floor. My heart bounced in my chest and my mind jumped back to the first time Mum and I went into the cottage and we saw the mess that it was in.

I'd been right. This wasn't normal, not even for untidy, easily distracted Uncle Jonah.

Something was definitely wrong.

Somebody else had made this mess. Somebody had damaged the door somehow and got into the office and turned it all upside down.

But why?

What were they looking for?

I walked into the room and around the desk before sitting myself in the soft swivel chair behind it. So, this was where Uncle Jonah spent his working days. His thinking days. Sitting in this chair, staring out of the window across the Trinity quad. Directly ahead, on the wall alongside the door, was stuck an enormous poster. It was glossy and was currently catching the light from the window on one side.

It was a photograph of some clouds. Large, thick black ones rolling across the sky with – what I assumed to be – hints of blue beyond.

I spun around in the chair a few times before standing up and turning to the fireplace. Nobody had cleaned it out recently and it was bulging with ash. Lots of the ash had spilled out onto the grate and the floor in front of it, and I found myself unavoidably treading it into the carpet. The ash was light and thin and I realised that it had once been paper. Tiny slivers of paper that had managed to avoid the flames stuck out of the mass of black and I reached for the poker and began prodding it into the mountain of ash.

I scattered some of the ash left and right until, underneath, I found almost half a sheet that had escaped being burnt. I knelt down and picked it out, dusting the dirty black bits from it. On it were typed the words 'PROJECT RAINBOW'.

'What are you doing?'

I jumped and looked over to the door. A tall, broad, dark-haired woman was standing just inside the doorway, her arms crossed and her face scrunched into a scowl.

'I said, what are you doing here?'

'I . . . er . . .'

Suddenly she spotted all the files and books that had been ripped from the shelves and thrown to the floor. She looked horrified.

'Why . . . you little vandal . . .' Her arms unfolded and she started marching around the desk to where I was standing by the fireplace. 'Disrespecting the dead. When I get hold of –'

I didn't wait around. I quickly jumped onto the desk and down the other side. The woman spun on her heels and watched me as I walked quickly to the door.

'Come back! Don't you just run away . . .'

I threw the door open and stepped out into the corridor.

'STOP!' the woman shouted.

I started running, my feet slapping hard on the stone tiles, and I jumped down a staircase and out into the daylight.

Up above me a window opened and the woman shouted from it, 'STOP THAT BOY!'

I raced across the quad, past the domed fountain thing towards the arch.

'STOP HIM!' I could hear her voice coming from somewhere far behind me.

To my left, one of the cloaked students on the grass seemed to be struggling to his feet, his eyes on me.

Realising he was going to try to catch me, I sprinted even harder and faster, my eyes fixed on that archway.

Thankfully the student was slowed down by his flapping cloak and I bolted through the room with the pigeonholes and out the other side, into the street with the quarter-mile-long vending machine. Without thinking, I turned right before quickly turning right again – shoppers and passers-by all lurching out of my way – and then slipped left down a tiny alleyway.

After a minute I slowed down and then – once I was certain that no one was following me – came to a complete stop. I wiped the sweat from my face and tried to catch my breath. My chest ached and I felt even more thirsty than usual.

I also felt stupid and foolish. It had probably been the noise of me kicking the door that attracted the attention of the woman in the first place. If I hadn't been interrupted I would still be in Uncle Jonah's office now. Who knows what I might have found? I swore to myself.

It was then that I remembered I was holding something. I lifted it up and looked at it once again.

The charred piece of paper.

PROJECT RAINBOW.

Along the bank of the river, a large truck was being unloaded and a second was being filled with plastic crates. On the side of the trucks it read: 'BARLOW'S INDUSTRIAL WASHING SERVICE'.

It was the day after my little visit to Trinity, and Mum had insisted we both take a trip into town. I wasn't exactly delighted by the prospect as I didn't want anyone to recognise me from the previous day. We stopped off in a small cake shop and Mum treated us both to a wholemeal scone. But later, as she steered me away from the shopping precinct towards the backs of the colleges, I'm sure my heart was thudding louder than usual.

'What are we doing here, Mum?' I asked, my eyes flashing from side to side in the hope of not seeing that woman again.

'You'll see,' she replied cryptically. 'We can't live off your uncle's money forever, you know.'

As we neared the pitiful stream that trickled its way past the tree-lined gardens, I could make out row upon row of washing lines strung across the river from one bank to the other. In the middle of the stream stood – wearing wellington boots – a whole crowd of women, many of them old. Each of them was pulling clothing out of a large basket that sat on the mud bank beside them and was dipping and squeezing it and rubbing it in the pathetic flow at their feet before reaching up and pegging it to the line. The lines were on pulleys at both ends, so that once something had been pegged, the washer simply had to give the line a gentle tug and the washing would move along, giving them a free stretch of line directly overhead.

'A very good morning to you!'

We turned to see a man with a little goatee beard and a walking stick approaching us.

'Hello.'

'Good morning. Are you looking to have some washing undertaken?' He spoke in a strange clipped way, like he could only really manage a syllable at a time. 'Best service on this stretch of the Cam, we are. No second-rate, overcharged robot jobs here – all washing lovingly done by human hand. Like in the old days. Twice winners of the Cambridgeshire Utility Service Award (Hygiene Section). Clothes guaranteed clean and intact or your money back. Cheap rates. Availability today.'

He looked at us like a living breathing advert, deliberately showing off his perfectly white teeth.

'Not at the moment, thank you.'

'Oh.' The teeth disappeared.

'But . . .' Mum was looking out at the long, busy row of women in the middle of the river. 'But I *was* wondering . . . I've done some washing in my time – not on such an industrial scale, I'll admit – but I was wondering if you were taking people on?'

I looked at her and raised my eyebrows. What was she on about?

'Taking people on?' The man stroked his goatee, now looking like some sort of villain in one of those silent movies – you know, the ones that were always tying damsels in distress to railway lines. Big waxy moustaches. 'I'm always looking for new people. How strong are your arms?'

Mum put her sack down and rolled her sleeves up, holding them out to him.

'Yes. Not bad. Not bad. Might be good for a few dozen kilos in the mornings. I don't pay much, mind you – 20k for a half-day's work. That's as much as I can offer.'

'That's all I need,' said Mum, covering her forearms again. 'When can I start?'

The man was stunned at how quickly this had all taken place. 'Er . . . What about tomorrow?'

'Perfect.'

'What do you think you're playing at, Mum?' I asked as we made our way back towards the Bot Job. 'You can't go washing. You've no idea about washing.'

'I can manage, don't worry about me. Anyway, we're going to need a bit of money coming in. We might not be paying any rent now, but Uncle Jonah's cash won't last that long. Besides –' she opened the boot to the car and lowered the sack into it – 'I'm going to need something to do while you're at school.'

6

Vivi Rookmini

The following morning found us both sitting in the headmaster's office at Hill's Road Primary. My mother kept glancing at her QWERTY, aware that she needed to arrive on time for her first day in her new job, and Mr Belsey – who was a big, Father Christmassy sort of man with a big Father Christmassy sort of nose – eventually waved her away and led me down the corridor to my classroom.

'Must be very difficult.' He seemed to have a stiff neck, and half swung his entire body around to talk to me as we walked. 'Being unable to see colour, I mean. Must make life very, very difficult. I can't imagine it myself. I just can't imagine it.'

And that's the thing. For someone who is able to see colours – who has always known of their qualities and their differences from day one – it is impossible to understand what it might be like to *not* see them. No amount of explanation can get that idea through. People can squint and squash their eyes together and try to cut out the colour. They can detune their televisions so that everything is in black and white. But nothing can really make them see the world as I – and others; there must be others, I'm sure – see it.

Then again, you can flip that argument. You could, of course, say that there was no way on earth that *I* could understand how *they* see the world. No clever device or tool to help me understand the – apparently – beautiful world of colour.

We are in two distinct camps. Two separate Venn diagrams.

Definitely no overlap.

Mr Belsey stopped outside a room, tapped on the glass window in the door and let himself in.

Inside, the teacher – an oldish woman with curly hair – turned away from the whiteboard.

'Ah,' the headmaster started, 'Miss Holbrook, this is our new pupil. Auden Dare.' He tipped her the wink. 'The one we talked about earlier.'

'Hello, Auden.' She came around the front of her desk, narrowly missing the large potted cactus perched on the edge of it, and beckoned me to her. 'Class!' The children sitting around the square tables stopped whatever it was they were doing and looked up at their teacher. 'We have a new member of the group joining us today. His name is Auden Dare. Please join me in wishing him a good morning.'

'Good morn-ing, Au-den,' the entire class said as one,

in a sort of bored, sing-song way. I gave an awkward little wave and as I did so the magnifying glass that I keep on a chain around my neck peeped out from under my jacket. I noticed one or two of the children look at it, so I lifted it and tucked it inside my shirt.

'Excellent!' Mr Belsey pulled his far-too-tight jacket even tighter around his large frame. 'I'll leave you in the capable hands of Miss Holbrook then, Auden.' Without a further look at me, he yanked open the door and left.

'Vivi –' the teacher caught the attention of a girl sitting on her own at the back of the class – 'perhaps Auden can sit with you. Perhaps you can be his New School Buddy for the next few days, hmm?'

The girl looked over and a spark of recognition ran through me. I knew her. But where from? Apart from the one trip to Uncle Jonah's house a few years ago I'd never been to Cambridge before. No, it must have been from some time more recent than that. Some time in the last few days since moving here.

'Yes, Miss Holbrook.'

I made my way through the classroom to the table and took a seat next to the girl.

'Hello,' she said, her questioning eyes almost burning into my face. 'I'm Vivi.'

'Hi, Vivi.' A hemp exercise book and a pencil suddenly slapped onto the table in front of me and I nodded a sort of 'thank you' to the teacher.

'So . . .' She seemed slightly nervous. 'You're new to the school.'

'Yes. Tell me –' I kept my voice down to a whisper as the teacher had found her way back to the whiteboard and was continuing where she had left off with the frightening-looking fraction question – 'what's a "New School Buddy"?'

From what I could tell, she was dark with long black hair pulled back into a wavy ponytail. Sparkly umbrella earrings shone in her ears, and her eyes were big and round and bright with cleverness.

'A 'New School Buddy' is someone who helps a new person at the school settle in. So, for example, I will show you where the rooms are, where the toilets are, where the dining hall is and so on and so forth. I will tell you the running order of the day, the start times, the end times. I will tell you who the other pupils are and who the staff are. I will tell you what days to bring in your PE kit and also which days you will require a specially prepared packed lunch.' She gave an enormously wide grin. 'Basically, I'm your best friend until you find a new one.'

'Vivi, shhh.' Miss Holbrook glared at the girl before turning back to the problem on adding two improper fractions.

Vivi went into a whisper just like me. 'I'm also the person who'll get told off for trying to answer your questions.'

It was during the break that it suddenly hit me in the head who the girl was. She was the one at Trinity who'd run past Mum and me into the courtyard. She'd obviously been visiting the college that day as well.

'Have you always been at this school?' I asked as one of the bigger boys fouled one of the smaller ones at football.

'Yes. Always,' Vivi answered. 'I've never been anywhere else. What about you? I mean, you're new, but what school did you go to before coming here?'

'One in London. Nothing much more to tell really. Wasn't very nice. The other children weren't really very nice.' I tried to deflect the questioning away from me. 'So, what sorts of jobs do your parents do?'

'My mother is the seamstress for the colleges,' she said. 'She fixes all of the Fellows' robes. Makes them too. She also adjusts some of the students' ballgowns – the bot-made ones are really very inferior, you see. They go to her to have them altered.' She looked proud. 'She's well known all across the university as the best sewer and stitcher there is.'

That would explain the visit to Trinity, I thought.

'What about your father? Is he away fighting?'

She shook her head and her ponytail gave a tiny wobble. 'No. He's dead.'

'Oh.'

'Don't worry. He died before I was born. I never knew him. It's only me and my mum now. And Migishoo.'

'Migishoo?' I asked.

'My parrot. He's a Senegal parrot actually. He lives with us. Do you have any pets?'

I told her about Sandwich and the way she likes to stretch herself across the bottom of my bed when I'm sleeping in it, and the way she licks all the juice off her food but leaves the meat itself.

'She sounds sweet.' Her eyes dipped to my neck for a second. 'Er . . . I couldn't help noticing . . . but you've got a magnifying glass around your neck.'

'Yeah.' I dug it out and waggled it about before tucking it back into my shirt.

'Why?'

I stared down at my feet. 'I don't have very good eyesight.'

'Don't you? Really? You would never know. You look at me OK. You've been watching the football OK. It can't be very bad, can it?'

'Well . . . I can't see colour.'

'What do you mean? You have red-green deficiency? Lots of people have that.'

'Red-green . . . what?'

'They confuse the colours red and green. It's quite common.'

I shook my head. 'No. It's worse than that. I can't see any colour at all.'

'What, nothing?'

'No.'

She stared away into the distance, her eyes not focusing at all on the football match. 'So everything's black and white, yes?'

I nodded.

'What's the name of your condition? What's it called? I love words. What's the word for it?'

'I never remember. It's a long word. Too many letters.'

She stood up and pushed her hand deep into her trouser pocket before pulling out a tiny notebook with an even tinier pencil stuck into the spirally wiry spine. She took the pencil, flipped the book open and scribbled something in it.

'There! Made a note to look it up later. Miss Holbrook's very strict about not using QWERTYs during recess.' She put the pad back into her pocket and sat down again. 'Doesn't really explain why you have a magnifying glass around your neck though, does it?'

'No.'

'So?'

'So, what?'

'Why *do* you have a magnifying glass? Are you keen on ants or spiders? Do you collect stamps?'

'No, I'm not. I don't.' I fished the glass out from under my shirt again and held it in front of my right eye, scrunching up the left one. 'Sometimes, in certain lights, I find it difficult to make out small details. When it's really sunny or really cloudy. Tiny print looks blurred. So I have to use this.' I wiggled it around on the end of the chain before tucking it back inside my shirt.

Suddenly a loud fluttering buzz filled the air. The football game stopped, and everybody looked upwards. Two Ariel drones eased themselves over the playground and landed on the electricity cable that passed overhead, connecting to the supply to recharge themselves. Their activity sensors looked like the curved beaks of a hawk, their two inactive light sources like a hawk's dilated eyes.

'I quite like the Ariels. They remind me of Migishoo,' Vivi said, shading her eyes from the dull sun. 'What's your favourite sort of drone?'

'I don't know. I don't think I've ever thought about it. Er . . . I suppose I quite like the Scoots. They're cool. They fly really high.'

'The Dodos are just stupid, I think.'

'Yeah. The way they bounce along the pavement. And they bump into lamp posts all the time.'

'I know.' She laughed, a high-pitched rat-a-tat of a laugh. 'They fall over too. Have you ever seen one fall over?'

I remembered seeing one topple just outside our block of flats, and snorted at the memory. 'Yeah. I have.'

'Believe it or not,' Vivi grinned, 'Cambridge is full of Dodos.'

'Oy!'

I jumped. Suddenly standing next to me was one of the footballers – the big one who'd just fouled the little one. He was tall and slim with black, spiky hair that stuck up above his sulky face.

'Oy!' he shouted again – slightly louder than before – despite standing so close I could smell him. 'What's that round your neck?'

'What?'

He seemed to go all flushed in the face. 'I said, "What's that round your neck?" You deaf or something?'

Two slightly shorter boys came alongside, their faces fixed with uncertain smirks. 'Go on, Boyle. Punch him.'

'Yeah. Go on.'

I looked at Vivi and grinned questioningly, but her eyes had a sort of scared look.

The big boy leaned in closer to me. 'What is it? I want to see.'

The stench from his breath nearly knocked me out, so I shuffled a little further along the wall before pulling the magnifying glass out again.

The boy stared at it. 'A magnifying glass? What do you want a magnifying glass for?'

I sighed. I'd only just explained to Vivi and I certainly didn't want to go through it with this big idiot right now.

'It's a long story,' I muttered.

'What?'

You deaf or something? I thought to myself.

'Go on, hit him,' the kid on the left with the fat nose repeated.

'Yeah. Go on,' the kid on the right with the swollen lips said again. 'He's asking for it.'

'Leave him alone,' Vivi suddenly blurted out before looking scared again.

The big kid leaned across me and glared at her.

'You shut your face, Rookmini. Or I'll throw you halfway up to those Ariel drones up there.'

I shook my head. I'd had enough. 'Look,' I said, 'I don't know who you are, but we've done nothing to you, so why don't you just leave us alone?'

The big kid's face screwed up into a ball of confusion and flushed even more. 'What did you just say?' he almost whispered in anger.

'I said –'

'No one talks to me like that.' His hand seemed to curl up into a fist. 'No one EVER talks to me like that. Least of all some magnifying-glass-wearing weirdo. I'm going to teach you –'

'Belsey at seven o'clock!' the one with the nose squawked before turning on his heel and walking away, closely followed by the swollen-lipped one.

The big kid straightened up and looked behind him, to see the headmaster on playground duty. He turned back to me and pointed at my face. 'Soon. I'll get you soon.

I'll find out who you are and I'll get you. No one EVER talks to me like that. Freak!'

And with that he twisted away and sauntered back towards the football game.

PROJECT RAINBOW.

I pinched the piece of paper between my fingers and held it up to the light, turning it over and over in the hope that some missing secret might just drop out of it.

But it didn't.

PROJECT RAINBOW?

Did it mean what I hoped it meant?

Sandwich jumped up onto the bed and started one of her dribbly purrs, trying to edge her way onto my lap. I let her and gave her a rough tickle around the chin – which she *looooves*. She pushed harder against my nails and rolled onto her side, her eyes half closed and dreamy. Then she began the terrible dribbling.

I lowered the burnt sheet of paper to the bed and tickled her with both hands – my mind a hundred miles away.

Was Project Rainbow what I imagined it was?

Had Uncle Jonah been working on a way of helping me see colour?

The first week of school shot past like a Scoot drone. Mrs Holbrook was nice. Vivi was nicer. But nobody else even approached me. It was as if the incident with Boyle had already damaged any credibility I might have had. He'd obviously been putting word around that I was a magnifying-glass-wearing oddball and everyone else seemed determined to stay away from me. To be honest it didn't bother me. Well, not much anyway. I'd had similar experiences in my old schools. I'd grown used to it. It was something I could just shrug off.

It probably didn't help that I was friends with Vivi. She seemed a bit on her own too. There was nobody you could really call her friend. OK, she might pass the occasional word or two with a couple of the other girls, but nothing much more. In a way, she was almost as isolated as I was.

One lunchtime, I decided to show off. Life's too short not to show off sometimes, don't you think? Now and again you just have to do it. You see, it might surprise you to find out that I was the East London Under-10s Gymnastics Club Champion. For three years in a row. I bet you thought I'd be a thin, pale, sport-hating boy who'd avoid all activity like some sort of disease, preferring to sit in a room playing computer games and feeling sorry for myself. But no. I'm not. I was the blond-haired king of the straddle jumps and double front soms. My box splits were better than anyone's and my work on the vault was – usually – spotless. For those three years I was pretty much top dog in my category.

But then I hit eleven and the competition suddenly got harder. Along with the fact that I was getting taller, and tall people never do very well in gymnastics. You see, to succeed in gymnastics you need to be short – I mean, *reeeeaaally* short – and as muscled as a full bag of nuts. That was never going to be me – I'm strong, but not like that. So a few months before moving to Cambridge, I gave it all up. I miss it a bit, it's true. All the evenings spent stretching and jumping and spinning around. You get used to it. Love it, in a way.

But in the end, it wasn't for me.

Also, you go through an awful lot of your weekly allowance of water when you're training, and Mum and I couldn't afford that. We had to hold back.

However, I'm still as fit as a fireman and a game of football would be a total *breeeeeze*. So if anyone had asked me to join in with their lunchtime game, they would have quickly realised that I was pretty neat with my feet.

But nobody did.

So that lunchtime, I thought I'd show off.

I got off the wall where Vivi and I usually sat, ran onto the pitch and launched into a quadruple round-off flick followed by a backwards somersault. Landing perfectly securely on my feet, barely out of breath, I looked around.

People were stood still, mouths and eyes wide open. I even saw appreciative nods coming from Putter and Keane, Boyle's two drag-alongs.

'Whoa!' said a particularly short Year Four boy. 'Did you see that?'

'Dat's cool.' A thin Year Three girl with a runny nose grinned.

But everybody else just stood and stared.

'Hey! Freakshow!' Boyle pushed his way onto the pitch and pointed his finger at me. Again. 'Freakshow! Did you grow up in a circus, eh? Is that what it is?' Putter and Keane snorted unconvincingly. 'Half man, half monkey, are you? Have to lock you up in a cage at night, did they? People pay a thousand quid to see you perform, eh?' He looked so bitter.

Meanwhile, the looks of awe faded away.

'You want to keep that sort of behaviour under control,' Boyle mumbled into my face. 'Nobody likes a show-off. Specially freaky ones that wear magnifying glasses. Ha!'

He turned and walked off the pitch, Putter and Keane fawning close behind. Everybody else tried their best to ignore me.

Not that I minded. Not at all. If that was the way they operated, then I wouldn't want to hang out with them anyway. They could carry on being scared of Boyle, keeping themselves to themselves and casting the odd untrusting, sideways look at me. Let them. That was their look-out.

I didn't need them.

I had Vivi.

You see, Vivi Rookmini was funny, smart – and I mean *reeeeaaally* smart – and honest. She knew almost everything, and the things she didn't know she enjoyed finding out about. Knowledge was almost as important to her as water, and not a day would go by when she wouldn't spill out a dozen newly learned facts like they were the most important things ever.

Besides, Vivi Rookmini was my friend – not just a New School Buddy.

And I liked her a lot.

7

History

Miss Holbrook was a decent enough teacher. Not particularly exciting or inspiring – she would feed you facts like they were vitamin pills – but her head was jam-crammed full of knowledge. And the sort of knowledge that seemed to take up most of the space was to do with history.

She knew all there was to know about the Romans, the Vikings, the ancient Egyptians. There was no one to touch her on the Tudors and Stuarts, the Georgians and the Windsors. And as for the First and Second World Wars . . .

'Please select a monitor and turn on your QWERTYs,' she would say, and we would all swivel around and position ourselves in front of one of the screens placed around the edge of the classroom. Then we would tap on our wrist computers – our QWERTYs – and get them to project the image of a keyboard in front of us, before receiving further instruction.

We all had QWERTYs. If you ever went to school without your QWERTY you would be sent home to get it. Some people had newer, better-quality QWERTYs than others (mine was a few years out of date, Vivi's was almost obsolete), but every single pupil in all the schools I've ever been to had a QWERTY strapped around their wrist. You could use them to access the Etherweb, to phone, to send messages, to project images, to tell you your energy requirements for the next twenty-four hours, to read your blood pressure, to tell you where you were, to tell you where you should be, to play your favourite music, to play games, to watch the news. Oh, and they could also tell you the time.

Everybody loved their QWERTY.

Anyway, Miss Holbrook would wait for us all to settle down before continuing. 'Today, class, I would like you to research the Battle of Agincourt,' or something like that. 'Find out as much as you can and then write a 700-word essay on what happened and the effect it had on the world and its development.'

We would sit there, using our QWERTYs to piece everything together, and type away on our virtual keyboards until we'd hit the golden figure of 700 words – very few people would have as many as 701.

This was something Miss Holbrook regularly made us do.

And I hated it.

You see, I'm not the greatest fan of history. I really do not see the point. I mean, what can some old war or battle from hundreds or thousands of years ago matter? I'm sure that, while it was going on, the Battle of Agincourt was an extremely important thing. For the people who were there, it was probably the most important thing in the world. No question.

But nowadays?

Time moves on. It always does. That's the point of it. It never stops.

And history is all around us. It is here and now. Everything that happens now is a part of history. Every little thing. It all contributes. It all rolls together and becomes something bigger.

So why waste our time on things long dead when we can discuss the world as it is now?

Why do we hide behind the past?

We are at war.

Over water.

The whole world is at war over water. That simple, wet, life-giving substance that everybody once took for granted. That beautiful, silvery, fragile stuff.

You see, there's not enough of it to go round. Since the rains started to dry up over twenty years ago, the only major source of water has been the sea. And you can't drink seawater. Nobody can. It has to have all its salt removed first. That's why the government and the Water Allocation Board took control of the coastline all those years ago. The entire edge of Britain is now a protected area (I've never even seen the sea; not many kids my age have) and huge desalination units are busy sucking up the undrinkable seawater, taking out the salt and turning it into something more pure. Something we can use.

We're lucky in this country. The sea is all around us. Because we're an island we are surrounded by it. However, there are lots of countries that aren't. Landlocked countries stuck between others. Countries that are completely dependent on the tiny drizzles of rain that happen once or twice a year.

It is this discrepancy (is that the right word?) that started the war.

Some countries have water. Others don't. Some need to get it. Others are unwilling to give it up. Some countries want to share. Others just want to take it all.

BOOM!

War.

That is why so many parents and siblings are away fighting right now.

So, excuse me if I don't get overexcited at the prospect of writing a 700-word essay on the Hundred Years War or the Battle of Hastings or something, because *this* war is more important. To me. To the rest of the class.

This is *our* Battle of Agincourt.

After all, not many members of the class had been left unaffected by the war. Sofia Meacham's father had only recently come back home in a coffin draped with a flag. Kai Everitt had had to move in with his aunt because both his father and his mother were killed fighting in Romania. Naomi Blackwell's older brother had lost both legs after straying onto a minefield in Barcelona. And everybody else had at least one close family member away fighting.

Everybody except Vivi, that is.

8

The Seamstress

One day after school, Vivi invited me back to her house for tea.

'Don't expect too much,' she said as we put on our coats and made our way out through the school gates. 'Mum's not exactly a brilliant cook. Whatever she gives you, just try your best to nibble it and don't pull a face. If you can manage to swallow it as well, that would be a bonus.'

We walked all the way into town, past the big hospital, past the big shops with the big 'closed down' windows, past the big vending machines and into the big area with the big old college buildings.

It was only when we turned onto the small road leading towards Trinity that I started to wonder where it was she was taking me.

'Er . . . Vivi,' I asked, 'where exactly do you live?'

We stopped and Vivi pointed up ahead. 'Here. Just here.'

She was pointing to Trinity College.

'Wait. Hold on. You *live* at Trinity?'

She smiled at me. 'Yes.'

'But . . . but you're not a student. And you're definitely not a . . .' I struggled to pick out the right word, '. . . a Fellow. So you can't live in the college.'

'Oh yes, I can,' she said, before turning around and continuing. I watched her for a second before rushing to catch her up.

'But I don't understand.'

She explained. 'Because my mother is the university seamstress we are allowed to live in some of the rooms on the top floor. It's part of the job. She mends the robes and we get to live there. Come on.'

It had been a couple of weeks since my little visit to Uncle Jonah's rooms, and I suddenly found myself getting all nervous and started worrying that someone would recognise me. I pulled the collar up on my coat, bent my head downwards a bit and marched on.

We passed through the pigeonhole area and stepped out into the quad. Our shoes tapped across the flagstones in the courtyard and we went in through a tiny door in the opposite wall.

The cold stone steps spiralled upwards and we came out onto a long, narrow corridor with windows on the right overlooking the quad. It wasn't far away from Uncle Jonah's rooms, I realised, and a horrible thought hit me.

What if –

'Come on.' Vivi waved me on before I could think any further. 'This is it here.'

At the far end of the corridor, Vivi pushed open a door and we stepped into her rooms.

The word 'busy' leaped to mind. If I could see colours, I'm sure I would have been hit in the face by an incredible rainbow of the things. For a start, small even patches of cloth had been sewn together and pinned up so that it looked like the ceiling itself was made of soft cushions.

A beaded curtain split the long room into two, hiding away whatever was beyond it from the front door. A scruffy, threadbare sofa sat in front of a smoky old fireplace, on each side of which was a large cactus, and a really old (and I mean *reeeeally* old) television set was positioned on top of what looked like a cardboard box covered in crêpe paper.

Near one of the dirty arched windows, a parrot swung on a perch, its head twisting as it watched me enter the room. Next to it was a table across which were spilled hundreds of cotton reels and scraps of silky cloth, and, dominating the far end of the table, a sewing machine, looking more like an instrument of torture than something used to join things together.

A dressmaker's dummy – headless and limbless with an adjustable waist, draped with some unfinished garment – stood next to a cluttered bookcase over-spilling with books.

And in an armchair, quietly stitching the brim of a hat, was Vivi's mother. She was darker than Vivi, but the shape of her face and her long flowing hair with the slight curl gave the game away.

My mouth went even drier than usual.

She was also the woman who'd discovered me in Uncle Jonah's rooms.

When we came in, Vivi's mum barely glanced up. Her eyes were focused on the job literally in hand.

'Mum,' Vivi said, dumping her schoolbag on the sofa. 'Mum, this is Auden.'

'Ah –' she still didn't look up – 'Auden. I've heard so much about you.'

Finally she stood up and propped the hat on top of the headless dummy before turning to me and shaking my hand.

'I'm Immaculata.' Her voice had an accent to it I now noticed. Something European, I thought. 'It's lovely to meet you.'

Her eyes squinted momentarily as if she recognised me.

'Hello,' I replied, trying to sound as if nothing was wrong. 'Good to meet you too.'

Behind the beaded curtain was a small kitchen and dining area where Immaculata had prepared some things for tea. Small triangular cheese sandwiches, quinoa biscuits, wholewheat muffins. Vivi was wrong about her mother being an awful cook. The food was amazing. We drank milk from plastic cups as we ate, and Immaculata watched me with her big dark eyes and asked questions. It made me nervous.

'Vivi tells me that you cannot see colour. Is that right?'

I nodded, spilling a few biscuit crumbs over the table.

'Achromatopsia,' Vivi said.

'Hmm?'

'Achromatopsia. I looked it up. An inability to see colour. Achromatopsia.'

I nodded again. 'That's it. That's the word. I always forget. Too many letters.'

Immaculata continued. 'Can the doctors do anything about it? Can they operate or put you on pills or something? Something that will help you see colour?'

'No. There's nothing they can do. I am going to see everything in just black and white for the rest of my life.'

'That's terrible.'

'Is it?' I gratefully accepted one of the muffins as Immaculata held out the plate to me. 'It's just as it is, I suppose. It's not important.'

Immaculata's eyes seemed to question my last statement and I tucked into the muffin to avoid having to look at her.

'Actually,' I said eventually, 'my uncle once promised that he would try to help me to see. He was a scientist.' I stole a quick look at her. 'He said he would try to work on something.'

'Is he still trying?'

I put the remains of the muffin back onto my small plate. It was quite dry and was making me thirsty; I didn't want to drink any more of their milk than I had to.

'No. He died.'

'Oh, I am sorry.'

I shrugged. 'It's OK. Just one of those things.'

After tea, we went back into the main room and Vivi introduced me to Migishoo.

'He loves to fly out over the quad at night. His favourite food is sunflower seeds.' She smiled at the bird. 'He'll repeat anything you say. Pretty parrot. I . . . am . . . a . . . pretty . . . parrot.'

Migishoo tilted his head as if he was wondering what the girl in front of him was on about. Then, after a few seconds he squawked.

'Priddy parod. I yamma priddy parod.'

We laughed.

'Go on. You try,' said Vivi.

'OK. Erm . . . Auden Dare is clever and handsome.'

The bird looked at me as if I was mad. And then . . .

'Or town tare is clerer ant ansum.'

'Ha!'

I sort of fell backwards, laughing, and as I did so my eye jumped onto something tucked away on a shelf. I suddenly stopped laughing.

'Auden?' Vivi asked. 'What is it?'

I walked across to the shelf and reached up. I grabbed hold of the thing I'd seen and pulled it down. It was cold and hard, smooth along its curved surface but jagged in the middle. And about a hundred different things slotted into place in my mind.

'What's wrong?' she asked again.

I turned it over in my hands, not able to believe my eyes. 'Snowflake,' I said mostly to myself. 'Snowflake 843B.'

Vivi jumped up off the chair. 'How do you know . . . ?'

Before she finished, I went over to where my coat was lying over the back of an armchair and reached into the right-hand pocket. I pulled out the small half of meteorite that Uncle Jonah had left me in his will and slotted it onto this new discovery.

They were a perfect fit.

Vivi stopped where she was.

'Vivi?' I said amazed. 'Six Six? *You* are Six Six?'

She looked stunned. 'And *you* must be the Golden Boy.'

Of course, it made perfect sense.

Vivi. Six Six. Break up her name into the Roman numerals VI VI. Six six. It was exactly the sort of cryptic crosswordy type thing that Uncle Jonah loved doing. Stripping words back to their basic elements and toying with them, piecing them back together – back to front, down then up.

'It's what Dr Bloom always called me. Six Six. I used to like Dr Bloom. He was really nice to me. Used to give me lollipops whenever I had to run errands to his rooms. Always asked me how school was going. Things like that.'

'And what was that you called me?' I asked. '"The Golden Boy"?'

Vivi nodded and got up from her chair. 'I suppose it must come from Auden. The chemical symbol for gold is Au. *Au*-Den. *Gold*-Den. Golden. That must be it.' She retrieved a folded sheet of paper from the same shelf as I'd found Snowflake 843B. 'He mentions you in the letter that went with my half of the meteorite.' She opened the paper and handed it to me.

I recognised the spidery, slanting scrawl straight away. Her letter was very like the one Uncle Jonah had left me. In fact, it said lots of the same things. A description of Snowflake 843B and of where it had come from. A small paragraph explaining just how tiny the chances of it hitting earth actually were. A mention of the fact that the meteorite looked just like a rock that could be found in the garden of Unicorn Cottage.

And then another paragraph.

By the way [it said], *its sister – Snowflake 843A – I have left to an extraordinary young man that I know. I like to think of him as the Golden Boy. The Golden Boy is one of the strongest and bravest people that I have ever met – he has had an awful lot to contend with in his life. I also have a feeling that after my death he might well move to Cambridge. If you should ever come across him then, do, please, make him feel at home. He will need a*

good friend, and I know for a fact you are one
of the best.

   Anyway, Six Six . . . Take very good care of
yourself and your dear mother, and remember
that your mind is bigger and sharper than any
number of universes squared.

Dig deep, my girl. Dig deep.

Always remember to dig deep.

Yours,

Jonah (Dr Bloom)

I didn't know how to feel. Uncle Jonah was referring to
me as the Golden Boy – which I think I kind of liked.

But then again . . .

Uncle Jonah – my uncle – had written a letter, just
like the one he'd written me, to someone else. Someone
he wasn't even related to. Vivi was just somebody who
happened to live in the same college as him. That's all.
What right did she have to the other part of the meteorite?

'That's weird,' Vivi said, taking the letter from me.
'Don't you think?'

'What?'

'Well, the fact that you were put next to me in school,
and then weeks later we find out that – without either of
us knowing – we have a connection. Dr Bloom.'

'*Uncle* Jonah,' I churlishly added. 'I didn't know him
as Dr Bloom. I knew him as *Uncle* Jonah.'

Vivi fell quiet and I suddenly felt guilty. She was my friend. A good friend. The best friend – as Jonah said in his letter. And as my best friend, I had a duty to take care of her. Not upset her.

'He must have thought very highly of you,' I said. 'To leave you the other half of Snowflake.'

Vivi smiled. 'He was nice. A very clever man. I liked him a lot.'

Suddenly, the bead curtain between the sitting room and the kitchen flew open and Immaculata marched in, pointing her finger straight at me.

'It just came to me! *You* are the boy who ransacked poor Dr Bloom's rooms!! You!'

'Oh goodness.' Immaculata fell back into a chair, her hand on her chest. Vivi had explained everything, and her mother calmed down almost immediately. 'Dr Bloom was your uncle? Dr Bloom was a gentleman. A real gentleman. Goodness! To think you're his nephew. The number of times I patched up his sub fusc . . . Well, well.' Her eyebrows suddenly got closer together. 'It was a terrible thing – him dying like that. Awful. Out of the blue. There he was, perfectly fit, and then . . . Terrible. Nobody saw that coming, I can tell you. '

'Yes.' I thought I'd better explain. 'You see, I went to his rooms to see if I could find something.'

'Well, did you? Find it, I mean.'

I shook my head. 'I don't know.'

'Only you seemed to make an awful mess in his office, throwing all the books and files all over the floor like that.'

'That wasn't me.'

Immaculata squinted closely at me. 'Wasn't it?'

'No. I think somebody else had been in his rooms before me. I think they might have been looking for something too.'

We all sat in silence for a few seconds, weighing up this information.

'Well, perhaps we'd better inform someone about it.' Immaculata shifted in the chair. 'The police or the Water Allocation Board or somebody. Let them know –'

'No!' I realised I had spoken too loudly. 'No.' Calmer now. 'I don't think we should.'

'Why not?'

'Because if somebody's taken something, then chances are it will be gone for good. The police won't be able to help now. They're far too busy as it is. Anyway, Uncle Jonah died months ago. Who knows how long his rooms have been like that?'

Immaculata nodded, realising that what I'd said was all true.

'It is true. After I found you in his rooms I had them cleaned up. I couldn't just leave them like that. It seemed disrespectful somehow. So even if there were fingerprints or anything like that, they'd all be swept away by now.

Oh dear.' She shook her head. 'Why would anyone want to break in? What were they looking for? He wasn't a spy, was he? Trinity has a great tradition of employing spies as lecturers.'

'Mum!' Vivi protested. 'Dr Bloom wasn't a spy.'

'How do you know?' Immaculata snapped back. 'You've never met a spy before, have you? How would you know what one looks like? That's the point of spies, isn't it, to be able to look normal. Fit in.'

Vivi tutted and sighed.

'I'm certain Uncle Jonah wasn't a spy, Mrs Rookmini,' I said. 'But whatever they were looking for must have had something to do with his work, I'm sure.'

Vivi's room was small but as busily packed as the main room. Her bed was jammed against a wall, and above it a large, open umbrella dangled from the ceiling.

'It holds all my old toys,' she said. 'All the ones I can't bring myself to throw away.'

Looking up, I noticed a couple of teddy bears and dolls peering over the edge of the umbrella.

'You can't *bear* to throw them away, can you? Geddit? Bear. Yes?'

Vivi shook her head and didn't greet my joke with the loud laugh it so clearly deserved.

Next to the window, a huge telescope was pointing upwards to the sky, and all over the room were posters and pictures of planets, moons and constellations. Books on space and space exploration were stacked up neatly on the floor, and a weird device that looked as if it was made of balls and wire seemed to have pride of place on top of a small table.

Vivi noticed me looking at it. 'It's an orrery.'

'A what-ery?'

'An orrery.' She went up to it and started winding a key. 'It's a model of the solar system. It shows how the planets rotate around the sun.' She let the key go and the thing started to whirr. The smaller balls all turned about the larger ball at the centre – the sun. Some of them revolved faster than others. After a few seconds it started to slow until it came to a complete stop.

'This particular orrery dates from when Pluto was still considered to be a proper planet – before it was reclassified as a dwarf.' Vivi gave the key an extra turn and watched the what-ery with fascination. 'Back then there were thought to be nine planets in our solar system. Nowadays there are only the eight.'

'Right.' I pointed to the ceiling. 'You've got a hole. In your roof.'

'That's not a hole, silly. That's a skyspace.'

'A what?'

'A skyspace is a window that looks out onto the sky. One of the old professors had it put in when these were his rooms.'

'What's it do?'

Vivi stared at me like I was some sort of irritating kid that kept asking questions just to wind the teacher up. Either that or she thought I was just stupid.

'It's to stare up through. The sky is always changing. It never stops moving. People can do it when they're thinking – it helps them concentrate. Focusing on the sky helps you relax and order your thoughts.'

'Sounds a load of rubbish.'

She ignored me. 'The clouds roll by, or I sometimes watch the stars at night. As the world rotates, the stars do too. Changing position. Within an hour you can have a completely different view. The whole sky changes.' She looked at me. 'Come on. Give it a go.'

'What?'

'I'll lie on my bed. You lie on the floor – you can have one of my pillows, if you like.' She picked one up and dropped it on the floor next to the bed. 'Try it. Just lie there and stare at the sky.' She hopped onto her bed and stretched out.

I sighed and got down onto the floor, resting my head on the pillow.

'I feel stupid.'

'Now just watch. Relax and watch the sky.'

I sighed again but did as I was told. I stared up through the strange perfect square of window that had been cut out of Vivi's ceiling. The clouds were thin and wispy and there was obviously a bit of a breeze outside as they appeared to be moving quite fast.

'They're moving fast,' I said.

'Scudding,' replied Vivi.

'Eh?'

'Shhh.'

We both lay there in silence as we gazed at the movement in the little pane of glass. After a few minutes it started to feel like I wasn't watching the sky at all. It was as though the square sheet of glass was a picture – a painting – pinned to the ceiling. And the picture was always evolving. Shut your eyes for a few seconds and, when you opened them again, you had a brand-new picture to look at. Your eyes homed in on the detail. The tiny bumps and ridges and puffs that made up the clouds. The way some clouds overtook others – barging past – or crept out from behind another, slower one. It was oddly . . . hypnotic. Soothing. Comforting.

So much so that I nearly fell asleep.

Thankfully Vivi spoke before I found myself snoring.

'Do you know the names for the different types of clouds?'

'Er, no.'

'Well, there's stratus – those are the low-looking patchy ones. Like cotton wool that's been pulled apart. The big fluffy kind are called cumulus. The ones which look really high up and wispy are called cirrus.'

'Which sort are they?' I asked, pointing upwards.

'Probably cirrus,' she said. 'Yes. Definitely cirrus.'

We fell silent again and watched the ever-changing sky.

'You know . . .' Vivi whispered eventually – the silence had clearly lasted long enough for her to feel like it would be wrong to break it with anything other than a whisper. 'You know, it was your uncle who originally got me interested in the stars. He gave me a star map for my tenth birthday and showed me all the different constellations. Kept testing me on my knowledge of them. He was the person who said I should get a telescope. Mum saved for ages to buy me one.'

I watched as a slightly thicker, bleaker cloud forced its way onto the canvas. It appeared to be shoving the other lighter clouds out of the frame. I thought back to the poster in Uncle Jonah's office. I thought back to the ashes. I thought back to the piece of paper with 'PROJECT RAINBOW' typed on it.

'When I was in Uncle Jonah's office,' I said quietly, 'I found a piece of half-burnt paper in the grate.'

'Oh?'

My eyes relaxed, watching the clouds.

'Yes. There were only two words on it: "PROJECT RAINBOW".'

'Project Rainbow?' Vivi asked, peering over the side of her bed.

'Hmm.'

'What is Project Rainbow?'

'I don't know. But . . .' I turned my head to look at her. 'Well, what's the first thing you think of when you think of a rainbow?'

'Atmospheric moisture content. Diffraction.'

'OK,' I corrected myself. 'What do *normal* people think of when they think of a rainbow?'

She thought. 'Colours?'

'Yes, colours.'

'Ah . . .'

'I think Uncle Jonah had finally started working on a way to help me see colour.'

'Project Rainbow.'

'Yes. Only . . .'

'What?' She rested her chin on her elbows.

'Why did he burn the papers? Why would he destroy all the work he'd put into helping me?'

Vivi didn't say anything.

'Perhaps . . .' I started, 'he'd given up. Couldn't do it. Found it wasn't possible.'

Vivi still didn't say anything.

'Perhaps . . .' I continued. 'Perhaps that was what the people who raided his office were searching for. Yes. I bet that's what they were after. I think they were trying to find his work on curing achromatopsia.'

PART TWO
BLUE

9

Trampoline

Pretty soon the summer came along and school wound itself up, stumbling to its inevitable end for the holiday. I've always loved the summer holidays. Six weeks of doing not very much whenever you didn't want to do it. Bliss! The only problem was that Mum's work didn't stop, so for most of the time off I was going to be alone in the house. So it was agreed that Mum would drop me off outside Trinity most mornings and I would spend the day with Vivi.

One of the best things about visiting Vivi was Migishoo. Once I tried to get the parrot to say something rude, but Immaculata heard and gave me one of her looks. So I apologised nicely and promised not to do it again.

Vivi and I spent most of the days exploring the town and the area of countryside that hovered just outside Cambridge. It was quite a flat landscape with not many hills but lots of lanes that twisted around on themselves through villages and small woods.

One of our favourite places to visit was the Sunny Vale Caravan Park.

The Sunny Vale Caravan Park had been badly named. For a start it was hardly ever sunny in this part of the world. Secondly it wasn't in any sort of vale or valley – it stood perfectly on display in the centre of a couple of fields two miles outside the city centre.

It had also seen better times. The flashing digital signpost under which visitors drove into the camp was actually rotting and buckled, with one of the posts supporting the sign having been knocked some way out of the ground. In the wind the whole thing swayed and squeaked like it was about to topple, and the lettering faltered and flickered until you couldn't read what it was trying to say anyway.

The camp consisted of about two dozen static caravans, all of them desperately needing a fresh coat of paint. If you peered through a window into one of the empty ones, you could see that the furnishings were old and beaten up and spider webs were starting to take over. Some of the windows were cracked and quite a few of them were screaming out for a good wipe with a damp rag.

However, even though the place was rundown and about as appealing as a pig in a Christmas pudding, Sunny Vale still had its fair share of customers. Holidaymakers from London and other cities who'd saved their hard-earned cash for a short break in the countryside. Three or four caravans at a time appeared to be occupied – some by young families, others by old people – but nobody ever looked especially pleased to be there.

Some days Vivi and I would walk out to Sunny Vale and spy on its current inhabitants. The way the caravans were placed across the fields made it easy to hide from view. We could skip along behind one and then dash across the overgrown path to another. It also became clear quite early on that the owners – who we never saw, even once, although they had their own battered little house on the edge of the site – only ever put people in the same few caravans. Obviously they could just about manage the upkeep of four or five caravans, while everything else was left untouched.

It was great fun sneaking about and hiding from everyone. In fact sometimes, when the camp was particularly quiet, we would run and hide from each other. We would play an elaborate game of hide-and-seek across the whole park, with the extra rule that nobody else was to ever see us. Both Vivi and I found ourselves to be experts at keeping out of sight.

Another place we liked to visit was the old scrapyard south of the city. All the thrown-out nonsense that people didn't want any more ended up here. Enormous hills of busted-up metal and crunched-down plastic littered the wide yard like an upside-down egg carton. A type of drone I'd never seen before – Sifters, I think they are called – were working their laborious way through the piles, sorting out the salvageable from the useless and dropping anything that could be saved into large buckets on their backs. They were slightly larger than the Dodos, with wheels instead of legs that propelled them easily across the bumpy, rubbish-strewn ground.

It was at the scrapyard that we found the trampoline.

'There's nothing wrong with it.' I rolled it out from the pile of discarded tat and prodded the springs and netting with my hand. 'Why would anyone want to get rid of this? There's absolutely nothing the matter with it.' A Sifter approached and, sensing our presence, wheeled itself around us.

Vivi shook her head and looked me up and down. 'You're not thinking of taking that, are you? Please tell me you're not.'

'But it's OK. Be a shame to waste it.'

'I just don't see the point of it. It's a bit childish, if you ask me. Bouncing up and down on a mat.'

'You don't see the point because you've never been sporty. You hate all sport. Apart from during PE at school, I don't think I've ever seen you run.'

'But a trampoline? Isn't it a bit like a bouncy castle? For kids.'

I nudged it even further away from the pile. 'No. When I was doing gymnastics I got really good at the trampoline – and I mean *reeeeaally* good. If we can get this back home I'll show you.'

Vivi folded her arms and huffed. 'Home? You think you're going to take this back to your house? But you live about a mile and a half away. You can't carry it that distance. In fact, you can't even pick it up. It's too big. Even with the two of us, it's too big.'

'Ah,' I said. 'But we can try rolling it.' The trampoline was one of those round ones with the safety netting all around the edge. 'There aren't many steep hills between here and home. It'll be a doddle.' As if to make the point, I gave it a big shove and it rolled a little way ahead of me. 'See.'

As it turned out, it wasn't a doddle. Far from it. The first problem we found was that trying to make it go in the direction you wanted was really difficult. You had to stop it rolling, then give it a bit of a push on one end to make it turn slightly, before shoving it onwards again. Soon enough you'd have to stop it once more and push the opposite end to readjust it. Left, then right, then left, then right again. Zigzagging along the road. It was really slow going.

Another problem was actually getting the thing to stop moving whenever it was going downhill, even on really small slopes. Vivi nearly got crushed on a couple of occasions as she jumped in front of it and tried thrusting it back. Being so light and thin, she had to lean all her weight into it to make any difference at all.

Unfortunately I'd badly underestimated just how uneven the road between the dump and Unicorn Cottage was.

There were significantly more ups and downs than I'd imagined. And the ups were the worst. It took both of us all our strength to get the trampoline up even the slightest of inclines, giving it bursts of energy in the hope that momentum would carry it further.

By the time we reached the cottage, both Vivi and I were half dead. I unlocked the door with my key, went into the kitchen and turned on the tap, filling two large glasses of water and – according to the flashing light attached to the tap – using up my personal allocation for the next two days. We sat on the drive, sipping our drinks and staring at the trampoline.

'Hope you're happy now,' said Vivi. 'Now that you've nearly killed me for a bouncy castle.'

I tutted. 'It's not a bouncy castle. It's a much more technical piece of equipment than that. It takes great skill and judgement to use it properly.'

'OK. Show me then.'

The problem was that neither of us had an ounce of strength left after pushing the trampoline all the way home, so we left it lolling on its side for the evening like a beached porpoise.

The next day, Vivi came back to the house and we lifted the trampoline onto its legs and adjusted it so that it was level. I tore the safety netting off – I didn't need any of *that*, thank you very much – and dusted it all over before climbing on and testing it for spring.

'Not bad. Not bad,' I said, finding a rhythm as I gently bounced. 'Pretty responsive.'

Vivi stood on the ground before me, not looking particularly impressed.

'Now watch this,' I blurted, before bouncing harder and higher and launching into a series of tuck jumps, straddle jumps, pikes and levers.

Still not very impressed.

So I went for it.

Forward somersault. Straight back. Double som.

As my body twisted and twirled in the air, I could see the look on her face change.

'Wow,' she said, her mouth wide. 'Wow!'

'You want a go?' I asked breathlessly as I brought myself to a tidy stop and jumped off the trampoline onto the grass. 'I'll show you some moves.'

'No. No. I don't think so.' She looked embarrassed. 'I'm not very good at that sort of thing.'

'Go on. It's easy enough.'

'No. It's all right.' She turned away and went over to stroke Sandwich, who was curled up on the kitchen doorstep.

'Please yourself.'

I caught my breath and looked around the garden. I looked at the tree with its tall branches overhanging the roof of the house. It was so close to my window that it blocked the sun every morning, and if my curtains suddenly disappeared I probably wouldn't notice any difference.

There was one branch – a really solid-looking one – that hung just above my window. As I stared at it, I had an idea.

I grabbed the trampoline by one of its legs and started to drag it towards the tree. As I pulled, it seemed to dig itself into the earth.

'What are you up to now?' Vivi sounded fed up. Sandwich was purring and dribbling under her fingers.

'Come on. Help me.'

She sighed and walked slowly over to the trampoline. She pushed and I pulled. Within a minute or two we had positioned it directly under the long branch near my window.

I climbed on and started to bounce, slowly building up height. Reaching upwards, my hands were soon just below the branch. A little extra oomph and –

Got it!

I held onto the branch, dangling like washing over the River Cam.

'Wahey! Look at me!' I could see right into my bedroom.

Vivi just stood there, shaking her head. 'I don't know why you always have to do all this physical stuff. It's dumb, if you ask me.'

I let go and bent my knees to absorb some of the bounce.

'Wait here!' I ran excitedly into the house and up the stairs to my room, where I opened the window as wide as I possibly could and pushed the bed so that it was directly under the window. I then fished about in a small bag and managed to find some of the gymnastics chalk that I used to use at the gym.

Back in the garden, Vivi had gone back to stroking Sandwich. I rubbed some of the chalk onto the palms of my hands before dusting off any excess.

I jumped back onto the trampoline and got going again. In a few seconds I had hold of the branch.

Now for the tricky bit.

I slowly rocked my legs back and forth, back and forth. Building up momentum.

Vivi could see what I had in mind. 'Be careful!' she called.

I ignored her. I needed to focus fully to get this right. My hands slipped easily around the rough branch as I rocked and my legs swung higher and higher. The window was only just below me. The power in my body slowly grew, until, feeling the moment to be perfect . . . I let go.

My body arced through the air and my legs slipped in through the window, closely followed by the rest of me. As my feet came into contact with the bed, I bounced slightly and the back of my head caught the very edge of the windowsill, smacking it hard.

'Ow!'

I lay on the bed for a few seconds, recovering. My skull felt bruised – probably turning blue – and my arms ached a little, but otherwise I was fine. I'd done it!

I got off the bed, ran downstairs and back outside and did it again. This time I increased the height of the swing before letting go. This meant my head had time to get through the window before my feet hit the bed. It was perfect.

After the fourth attempt – by which time I could have done it with my eyes closed – Vivi got up and walked towards the lane. 'Perhaps I'll just go home.'

'No, don't. Please don't go,' I called out from my bedroom window. 'Let me try just one more thing and then we'll find something else to do.'

'One more thing?'

'Yes.' I climbed out of my window and sat on the ledge.

'What are you doing?'

I placed my feet flat against the outside wall and pushed, my arms reaching out for the branch. I grabbed it and held on tight until my body rocked itself to a stop. I hung there for a few seconds just looking around, taking everything in. The fields that swept away into the distance looked strangely regular and square. They reminded me of the pieces of cloth pinned to Vivi and Immaculata's ceiling. The rough uneven hedges that ran alongside the uncared-for lane looked like a long line of wild-haired men, queuing up for something or other. Across the fields you could see the irrigation pylons dotted here and there like tall, thin pyramids. For a few minutes every morning and evening the farmers would be allowed to blast the crops with water, spraying the fields with a fine mist. Once or twice – when the farmer wasn't looking – I had crawled in and stood beneath one of the pylons, allowing myself to get soaked and licking up the drips that ran down my face. I could probably be arrested for it – I'd seen the Water Allocation Board violently arrest people in the street for less – but it felt so good to wipe the grime from my face and hair; the allowance of four minutes per week in the real shower was never enough. Not for anyone.

I looked down across the garden of Unicorn Cottage. Like most of the things that had belonged to Uncle Jonah, it was messy and neglected, the lawn hopelessly patchy. In fact the lawn seemed to sort of bubble up in parts, like it wasn't sitting properly.

Then suddenly . . . *click!*

It was at that moment that a number of things shot through my head.

When I think back on it now, it almost seems like I was meant to be hanging from the tree facing that particular direction at that particular time having those particular thoughts.

Not that I believe in fate or anything like that. I mean, how can anyone believe in fate when so many random things seem to happen in the world? Try telling Sofia

Meacham or Kai Everitt about fate. Try telling the millions of people whose relatives have died or have lost limbs in a war over water that it must all have been fate. People who believe in fate just don't want to accept responsibility for anything. They'd rather see the world in black and white with no greys in between. You're alive, you're dead, end of, in their opinion. People who believe in fate have already given up.

Had Uncle Jonah given up?

So, no. It wasn't fate. It wasn't *meant* to happen. It just did. A lucky chance that my thoughts all came together at that moment.

It was the letters that I found myself thinking of.

The letters that Uncle Jonah had written to both Vivi and me.

Do not be put off by the fact that it looks like any other lump of stone or rock that you can find on any hillside or in any quarry or even in the garden at the rear of Unicorn Cottage.

That's what he'd written in both the letters. About the two parts of the Snowflake meteorite.

. . . or even in the garden at the rear of Unicorn Cottage.

And later in the letters . . .

Dig deep . . . Dig deep.

Always remember to dig deep.

I remembered now, when I first read the note that came with Snowflake 843A, how strange and odd that sounded.

Dig deep. I had assumed that Uncle Jonah was telling me to be brave, to try and stay true to the sort of person I was. Same thing with Vivi.

But what if it was something more than that?

What if it was a code? A clue?

I scanned across the lawn and my eyes were drawn to a spot at the back of the garden, just in front of one of Uncle Jonah's rubbish-stuffed sheds. The grass seemed especially bumpy just there.

I let myself drop from the branch and climbed back down onto the ground.

'Finished now?' Vivi asked, turning back from the lane and following me.

I picked my way across the dead grass towards the shed.

'What is it? What are you doing now?'

I knelt down. The lawn felt oddly buckled and it shifted slightly under my knees. I dug a couple of fingers into the soil and tried ripping up a clod. To my surprise, it came up incredibly easily. I threw it behind me and did it again.

Vivi laughed. 'What *are* you doing, Auden?'

I ignored her and pulled up a few more lumps of the knotted, rooty turf.

Suddenly, something shone back at me from beneath the lawn.

'There's something metal in the ground,' I blurted out. I brushed some of the dark grit out from the hole I'd just made.

'What's that?' Vivi stood over me.

'I don't know.'

I tried grabbing another part of the turf and pulling it up, but this area was tightly packed after years of knotty roots had tied it all together. If Uncle Jonah had been a little bit negligent with the house, then he had been completely abusive with the garden. The lawn hadn't seen a fork or a rake or a hoe in many long years. The discarded boxes and bins that littered it were almost deliberately placed to make the whole area look (and smell) as awful as possible.

'Is there a spade? Or a fork? Can you see one?'

Vivi looked around. 'No.'

'Have a look in one of the sheds.'

She went to one of the doors, and sprang backwards as a ton of rubbish seemed to spew out. She poked about for a bit and then came back with something in her hand.

'No fork or spade. But I found this.' She held it out to me. It was a small gardening trowel. 'That's all there was.'

'OK.' I took it from her and started hacking at the earth, digging away until the matted roots loosened. After a couple of minutes of hard work, I dropped the trowel and grabbed at the turf with my hands again. This time it all came away easily. I pulled clumps up and threw them over my shoulder behind me.

Whatever the metal thing was, it was long. And wide. Over the next ten minutes, I managed to expose a couple of square metres.

I tapped on the metal. It clanged, the sound almost bouncing back at me. I did it again. I looked up at Vivi, who was frowning. She was clearly thinking the same thing I was.

'It's hollow,' she said. 'It's not solid.'

'What do you think it is?'

She shook her head. 'I don't know. An old pipe?'

'But pipes are curved. This is flat on the top.'

Vivi dropped to the ground and joined in, clawing away at the earth and roots surrounding the thing. At one point, we changed direction. Instead of working our way along the garden towards the house, we dug back towards one of the sheds. I loosened the turf with the trowel before we both ripped it away with our bare hands. Soon we'd removed all the soil up to the base of the shed, and the metal thing still hadn't come to an end.

'It goes under the shed,' I realised.

'What does that mean?'

'I'm not sure.' I sat there for a second, thinking. If it went under the shed, then it must have been put there before the shed was built. It wasn't that deeply buried, so whoever put the shed on top *must* have known the metal thing was there. The shed wasn't that old – the bitumen didn't look at all faded – so, presumably, Uncle Jonah must have put it there. 'We need to empty the shed,' I said, suddenly jumping up and brushing the earth from my trousers. 'Come on.'

This shed was also full of junk Lots of discarded cardboard and technical-looking metal things seemed to fall out as we opened the door wide, and the stuff that didn't fall out remained utterly jammed to the roof, the little plastic windows of the shed barely detectable in the mess.

'You want to get all of this out?' Vivi asked.

'We need to see what happens under the shed.'

'There's an awful lot of it. And I don't think your mum's going to be too happy when she sees it all spread out on the lawn.'

I gave her a wink. 'Don't worry about my mum. I can handle her.' Although, to be honest, I was a bit concerned myself. Still . . .

I reached in and pulled something large and wooden out and dumped it on the lawn. Vivi grabbed something smaller – a black bin liner full of rubbery bits and pieces – and put it down next to the wooden thing. Some of the stuff was heavy enough for us both to have to carry it, and within an hour we had almost emptied the shed.

There was one last item that needed to be removed. A large pram-sized rectangular thing against the far wall that was covered in a tight-fitting tarpaulin. The tarpaulin didn't reach all the way to the floor, and at the bottom you could see that the thing had wheels. Four big fat wheels.

'What is that?' Vivi asked.

'Not sure. Let's get it out first and look at it outside.'

The thing was heavy but rolled easily enough. I turned it around in the tight confines of the shed before pushing it out over the lip of the door and onto the grass.

The sheet of tarpaulin was tied tightly around whatever it was, so we got on our knees again and started working at the knots with our fingers. Eventually they were undone and we yanked the tarpaulin off with some difficulty.

It was some sort of machine. Like a huge black box on wheels. On the top of the box, towards what I assumed to be the front, was a wide hole that seemed to funnel downwards into its centre. Slightly further back on the top was a kind of flap. Vivi unclicked the latch and opened it up. We both leaned over and peered inside. There was nothing. Just an empty cube-shaped space about the size of a football.

On one of the sides were two huge square plastic buttons. I punched one of them. Then I punched the other. Nothing happened.

'Is there a lead? Do we need to plug it in?'

Vivi pointed back at the cube-shaped space under the flap. 'I've a feeling that this is where the battery is meant to go.'

'What sort of battery is that?' I said. The space was

much, *much* bigger than the ordinary batteries you could buy in shops. But it wasn't as big as a car battery. It was somewhere between the two.

'Perhaps Dr Bloom hadn't got around to inventing the battery for it when he died,' Vivi suggested.

'No. That doesn't make any sense. You build something around a battery. Not the other way around.' I inspected the junk we'd spread out over the garden. There was nothing that looked as though it would fit the space. 'It must be here somewhere.'

I went back to the black box on wheels and punched uselessly at the buttons again. Walking around to the other side, I noticed something written on it. In chalk. Some of the chalk had rubbed off – possibly when we pulled off the tarpaulin – and some of the letters were smudged into a blur. I squatted so that I was level with the writing and dug out my magnifying glass to focus. Holding it in front of my eye, I could just about make out, in Uncle Jonah's scratchy handwriting, the words:

Ra
Machi

'Rainbow machine!'

'What?'

'This is his rainbow machine. The one I think he was building. For me.'

* * *

Instead of being annoyed, Mum was delighted when she saw that we'd cleared out the two sheds at the end of the garden.

'That was a job desperately needing doing,' she said when she saw all the tatty old rubbish covering the lawn. 'Thank you both. Now –' she looked across the garden – 'if you could pack it all into black bin bags and put it out front for the Junker drones, I would be exceptionally grateful.'

We both groaned, but got to work, carrying the awkwardly shaped bits and pieces between us and leaving them all out on the scrappy patch of grass in the lane until the garden was cleaner than it had been even before we began.

There had been no battery in the second shed either. Nothing at all. We'd picked through everything but couldn't find it. Not a sign.

'Perhaps it never did work,' Vivi said as we pulled the tarpaulin back over the machine and wheeled it to the back fence, tucking it away under the overhanging braches of a tree in the field behind the house. 'Perhaps he used the battery for something else because the rainbow machine wasn't ever going to work. After all, he burned all his notes on it, didn't he? Why would he do that if it was something that was going to work?'

'I don't know,' I answered, a bit irritated with her. 'I don't understand any of it. But if we can find that battery, we can *see* if it works or not.'

Vivi gave her head a little shake.

'What?' I asked.

'Well . . . the thing is . . . I don't really understand what it could do to help you see colour. Does it make a rainbow? If you turn on the machine, does it make a rainbow in the sky? Because, if that's all it does, you're still not going to be able to see any colours, are you?'

'Perhaps the rainbows are more vivid . . . stronger or something, so that I *can* see them.'

'You can't make rainbows stronger than they are. That doesn't make sense. Rainbows are just rainbows. You can't just turn up the volume on them.'

'How do *you* know?'

'I just do. It's obvious.'

'Well, perhaps it doesn't *make* a rainbow,' I spat. 'Perhaps I have to put my face in the funnel part and it will cure me.'

Vivi smiled.

'Anyway, what do you care?' I ducked, avoiding the branches. 'It doesn't matter to you. You can see every colour there is. You don't care about whether or not I can see colours. It doesn't bother you. You can just go through your life admiring the sky and the sun and the flowers. I can't.'

'That's not fair!' she said, her eyes beginning to fill with tears. 'Of course I care.'

'No, you don't! You sit up there in your room, watching

the sky flying past, poking your telescope into the stars and talking to no one but your bloody parrot.'

Vivi marched quickly off into the lane, her shoulders high and tight. As she went around the corner she didn't even bother to look back at me.

10

Invisible Ink

I hardly slept that night. I felt so guilty that my pillow seemed to become shapeless and lumpy and impossible to rest my head on. I wondered about going down into the garden and investigating where the pipe went, but I realised that I would probably wake Mum and then I'd have to own up about the rainbow machine. So in the early hours – having finally given up on sleep altogether – I grabbed my QWERTY and swiped it out of standby mode. I sat up in bed and projected news bulletins onto the wall. The scrolling headlines didn't do anything to cheer me up.

ONE HUNDRED AND TWENTY BRITISH SOLDIERS KILLED DURING SKIRMISHES IN NORTHERN HUNGARY.

BRITISH TANK REGIMENT ALMOST COMPLETELY WIPED OUT AFTER AMBUSH BY ENEMY TROOPS IN MAASTRICHT.

DESALINATION UNIT IN EASTBOURNE RAIDED AND DESTROYED BY NORTH AFRICAN PIRATES.

UK WATER PRODUCTION DOWN BY 12% SINCE LAST YEAR.

I kept the sound low and watched footage of soldiers under attack in the centre of Turin. Huge smoky explosions followed by lots of shouting and running. Guns and helmets. Armoured vehicles scrunching over rubble. Women shielding young children in corners of derelict buildings.

I turned my QWERTY off.

Miserable stuff.

As usual.

I hadn't heard from my dad in nearly three months. The last time I talked to him, he was on three-day leave in Zurich. He buzzed me on my QWERTY and kept telling me how much he missed Mum and me. I couldn't see his face clearly – the signal kept being interrupted because of the army's encryption software – but he looked OK. A bit sadder around the eyes than normal and with more stubble on his chin than he usually had – which is understandable when you think he's been off fighting for nearly two years now – but otherwise he looked OK. I asked him what it was like, fighting in places he'd never even heard of before. He said that it was weird but that you got used to it. I asked him what food and water they were giving him, and he insisted that the army fed and watered its troops well and that Mum and I didn't have anything to worry about. I wanted to ask him loads of things, but I didn't get the chance because the encryption software cut us off and wouldn't allow us to reconnect.

That was three months ago and I haven't heard from him since.

What if he doesn't come back? I ask myself sometimes. *What if he never comes back?*

Then I tell myself to stop asking myself stupid questions.

I must have eventually dropped off because, before I knew it, I was waking up with a *reeeaally* terrible horrible thirst.

Of course, everybody wakes up thirsty. Well, everybody's *always* thirsty. All day long. Twenty-four/seven, three-six-five. Everybody talks with that click in their voice because of the dryness of their mouth and lips that look like jigsaws. Tongues are always darting in and out, trying to spread around what little moisture there is. And everyone's dirty. Don't forget dirty. And smelly. Nothing and nobody is ever truly, properly clean nowadays. Restricting water supplies does that to you, you know. Makes you thirsty and dirty. Thirsty, dirty, smelly and desperate.

But on this particular morning, my throat was even drier than it normally was. Perhaps I'd sweated more than usual in the night. Yes, that must have been it. I'd lost water in the night through sweating. In fact my pillow seemed especially damp with sweat.

Downstairs, Mum had to let me have some of her allocation since I'd used up so much of mine just the day before, and I stuffed down my breakfast of eggs and potato fritters before we jumped in the car and she drove us to the city centre.

At Trinity, Vivi was perched on the weird fountain thing reading a book that looked way too complicated for someone of our age. She glanced up when she saw me approaching, then her eyes seemed to quickly jump back into the book.

'I like your nail varnish,' I said. I wasn't entirely sure she was wearing any, but I thought girls liked you to say that sort of stuff.

'It's edible.' She waggled a finger at me. 'Blueberry flavour.'

'Not good if you're a biter then!'

'True.'

'I'm sorry,' I said. 'I'm *reeeeally* sorry. I was an idiot yesterday. I didn't mean any of it.'

Slowly she closed her book and put it down on the crumbling wall beside her. 'I know,' she said, sounding the same as she always did. 'You were just kicking out because we couldn't find the battery. You were frustrated. I realise that.' She hopped off the wall and took the book down. 'Anyway, I was thinking . . .'

'What?' I was amazed. I'd thought I was going to have to do some really quite serious begging to win her round.

But she appeared to have got over it already. Was she pretending? I wasn't sure. I watched her closely.

'I was thinking that you were right. There must be a power source for that machine somewhere. Must be. Anything else just doesn't add up.' We walked across the courtyard. 'And I think I know where it might be.'

'Where?' I asked. Looking at her face, I could see that she had spent a good part of last night thinking this all through. She'd put the argument aside, not necessarily because she wasn't hurt by it, but because there was something more interesting – more enthralling – to think about. A puzzle. Vivi's brain had knocked Vivi's emotions away like an irritating buzzing fly.

'Under the ground,' she replied. 'In that pipe thing under your garden.'

We stood in the empty shed, looking at the floor. It wasn't like the floor in the sheds that I'd seen in other places. Other sheds had a rubbish rectangular piece of cork as a floor, something that would start to rot as soon as it got even the slightest bit damp. But the flooring in this shed was more solid – actual real planks of wood that ran all the way along its length. They were secured in place with screws, so I had to borrow one of the screwdrivers that I found in a pot in the utility area of the house.

The pipe seemed to run under the far end of the shed, so I started there. I notched the screwdriver into the head of the first screw and twisted. It came out quite easily so I got to work on the other screws, one in each corner. A couple of minutes later I'd removed all of the screws in the first plank, so I wedged the end of the tool into a crack and levered it out of position.

A hole. A gap. Beneath the shed. A deep, dark hole into which I could extend my arm and still not touch the ground below.

'What is it?' Vivi asked, somewhere behind me.

'It's a sort of . . . a sort of chamber.'

I quickly unscrewed the next plank and the next one. Now I could push my head down into the hole. The air beneath felt cold on my face and I looked around. Now, most people would have needed a torch to see into that black pit. Not me. As I'm sure you remember (because I've already told you!), my eyes are brilliant in dim light. I can make out shapes and detail that not many people can.

The chamber turned out to be a small room with a brick floor and brick walls to which moss was clinging. I peered down into each of the corners (having to almost twist over onto myself to see into the corners still under the floor of the shed) and could see nothing at all. It was completely empty.

Then, suddenly, a flicker in my left eye. I turned to see where it had come from and I could just about make out a box shape on the wall. The battery? I tried to focus on it and then – flash – another flicker came from the box.

I pulled my head out of the hole and hurriedly started removing the next few planks of wood.

'What's down there?' Vivi asked impatiently.

I dumped another plank near her feet and ignored the question. 'Go round the side of the house,' I said. 'Against the wall is a rusty stepladder. Bring it here.'

Without any more questions she ran out of the shed.

The boards came up easily and eventually I lifted the last one covering the pit.

Vivi bashed the stepladder into the shed. There was very little space in which to manoeuvre, so the first time she brought it in we had to take it back out into the garden and turn it so that we could lower it into the hole the right way round. I wedged the bottom end of the ladder into the far corner and wobbled it to make sure it was secure. It was, so I went down first and Vivi followed.

'It's dark. I can't see.'

It was true. It was definitely dark. The roof of the shed above blocked out most of the sky and only a little light got through the grubby windows.

'Use your QWERTY,' I told her.

Vivi tapped the screen. Then she tapped it again.

'It's not working,' she said.

'The torch function?'

'No. All of it.'

I tutted. 'You need to get a new one. Here, use mine.' I unstrapped my QWERTY from my wrist and handed it to her.

'Yours isn't working either.'

'What?'

'Look.' She handed it back to me and I swiped my finger across it. Nothing. It was utterly dead.

'I don't understand. It was fine last night.'

'Well, it's not now.'

'Weird.' I slipped it back onto my wrist.

The little light on the box flickered again. Vivi noticed it too. I leaned forward and touched it. Suddenly the whole box seemed to glow, filling the chamber with light.

The box was a numerical keypad, with a small screen above it with a flashing cursor. It was then that I noticed that most of the fourth wall was not a wall at all. It was made of the same shiny metal that we'd discovered beneath the lawn, but with a slight, almost infinitesimal, gap straight down the middle.

'It's a door,' I spluttered. 'It's a door into the pipe . . . No, wait. It's not a pipe. It's a tunnel.'

Vivi's mouth had fallen wide open but her eyes were bright with excitement.

'We need the code,' she said. 'What's the code?'

I tapped some random numbers into the pad just to see what would happen. After the sixth digit the pad gave a long, critical beep like it was telling me off.

TWO ATTEMPTS LEFT . . . scrolled across the screen.

'Oh no.'

'If we don't get the right code, it will shut itself down, won't it?' Vivi asked. 'And then we'll never open the door.' She gave me a glare. 'Why did you have to go and waste one of the attempts?'

'Er, possibly because I didn't *know* I was wasting one of them!' I replied sarcastically. 'Possibly because the rules aren't exactly scribbled on the wall.'

'No need to be like that,' she said grumpily.

I ignored her and tried to think. What would it be? Assuming Uncle Jonah had been the one to put the door here, what code would he have set? It could have been anything. I didn't exactly know how Uncle Jonah's mind worked – I hadn't known him that well. Without more information, the random numbers I'd just punched in were as likely as anything else. Surely he must have left a clue somewhere.

In desperation I looked around the walls in the hope that I might find a small strip of paper with the numbers on. There was nothing. No clue. Nothing to point you in the right direction.

'Don't put any more numbers in until we know what it is,' Vivi said, coming in closer and looking at the blinking box herself. 'We can't waste any more chances.'

'I realise that now.' I turned to go back up the ladder.

'Where are you going?'

'Outside. Standing around down here isn't going to help us, is it?'

In the garden, I walked the length of the metal strip.

'How far back do you think this tunnel goes?' asked Vivi as she came up next to me. 'Do you think it goes all the way under the house? Or even further?'

'I don't know,' I mumbled. The last couple of days had started off like an adventure but had just become frustrating. Everything seemed to just fall apart the more you looked at it. 'Perhaps it's all just a complete waste of time. I mean, is there even anything under there?'

'Of course there is!' she almost screamed. 'Why would Dr Bloom go to the bother of hiding that tunnel away? There must be something incredibly important the other side of the door. Can't you see?'

I kicked at a loose edge of grass with the tip of my shoe.

'Come on.' She softened her voice. 'Let's go back down and look at it again. There must be a way of working it out.'

I sighed and walked over to the shed. As I got closer I looked up. On the thin strip at the top of the door frame somebody had written something.

'What's that?'

'What's what?'

'That.' I pointed. 'Something's written there.'

'I can't see anything.'

'Look. Just there.' I got on tiptoe and tried to see. Struggling, I fished the magnifying glass out from inside my shirt and held it up. The word *ADDOBUS* – all capitals – was scrawled in fine wiry handwriting across the rough-cut wood. 'See?'

'There's nothing there.' Vivi held her hand up to shield her eyes from the light.

'Yes, there is. Look.' I spelled it out for her. 'A.D.D.O.B.U.S.'

She looked at me as if I was mad. 'Auden, there's nothing there.'

'You can't see that?'

'No. Honestly, I think you're seeing things.'

My mind suddenly jumped back to something that happened a couple of years before. A kid at school brought in a spy kit. Just lots of stupid plastic junk designed to occupy an eight-year-old for about half an hour. See-behind-you shades; an earpiece that claimed to help you listen in on conversations the other side of the yard; sheets of codes to decipher. That sort of thing.

And a pen of invisible ink. Ink that could only be seen after being exposed to a blast of hot air.

I remember everyone gathering around as he scribbled something down on a sheet of paper and then held it up for us all to see. Of course, nobody could see what he'd written. Except me. I could see it. As clear as the tip of my nose. Yet another of the peculiar benefits of my condition, I suppose. Stupidly, I told them all what it said. If I'd had any sense at all I'd've just kept my mouth shut and pretended to be normal like everyone else. But I didn't. The kid who'd written it looked at me like I was some sort of cheat and then, when everyone else had found out that I was right, they all looked at me like I was some sort of freak. Which is a bit odd, because if you saw that happen in a comic or a film it would be obvious that the person was a superhero. But in real life, nobody believes in superheroes. Only weirdos. Weirdos are easy to believe in.

'It's invisible ink,' I said.

'You mean there *is* something written there?'

I smiled, remembering telling Uncle Jonah about the incident at school, and him finding it incredibly funny. 'Uncle Jonah put it there because he knew I'd be able to read it.'

'What does it say again?' I could see the spark in Vivi's eyes flaring up again.

'ADDOBUS.'

'What does that mean? It's a pity our QWERTYs aren't – oh. It's working again.'

I looked at mine. The screen was glowing away. 'Mine's working too. Strange.'

Vivi tapped on her QWERTY. 'ADDOBUS doesn't mean anything. Not according to this.'

We stood there in silence for a minute.

'There must be a way of working out what it means,' Vivi said. 'Do you think it might be an anagram?' She used her QWERTY to run the letters through an Etherweb anagram checker. 'No. Nothing. Gah! This is annoying!'

We both stood at the door to the shed and stared up at the strip of wood.

'Hold on.' It was Vivi again. 'You said it was written in capitals, yes?'

'Mmm.'

'Well . . . that might mean the letters stand for something.'

'Yes, but what?'

'I don't know . . . Wait . . . DOB. You see that all the time, don't you?'

'Do you?'

'Yes. D.O.B. Date of birth. You always see it on forms.'

She was right. 'So what do the other let—'

A light-bulb moment.

'What?'

'A.D. Auden Dare,' I said. 'Auden Dare's date of birth. My date of birth!' I rushed into the shed and practically jumped down the ladder.

'Wait, Auden . . .'

I punched my date of birth into the keypad. The pad gave another long critical beep and *ONE ATTEMPT LEFT* . . . scrolled across the screen.

'No!'

Vivi came down the ladder after me. 'Wait! We need to think it all through.' At the bottom of the ladder she dusted some rust off her hands. 'ADDOBUS. Auden Dare. Date of birth. What about the U and the S? You rushed in too quickly and forgot about the U and the S?'

I thought. 'The only thing I can think of is the USA. The United States. Of America.'

'That's it!' Vivi cried.

'What is?'

'In the US they write their dates all awkwardly. In this country we always write the day then the month and then the year. Over there they swap the day and the month over.'

'Why'd they do that?' I asked.

'No idea. But surely that's what it means. Auden Dare's date of birth in the US format. Go on, try it.'

'It's our last attempt. Are you sure?'

Vivi looked doubtful for a second.

Before she had time to answer I tapped it in, swapping the month and the date around.

A beep. A much nicer beep, almost like it was congratulating me.

OPEN . . . filled the screen and –

The doors separated, withdrawing into the walls on either side.

'You did it!' Vivi squealed.

'*We* did it,' I corrected her.

However, our joy didn't last very long. Beyond the doors was a squarish metal tunnel and we stepped into it, the clanging sound of our feet echoing around the space. The tunnel was only about three metres long and ended . . . at another door! Another *closed* door. With another number pad on the wall next to it.

'Oh no.'

'Not again!'

This pad was slightly different. There were no numbers or letters to press. It was just a screen. And on the screen were sixteen glowing dots. The dots were not in any sort of order, they seemed to just be randomly thrown all over the place, and some of them were slightly bigger than the others.

'What's all this about now?' I asked, barely managing to hide the fed-up tone in my voice.

But Vivi didn't answer. She was staring hard at the arrangement of dots on the screen.

'Don't tell me you can see a pattern in them!' I laughed. 'They're just random, aren't they?'

Still she didn't answer. After about a minute she grinned. 'In the letters that Dr Bloom wrote to us . . .'

'Yes?'

'Well, he gave us the clue for finding this tunnel, didn't he?'

'So?'

'Well, he also told you that if you needed to find out anything about stars and space to ask Six Six, yes?'

'Uh-huh.' I nodded.

'When did you say your birthday was?' Vivi asked me.

'The second of March.'

'March second . . . That makes you a Pisces.' She squinted at the screen again. 'Pisces. Yes!'

She moved closer to the screen and put a fingertip on one of the dots, then slid it across to another. A line appeared on the screen tracing her movements. 'This is the constellation of Pisces.' She dragged her finger across the screen to another of the dots, then another, like some sort of dot-to-dot puzzle. 'You know what a constellation is, don't you?'

'Of course I do. It's all about the stars, isn't it?'

'It's a collection of stars. This one – the one connected to your birthday – is Pisces. It's supposed to look like two fish jumping out of water.'

The shape she was drawing on the screen looked nothing whatsoever like two fish jumping out of water to me. If anything it looked like a bent stick. With a leaf still attached to one end.

Vivi did a sort of loop at the bottom right-hand side of the screen, linking up the last of the dots, and then stood back. The image remained fixed on the screen before . . .

Beep.

OPEN . . .

The doors pulled apart.

'You, Vivi Rookmini,' I said, laughing, 'are a genius!'

'Oh, I don't know about that. It was obvious really.'

Beyond this door was another small room. There were still no lights, and when Vivi tried to access the torch function on her QWERTY it wasn't working again. I looked at mine – nothing.

We stepped into the room and I suddenly froze.

'What? What is it?' Vivi couldn't see a thing.

But I could.

Something was sitting on the floor at the far end of the room.

'Tell me,' Vivi asked again. 'What is it?'

I turned to look at her and found myself whispering my reply.

'It's a man.'

PART THREE
RED

11

Paragon

Vivi shone the torch that she'd found in the utility room over the figure slumped against the metal wall.

'What is it? Is it alive?'

I knelt down beside whatever it was and looked it up and down.

'Is it a drone?' Vivi asked.

'Funny-looking drone,' I said. 'I've never seen a drone shaped like a human being before. Have you?'

'No. Perhaps he's a new sort of drone. One they've not brought out yet.'

'Perhaps.'

After the shock of seeing a man lying in the small chamber, I had edged myself forward carefully and seen that it was, in fact, not a man at all. It was man-shaped – that was true – but it was made of metal and wires and lights. Its 'back' was resting against the wall, and its 'head' was nodding forward onto its 'chest' as if it was asleep. Vivi had run off to get a torch and returned waving it around like an excitable swordfighter.

'What's it doing here?' The day seemed to be filled to the top with questions.

'I don't know,' I answered, nudging the thing with my finger.

'Why hide it away down here? Why keep it under the ground in a secret tunnel, with two sets of security doors to protect it? Come to think of it, there's obviously something creating an electro-magnetic disturbance down here, stopping our QWERTYs working. That can't be a coincidence. Why? Why go to all this trouble to hide a drone?'

'I don't think it is a drone. I think it's more than that. I think it's a robot.'

'A bot? But bots build cars and boats and planes. They stitch clothes together – very badly. They're machines bolted to the floors of factories. They don't move. They're unthinking things with a single job that they're designed to do. And they certainly don't look like humans.'

I poked its arm again. Nothing happened. The metal was bright and cold and I could see my face in it.

'Is it . . .' Vivi struggled to find the right word, '. . . dead?'

That was when I noticed the button. Big and round and positioned somewhere you might describe as being just under the collarbone. I imagined it to be green – whatever green is. Green for go.

'Should you be doing that?' Vivi watched as my finger headed towards the button. 'Shouldn't we tell someone about this? An adult?'

I was excited. This whole situation was set up for *me*. Not anyone else. Uncle Jonah had known that when he died Mum would inherit the house and that I would be with her. He used *my* birthday as the code on the first door and *my* star sign on the second. It was all set up for *me* to find. Me. Not some random adult.

I looked up at Vivi. 'Er . . . no!'

I hit the button.

The robot started to whirr – a high-pitched whirr a bit like when Etherweb boxes at school are activated. It whirred and then it hissed slightly. Lights flickered on the front of its 'chest' and along its 'arms'.

'I think I found the on switch.' I grinned at Vivi who had taken a step backwards.

Suddenly, lights where its eyes would be flashed into existence and it turned to 'look' at me. It felt weird to have this thing with its bright inhuman eyes staring at me and, for a brief moment, I was scared. What had I done?

The head swivelled slowly and took in Vivi who gave a sort of tiny dog-like whimper, her trembling hands making the torch shake – the light twitching in the tiny room.

Then the robot's body shifted, easing its weight forward until the legs bent back on themselves before straightening again, pushing it upright. All accompanied by hisses and whirrs and tiny internal bleeps that bounced loudly around the walls.

Soon it was standing up. And – *whoa!* – was it tall. The top of its head was only a few inches below the ceiling, making it six foot five at the very least.

I got up from the floor and went over to Vivi.

'Perhaps you'd better . . . turn it off now . . . don't you think?' Her anxious eyes seemed to be begging me. 'Perhaps we'd better stop . . . now. Yes?'

'Not yet,' I whispered. 'Please. It'll be OK.'

The robot's head twisted and tilted as it took in its surroundings.

'Hello!' I said, and it jerked back to look at me. 'Er . . . hello.' I don't know why – I'd never even done it with a real human being before – but I extended my hand towards the bot to shake its 'hand'. 'Hello.'

Its glowing eyes stared at me for a few seconds before . . .

The pneumatic or hydraulic pistons or whatever they were in its arm lifted the hand up towards me, and the fingers curled around mine. For a moment I was worried that they were going to crush my hand, but the fingers stopped moving and the hand felt gentle wrapped around my own.

'Hello,' I repeated, and tried shifting my arm up and down – shaking hands. To my surprise the robot's forearm moved too. Easily. Softly.

'Hi,' the robot said.

I don't know what I was expecting. I suppose I was expecting it to be a bit like Migishoo – copying, repeating back whatever I said and not properly understanding. The fact it didn't – it said 'Hi' not 'Hello' – surprised me. Unnerved me.

Vivi came forward a little.

'My name is Auden Dare. And this is Vivi Rookmini.'

The robot lifted its own hand and stared at it, twisting it around in front of its face like it was trying to understand what it was.

'Hi Audendare,' it said, still inspecting its hand. 'Hi Vivirookmini.' It said our names like there was no gap in between them.

'What is *your* name?' Vivi asked, trying to be brave but the shiver in her voice came through.

The robot dropped its hand to its side and looked straight at us.

'My name?' it asked. It seemed to be thinking, like it wasn't sure. Perhaps it didn't have a name. I mean, why would you give a bot a name? I could see Vivi was thinking exactly the same thing and clearly felt a bit foolish for asking, her eyes dancing between the robot and the floor.

'My name,' said the robot, 'is Paragon.'

'Paragon?'

'Yes. Paragon. My name is Paragon.'

It spoke (if that is the right word to use for a mechanical, automated lump of metal with a grille for a mouth) in an American accent, like it had just walked out of a movie.

It took a small step forward and twisted its torso about to take in the small room in which it had been left.

'Good to meet you, Audendare and Vivirookmini.'

Vivi gave a small laugh. The voice wasn't the sort you would imagine coming out of a robot. You would think that a machine would talk with a stuttering monotone. Some-Thing-A-Lit-Tle-Like-This. But it didn't. Its voice was smooth and clear and kind of . . . normal.

'Paragon,' Vivi said. 'What a lovely name.'

'Is it?' I looked at her.

'Yes. A paragon is a perfect thing. A shining example. A model for others to follow.'

'Thanks, Miss Dictionary.' I turned to the machine in front of me. 'Who made you? Was it Jonah Bloom? Did he put you here?'

A couple of lights flickered on the face.

'I,' Paragon started, 'do not know. I do not have that information. Sorry, Audendare.'

'That's all right.' For some reason – even though I knew that this thing in front of me was nothing more than wires and circuit boards – I found myself not wanting him – sorry, *it* – to feel as if it had anything to apologise for. Doesn't make much sense I know, but if something looks and acts like a human being, it feels as if you should treat it like a human being. I tried to shake the silly idea out of me. This was, after all, something manmade. A tool. That's all. Just a tool. A tool with pretend arms and pretend legs.

138

'What job were you built to do?' I asked. 'What is your purpose?'

It paused like it was thinking again. 'I do not have that information, Audendare. I do not know my purpose.'

'But you must do. There must be something in your computer brain that tells you what it is you are meant to do. Every bot has some kind of role.'

The machine in front of me seemed to stiffen slightly. 'A *bot* is a device created by humans to undertake simple construction tasks. I don't believe I am *that*.' It sounded offended. 'I do not know for what reason I was created . . . but I am certainly not a bot.'

Vivi smiled at me.

'What about a drone then?' I said. 'Are you just a drone?'

It tilted its head like it was thinking the idea over.

'Nope.'

Nope? What sort of a word was 'nope' for a robot? 'Negative' or something would be more appropriate, wouldn't it?

'Well, what *are* you then?'

'I don't know.' It looked around again. 'Tell me, Audendare and Vivirookmini . . . where am I?'

The thing climbed the ladder with ease and had to duck as it made its way out of the shed into the bright light of late morning. It scanned around, taking everything in – the house, the garden, the sky. Hopefully no nosy neighbours.

'There is another sky,' Paragon started. 'Ever serene and fair. And there is another sunshine. Though it be darkness there.'

'What?' I asked.

'It's poetry,' Vivi said, staring up at the strange creature revealed in all its metallic wonder before us. I didn't know the first thing about engineering, but you could see that it was lovingly and precisely crafted. 'He's reciting poetry. Aren't you?'

'Emily Dickinson,' Paragon answered.

Poetry? Why bother programming a machine with poetry? What's the point of poetry? Poetry doesn't collect your rubbish. Poetry doesn't fix your TV. Poetry doesn't pump up the tyres on your car. A machine that recites poetry is a waste of vital electronic equipment, surely? A waste of valuable resources.

I didn't say anything. There were things I wanted that I thought Paragon might be able to give me.

'Do you recognise this place?' I asked it.

'Er . . .' It seemed to doubt itself. 'Er . . . nope.'

'You sure?'

'I . . . don't . . . think so. Nope. Definitely not.'

Again I was confused. A true machine would instantly know and would be able to instantly tell you. That's how computers work. There's a YES. There's a NO. And nothing in between. Definitely no Er . . . So why the element of doubt in its 'voice'?

Paragon wandered away from us, peering about at some of the rubbish still left in the grass, picking it up and turning it over and dropping it. I turned to Vivi and told her my thoughts.

'There's a thing called fuzzy logic,' she said. 'I read about it once. It's where you give a computer a chance of getting things wrong. It's a way of making a computer's brain more like a human brain.'

'What's the point in that?' I asked. It didn't make much sense to me.

She shrugged.

'So even though it's acting like it's human . . . it's still just a robot.'

She shrugged again.

I led Paragon into the house – luckily Mum was at work. I showed it the sitting room and the kitchen and the utility room.

'You're certain you've never been here before?' Perhaps – at some point – the fuzzy logic might turn in my favour and reveal the truth.

'Nope. I do not recall ever having been here before. In fact . . . I do not recall ever having been *anywhere* before.' He stressed the 'anywhere' perfectly. 'This is the first place I have ever been.'

'What do you mean?'

'He's been reprogrammed,' Vivi said somewhere behind me. 'Your uncle must have wiped his memory before putting him down below the shed.'

'And you've never heard of Jonah Bloom?' I asked again.

'Nope. No idea. I know the tale of Jonah and the Whale. Do you know it?'

I sighed. 'No, I don't, and to be honest I don't care. What about the rainbow machine? Have you any idea where the battery for the rainbow machine is hidden?'

'Sorry, Audendare . . . I don't know anything about a rainbow machine. I can tell you how rainbows are made –'

'No.'

Paragon straightened again, as if it was slightly taken aback. 'O-kay.' It turned to look at Vivi and, even though it didn't have eyebrows, it appeared to raise them.

I marched over to Paragon and punched the button that had started it up in the first place. The electric hum died along with the flashing lights and the machine stopped dead still where it stood.

'What did you do that for?' Vivi frowned.

I didn't have an answer.

'Just because he doesn't know what his purpose is, doesn't mean he hasn't got one.'

'Will you *pleease* stop referring to it as "he". It's a thing. Not a person. It's a mass of wire and metal acting like it's human. That's all. Just a slightly more advanced lawnmower or something. Stop calling it a "he".'

Vivi went quiet. We both stood there staring at the robot, stuck completely still, halfway through a movement.

'Anyway,' Vivi said quietly, 'why does it have to have a purpose? Is that the reason why everything exists? Because it's useful? And if it's just a machine, why did you shake its hand down there?'

'I was confused for a second. I wasn't thinking properly.'

'Well, what are you going to do about him? You can't just leave him here in the middle of your utility room. Your mother will be back from work later and I don't think she'll be all that pleased to see a robot blocking up her access to the back door.'

Mum. I thought for a second. Should I tell her about Paragon? Should I show it to her? What would she say? She would probably say that we should let the authorities know. Then it would be taken away. And even though it said that it knew nothing about a rainbow machine or its power source, I wasn't convinced. Perhaps it had orders from my uncle to hold back on certain pieces of information and not to reveal them for some reason. Perhaps, even though it had – according to Vivi – been reprogrammed, the information might be still there somewhere, deeply scratched into its memory bank. All I knew was that if the authorities took this . . . thing . . . away, I would probably never find the battery and never get the rainbow machine to work.

'We'd better take it back underground. For now,' I said. 'I don't think we should tell anyone about this.'

'No,' Vivi agreed. 'But I was thinking . . .'

'What?'

'Perhaps it's true that he has never been here – to this house – before. I mean, it's unlikely that Dr Bloom actually built him here.'

'*It*,' I corrected her. 'It's a *thing*.'

She ignored me. 'But perhaps he might remember *another* place. If we were to take him to places he might have a memory of, then it's not impossible he might have some idea of why he was built. Yes?'

'Yes. I suppose.' I stopped and thought. 'Hold on – you're not suggesting we take it to Uncle Jonah's rooms in Trinity, are you?'

'Well . . . ideally, yes.'

'But . . . look at it. It's massive. How are we meant to get it there?'

She thought for a minute. 'OK. You're right. Perhaps instead we could show him Cambridge from a distance. If we go up one of the hills not far from here, we might be able to show him the city and hopefully he'll remember why he was built.'

'OK. But tomorrow. Not now. For now I think it'd better go back into its room under the shed.' I hit the on switch and the robot seemed to immediately continue the movement it had started before I'd turned it off.

'Hi again Audendare and Vivirookmini. How are you both?'

'You're going back underground,' I said.

'Hmm?'

'You heard.'

Vivi stepped towards Paragon. 'We'll come back and see you tomorrow. We're going to take you out and see if we can work out what your purpose is.'

'*Tomorrow, and tomorrow, and tomorrow,*
Creeps in this petty pace from day to day.'

'Poetry?' asked Vivi.

'Shakespeare,' replied Paragon.

'Will you please pack it in with the poetry!' I sighed. 'And get yourself back into the shed. Now.'

The machine made its way without complaint back to the hidden room under the garden.

'You promise you will return tomorrow?' it said in the gloom of the chamber, and it almost sounded pitiful. 'I think I would like it if you were to help me find what it was I was built for. That sounds good. And in exchange perhaps I could –'

'Yes, yes,' I said dismissively, and punched the off button one more time.

12

Purpose

'Good morning, Audendare.' The robot seemed to be grinning out of the darkness at me.

'Look . . . er . . .'

'Paragon.'

'Yes. Paragon.' Giving a thing a name felt funny. 'Look, my name isn't Audendare.'

'Isn't it?'

'No. It's Auden.'

'Oh, I see.' It nodded like it understood. 'Your first name is Auden and your last name is Dare. Am I right?'

'Yes. That's right.'

'That makes sense.' It moved its head closer as if it was sharing a secret with me. 'To be honest . . . I did think that Audendare was quite an unusual name. And I suppose Vivirookmini's name is really Vivi . . .' it paused for a second,' Rookmini. Yes? Two separate names again?'

'Yes.' I was having a conversation with a tin can.

Paragon crawled up the ladder and stepped back out

146

onto the patchy lawn where Vivi greeted it like it was a long-lost uncle or something.

'So?' it said. 'What's the plan?'

'Well,' Vivi began, 'I think that it might be a good idea to just see if it becomes obvious what you were constructed for.'

'And to try to see if you really do know anything about the rainbow machine and how to work it,' I added quickly. That, to me, was much more important than finding out what this glorified wheelbarrow was for. If Uncle Jonah had *really* found a way of fixing my problem, then obviously I was keen to try it out. After all, Paragon had probably just been a little side project for Jonah – a hobby – like the way some people rebuild old cars or weave willow baskets. No, Paragon itself wasn't important in my eyes (so to speak). It was what it might know or be able to do that was exciting to me.

You see, I know I rather go on about how it doesn't matter not being able to see colour, and how it makes me special in a way. Like I'm a superhero. And sometimes I really believe that. When I'm happy and things are going right, I feel like it's kind of a good thing not to know the difference between red and green. I can persuade myself that things for me are simplified and, in a sense, colour is just a complication. Those are the good days.

But there are many other times when I don't feel like that at all. When all I can think is how incomplete I actually am. How much I'm missing out on. Those are the bad days. The days I feel depressed or angry. Sometimes the anger slips out and I might punch my pillow or kick a wall. And sometimes the anger turns in – and that's a lot worse.

I don't like those days.

'And how are we going to do that?' Paragon replied, its head tilted a bit.

'Vivi thinks we should go for a walk,' I moaned.

'A walk?'

'I know. Mad, isn't it?'

Vivi stuck her tongue out at me. 'Yes. Just to see if it gets you thinking. Try and tease out what it is you were designed for.'

'And if you know about the rainbow machine,' I repeated quickly.

'O-kay! Let's get going!' It started to walk.

'Hang on, hang on,' I stuck my hand up in front of its chest and it stopped. 'We can't exactly take you out looking like that.'

'Like what?'

'Like *that*. Like a robot. Everyone will be staring at you. Then the authorities will probably take you away from us.'

'Yes. And we can't risk any of the Scoot drones or the Ariel drones spotting you either,' added Vivi.

'Oh, I wouldn't be too worried about any drones,' said Paragon. 'I can take care of them.'

'You can take care of them?'

'Yep.'

'How?'

'Whoever it was that built me gave me an EMD – that's an electro-magnetic disabler. I can block any electronic device within two hundred metres. Any drones that pass by will simply stop functioning correctly. So don't you go worrying about drones.'

Both Vivi and I glanced down at our QWERTYs at exactly the same time. I don't know about Vivi's, but mine certainly wasn't working properly.

'Yes, well, that's good news about the drones,' Vivi said, 'but we also have to worry about any people seeing you.'

'So? What do you suggest Vivi . . .' he paused, 'Rookmini?'

'Ta-dah!' She pulled a long dirty-looking trench coat with a big-buckled belt from behind her back. 'This used to belong to one of the professors at Trinity. He didn't want it any more so he gave it to my mother in case she could find some use for it. That and –' she revealed the contents of her other hand – 'this!' It was a hat. A large, wide-brimmed thing that would shade your eyes from even the sunniest of suns. 'I thought you could wear them.'

I shook my head. I couldn't believe we were about to put clothes on a walking tumble dryer.

'I . . . don't think I'm designed to wear clothes,' Paragon said, looking from Vivi to me then back again. 'Am I?'

'No. You're not,' I answered. 'You're a machine. You're not human.'

'Oh.'

Was it just me or did it sound hurt?

And why did I feel a teeny bit guilty?

'Anyway –' Vivi came forward and held the coat and the hat out to Paragon – 'we can't go out without you wearing something, so . . .'

Paragon took the clothes from her. It dropped the hat on the floor and seemed to throw the coat around itself. Considering it had never before put a coat on, it did so gracefully and slickly with not even a single struggle around the shoulders. I was impressed.

Then it bent to the ground and kind of flicked the hat, which rolled itself up the length of its outstretched right arm, bounced off the shoulder and onto the head, where it fell softly and securely.

'Wow.' Vivi was open-mouthed.

'Cool,' I found myself saying with a smile on my face.

Paragon tugged the hat down gently. 'Any good? How's it look?'

'Suits you,' said Vivi, before popping together the buttons on the coat and pulling the belt tightly around Paragon's torso. 'You look very smart.'

We walked across the patchy fields of wheat that bent in the slight, warm breeze, past the tall pyramid-shaped irrigation pylons and along the unkempt, unused tarmac roads. Both Vivi and I thought it best to avoid people if we could; even clothed, Paragon looked a bit odd and we were sure to get the occasional funny glance. So we headed out away from the city and into the countryside.

'Perhaps you were designed to fix the roads,' I said after almost twisting an ankle in one of the many potholes that littered the lane along which we were walking. 'And even if you weren't, they need to design *something* to fix the roads.'

'Nope,' Paragon answered. 'Definitely not fixing roads. That's not me. I feel I have a greater purpose than that.'

'You don't *feel* anything,' I said, slightly irritated once again by the way this machine was pretending to be human. 'You just *think* you feel. Well, actually, you don't even think. You just turn switches on and off in your computer brain. That's all. It's just combinations of switches and pistons and stuff.'

Paragon stopped walking and turned to face me. 'I have to say, Auden, you really are horribly analytical.'

'What?'

'Well,' it continued, 'you seem intent on reducing everything to its basic, unimaginative, constituent parts.'

'Hold on, are you –'

'Don't listen to him,' Vivi interrupted, grabbing Paragon by the sleeve. 'He's just a misery-guts. Come on.'

They both walked off, leaving me standing alone in the middle of my pothole.

* * *

The countryside around Cambridge is mostly flat and even – a bit like somebody has taken a massive rolling pin to it, or stamped their huge boot across it – with only the occasional hill or valley, and as the morning eased on we slowly made our way towards one of the hills, topped with a spiky crown of trees.

At one point a pair of Ariel drones drifted by above us, their usually blinking eyes dull and dead, before carrying on into the distance.

'Did they see us?' said Vivi.

'Nope. They didn't see a thing,' Paragon replied. 'Trust me.'

The hill looked quite gentle from the lane and we climbed over the rotten stile into the field of lifeless grass and made our way towards the gritty path that wound its way upwards.

Halfway up, we stopped and turned around to look at the spread of the land below.

'OK.' Vivi – who wasn't as fit as me – struggled to catch her breath. 'So . . . in the distance there . . . you can see Cambridge. Some of those spires belong to the colleges of the university. Which was where Dr Jonah Bloom worked – the man who built you. He was a Fellow at Trinity College . . . ?' She looked at the machine in the hope something might click. But no. There was nothing. 'OK then. All around us you can see the fields. Some growing the corn and wheat for food – those are the ones with the irrigation pylons. Other fields are growing succulents and cactuses . . . cacti . . . er . . .'

'Cacti. Cactuses. Either one's fine,' Paragon confirmed.

'. . . OK. So some of the fields are growing succulents and cacti because they don't require much water and people can buy them to have in their houses. Nobody buys actual flowers any more.' She shielded her eyes against the sun and pointed into the distance. I didn't even bother looking. When it's particularly sunny my eyes struggle to see anything – everything just seems to blur. 'Over there you can see transportable water-storage units. Next to them you can see the recycling plant. Just in the distance on that side there are grain-distribution centres – those warehouse buildings right there – can you see? And if you really squint, you can just about make out the thin line of where the River Cam used to flow. It's not much now of course.' She looked up at Paragon, who was scanning the whole of the horizon. 'Now, does any of that mean anything to you?'

'Nope.' It turned its head and looked slightly further up the hill. 'Although . . .' It stumped up the hill towards a large patch of weeds and grabbed one of the stalky plants, yanking it out of the ground so that its roots dangled uselessly and clods of earth dropped onto the dry path. It came back down and held the plant out towards us.

'What?' I asked.

'Do you know what this is?' it asked back.

'Of course,' I replied as sarcastically as I could manage. 'I'm an expert on useless weeds.'

'Hmm. Sarcasm. Nice.' Paragon gave the long stem with the pointy flower at the top a bit of a shake. 'This is *Verbascum thapsus*. Also known as Aaron's rod. Comes from the family Scrophulariaceae. Biennial. Native to Britain although quite uncommon in both Scotland and Ireland. Generally grows on wasteland – like this. Was once used to treat bronchial difficulties. People would crush it up and put it in a pipe to smoke. Herbal medicine.'

It stood there like it was waiting for us to comment. It was me who broke the silence.

'So?'

'So, what?'

'What's the point in knowing that?'

It looked slightly flustered.

Vivi went alongside Paragon and took the long stem from it. 'Medicine. Perhaps that is why you were made. To treat people. Like a doctor.'

Paragon gave its head a shake. 'I don't think so. I know an awful lot about plants. Not all of them are used for medical purposes.'

'If you know about plants,' I started, 'then you might have been designed for farming.'

Its head carried on shaking. 'No. I know about lots of things. Not just plants.'

154

'What other things do you know?' Vivi said.

'There are too many to list right now. Far too many.'

'Name some,' I ordered.

'Some?'

I sighed. 'Yes. *Some.*'

It gave the impression of thinking for a moment or two. 'OK. I can tell you the Latin and common names of every bird native to Britain and mainland Europe. I can tell you the Latin and common names of every *tree* native to Britain and Europe.'

'You can recite poetry,' Vivi added.

'Yes. I can recall every poem written by all the major European, Asian and North American poets since approximately 3000BC. I can identify and comfortably discuss every single significant piece of art – in all its forms – created over the last two thousand years. I can provide you with a list of constituent gases that make up the atmosphere of every planet in our solar system. I can tell you the quickest route between two places. I can list the members of every single government that held power in every single country of the world over the last three hundred years. I can also tell you the best way to make Welsh rarebit.' It paused. 'That sort of thing.'

'So you can tell us lots of stuff that we can just look up on the Etherweb?' I sniffed. 'Things that I can find out from messing about on my QWERTY.'

'Ah, yes,' Paragon replied. 'But can your QWERTY do

it with a smile on its face?' Paragon pointed comically with both hands to its shiny, metal, unmovable mouth.

'Is that meant to be a joke?' I found myself grinning.

'Of course. As well as being extraordinarily clever I have also been blessed with a tremendously advanced sense of humour!'

'Advanced, ha!' I spun around and stared up at the rest of the hill above us.

'Yes.' Paragon came alongside me and leaned in close. 'A sense of humour that doesn't rely as heavily on sarcasm as that of *other* people I could mention.'

I ignored it and carried on up the hill.

At the top I pushed into the thick, dark wood, picking my way over the fallen rotting timber and slippery moss until I stepped out into a small clearing where brambles seemed to be taking over, snatching at the bottom of my trouser legs like the fingers of a Flute drone. A minute or so later Vivi and Paragon came into the gap, Paragon turning aside and tapping the bark of an ancient-looking tree.

'Engish oak. *Quercus robur.*'

I tutted and Vivi frowned at me.

'What?' I perched myself on the edge of a half-toppled log.

'It's all right, Vivi.' Paragon picked its way over to where I was sitting. 'I'm getting used to him now. I don't think he's particularly impressed by all the things I know.'

'Yes, well –'

But Paragon cut me off – a shockingly rude thing for a robot to do, to my mind. 'I don't think Auden Dare has any time for flowers or trees or poetry, do you? I think he finds it all a little –' it pretended to struggle for the right word – 'useless. Yes. He finds all my knowledge a tad impractical.'

'It's not that –'

But it cut me off again. This time with an enormous flourish and a flick of the trench coat. Within a second the coat was on the floor at the machine's feet.

'Excuse me,' it said, 'but I really feel I need to get this off my chest – if you'll pardon the pun. I've tried to put it off but I just can't any longer.' It jabbed a finger towards the point a little below the on/off button. 'There is a light – just here – that appears not to work. I've a feeling it should be red. Every other light on my body works, but this one does not. I've run diagnostics to try to isolate the problem, to no apparent avail. I initially assumed it was merely a faulty LED, but alas no. I can't even work out what it is connected to. And I'm starting to feel a touch frustrated by it, to be honest.' It turned and took both Vivi and me in before whispering, 'I'm a bit worried about it.'

'It's probably not important.' Vivi talked in the sort of smooth, soothing voice that I used on Sandwich whenever she got a thorn or a piece of glass caught in her paw. 'It's probably something that doesn't *need* to work, or something small that just wasn't finished. I wouldn't worry about it.'

Paragon seemed weirdly reassured. 'You think so, Vivi? Yes, perhaps you're right. It might be just nothing, don't you think?'

A small light that didn't work?! A tiny, almost insignificant thing that didn't seem to stop it from functioning correctly! A *red* light! I found myself virtually hissing in anger. Perhaps it was going to be one of the bad days after all. Paragon noticed.

'Auden? Are you OK?'

'Oh yes, I'm OK. Perfectly fine.'

'You don't sound OK.'

'Oh yes, don't worry about me. Just keep worrying about whether that little light is pink, purple, fluorescent orange with green spots . . .'

'Auden, Auden –' Vivi was clambering towards me.

I was close to tears. 'Maybe it's blue like they say the sky is, or gold like my dad's hair. I should like to see the colour that belongs to my dad's hair. My mother's eyes.'

'You can't see!' The robot sounded almost as upset as I did. 'That's what it is, isn't it? You can't see colour. You have –'

'Achromatopsia,' I blurted out.

Upon hearing the word 'achromatopsia', Paragon did something strange. Something it hadn't done before. It suddenly jerked to attention. Not with the smooth human-like movements that it had always used so far, but with stiff, quick and regular actions. Like a robot. Like a *proper* robot designed for building warships or something. It locked its arms at its sides, pulled its legs straight together and fixed its head level and staring into the distance.

'Paragon?' I found myself asking.

Then it spoke. Not with the easy fake human voice that it had been fooling Vivi with since we found it, but with a dull, monotonous robot voice.

'My . . . name . . . is . . . Paragon . . . I . . . was . . . created . . . by . . . Doctor . . . Jonah . . . Bloom . . . Fellow . . . in . . . Physics . . . and . . . Mathematics . . . at . . . Trinity . . . College . . . Cambridge . . . and . . . of . . . Unicorn . . . Cottage . . . Cambridge . . . Doctor . . . Jonah . . . Bloom . . . has . . . no . . . children . . . of . . . his . . . own . . . His . . . nearest . . . living . . . relatives . . . are . . . his . . . sister . . . Christabel . . . Dare . . . and . . . her . . . son . . . Auden . . . Dare . . . of . . . Forest . . . Gate . . . London . . . Auden . . . Dare . . . suffers . . . from . . . achromatopsia . . . a . . . rare . . . inability . . . to . . . see . . . colour.'

It stopped its chant and remained completely still. Vivi and I just stared as the breeze battled its way through the trees and into the clearing.

13

Threats and Menaces

Then Paragon resumed its normal free-flowing, almost natural movements. It was a bit like it had been holding its breath and had suddenly exhaled, relieved to do so.

'The word unlocked him,' Vivi said. 'The word "achromatopsia" actually unlocked him.'

'Eh?' I asked.

Vivi shook her impatient head at me. 'That word was obviously used as a key by your uncle. Hearing the word triggered some information.' Vivi stood in front of Paragon – ridiculous now with the hat half-dangling off the side of its head – and stared straight up into the face. 'Did it release any other information? Did you find out anything else?'

Paragon seemed to stumble before adjusting the hat. 'No. I don't think so. Perhaps a little of the nature of Dr Bloom's work, but nothing much.' Vivi picked the trench coat up from the musty ground and held it out to the machine. Paragon took it and, this time, slowly swung it onto its shoulders, less enthusiastic than before – maybe even a little shaken up. 'A bizarre sensation,' it rather mumbled to itself. 'Very, very odd.'

I got up from the log. 'So you *did* know my uncle.' I smiled. 'Did you know him well? Can you remember him?'

'I remember . . . a little.'

'Like?'

'Like the way he hummed to himself as he fitted my central flange cooling system. Or the time he was adjusting my lower carotid piston and he nearly lost one of the primary T-junction valves. Things like that.'

I laughed. 'Not exactly tales to tell the grandchildren, are they?'

'Nope. Perhaps not.' It seemed subdued. Quiet. 'I only knew him whenever he switched me on, I suppose.'

'How many times was that?' Vivi asked.

'Seventeen times. Fifteen if you ignore the two accidental bumps from his elbow.'

Fifteen times? And each of them for just a few minutes?

'What about the rainbow machine? Project Rainbow,' I asked. 'Do you know where the battery for the machine is? Do you know how to operate it?'

Paragon shook its head.

'But don't you see, Auden?' Vivi was acting rather overexcitedly. 'If he was triggered by a word, he might be triggered again. By another word. Or by many different words.' She stopped directing her speech at me and aimed

161

it at Paragon instead. 'Who knows what information you've got hidden away inside you?'

'Can you read me, Six Six?' I whispered. The walkie-talkie function on a QWERTY was pretty basic but good enough for the corridors of Trinity College.

'Loud and clear, Golden.' Vivi's voice came back all squeaky and a little bit melodramatic and I tried not to smile. 'Over and out.'

An old professor stumped past and I leaned against the wall with charismatic nonchalance, pretending to check the time. Thank goodness we'd left Paragon tucked away in its shed, I thought.

'What is your status, Six Six?' I whispered again, once the old guy had moved out of earshot.

Silence.

'Vivi, where are you?'

'You didn't say "over and out". You're meant to say "over and out" when you finish.'

'All right. All right. What is your status, Six Six? Over and out.'

'I'm in. The eagle has landed. Alpha, bravo –'

'Yes, yes.' I cut her off, negotiated two corners and a bunch of students, then sped for the open door.

The room was much neater than the last time I was here – Immaculata had been right about that. After she'd discovered me in Uncle Jonah's rooms she had arranged for college cleaners to straighten the place up. So now all the papers and books and folders and files were neatly stacked in no particular order on the desk and on a couple of the shelves. Even the hearth where I'd found the 'Project Rainbow' sheet had been emptied and brushed beautifully clean.

We set to work.

'There must be something here,' I muttered. 'Something that will tell us . . . something. Anything.'

Vivi positioned herself behind a teetering pile of folders. 'Do you think Dr Bloom left information on Paragon in one of these files?'

I shrugged. In all honesty my mind was mainly on the rainbow machine. That was the ultimate prize as far as I was concerned. And I hoped I was going to find it in Uncle Jonah's rooms.

We stood side by side, working our way through tons of scientific waffle that meant absolutely nothing to me. Once or twice Vivi gave a little appreciative noise as if she'd read something that impressed her, her massive brain obviously understanding a lot more of this stuff than mine ever could.

After dismissing a file we would dump it heavily onto the floor before picking up another and flicking our way through the pages in that. It was in file number seven that I came across something.

Tucked into a plastic pocket on the cover was a sheet of A4 paper folded in half. I eased it out and opened it up.

It was a letter – or a copy of a letter, at least. A handwritten note to Uncle Jonah. I flattened it on the desk and started reading to myself.

Dear Dr Bloom, [it began]
Thank you for your letter dated 2nd November.
I need you to understand that failure to
complete the allotted work will result in
your prosecution at the very least. These are
dangerous times, Dr Bloom, and we must all do
our very best to keep our country safe and our
citizens protected.

And then, a slightly menacing last line.

I do hope you take very good care of yourself.

At the bottom was a signature I couldn't fully decipher. The first word clearly started with an *H* before becoming illegible, and the second initial was either an *M* or a *W* – it was difficult to tell.

I showed Vivi.

'What does that mean?' she asked frowning. 'You don't really think he *was* a spy, do you?'

I shook my head and looked around the room.

'There's no QWERTY screen,' I said, suddenly noticing. 'Where is his QWERTY screen?'

Vivi looked. 'That's strange. I'm certain he did have one. Perhaps the university authorities took it away. Gave it to another lecturer. They do that sort of thing sometimes.'

But I wasn't so sure.

Walking back home alone from Trinity that afternoon, I couldn't help feeling that someone was following me. All the sneaking around was making me jittery.

As I turned a corner and passed one of the enormous and scary Water Allocation Board posters that warned everyone to 'BE ON THE LOOKOUT FOR BLACK-MARKETEERS. THE WATER THEY SELL YOU WILL **KILL YOU!**' I glanced over my shoulder to check.

Bam!

I walked straight into someone, my shoulder knocking solidly into the arm of another boy, who twisted and half fell into the road.

'Aaargh!' the boy barked.

One of his two companions – the one with the fat nose – lurched forward to try to catch him.

'Careful!' cried the other companion – the one with swollen lips. 'Watch where you're going.'

'You OK, Fabius?' said the one clutching onto the fallen boy's arm. 'You aren't hurt, are you?'

'Get off me!' He jerked his arm away from fat nose and straightened up. 'I don't need your help.'

It was Boyle.

He looked angrily at me and then, as recognition slowly squeezed its way into his thick skull, he smirked.

'Oh, look who it is! The kid with the magnifying glass! What's his name again? Dare. That's it. Dare.'

'What do you think you're playing at, Dare?' said Putter, positioning himself a little behind Boyle.

'Yeah. Running into Fabius like that,' said Keane, shuffling alongside Putter. 'Could've caused an accident.'

'Shut up, Keane,' Boyle growled. 'I'll deal with this.'

I looked past the three boys. There was nobody else in the lane.

'Look, Boyle,' I started, 'I'm sorry I nearly knocked you over, but –'

'Sorry?' Boyle frowned. 'Oh yeah. You'll be sorry all right.' He reached out and grabbed me by the collar before lifting me up and pinning me against a wall. He glanced around and started whispering. 'See, I don't like little freaks like you who think they're better than everyone else. Weirdos who have . . . magnifying glasses dangling around their necks.' Holding me in position with one hand, he felt for my magnifying glass and ripped it away with the other. He looked briefly at it before tossing it away to Putter. 'You see, I think you need to be taught a lesson. Anyone about, lads?' he asked Putter and Keane.

'No one, Fabius,' one of them said.

'Go on. Hit him,' said the other.

'Yeah, smack him around. He deserves it, the little freak.'

Boyle pulled his arm back into position and clenched his fist.

'You're gonna be sorry you ever came to Cambridge, Freakshow,' he hissed smugly through his rotten teeth. 'This is gonna be the worst beating you ever had.'

I smiled. 'I doubt it.'

'Wha—' He looked confused.

And that was my moment to strike. With lightning reflexes, I pushed hard off the wall and launched into a double back flick, my left foot kicking Boyle's head as I went. He staggered backwards, dazed and groaning. Putter and Keane, as slow-witted as their leader, both stood there stunned as Boyle stumbled out into the middle of the lane.

I took my opportunity and leaped over Boyle's hobbling body, before shooting off past the two mindless henchmen – snatching my magnifying glass out of Putter's slack hands – and running as fast as my quivering legs would allow. Halfway along the lane I heard a loud voice booming behind me.

'I'LL GET YOU, DARE! I'LL GET YOU AND I'LL GET THAT LOSER *GIIIIRRRL*FRIEND OF YOURS!! JUST YOU WAIT!!'

I didn't even bother to look back.

* * *

Arriving back at Unicorn Cottage, I immediately closed the curtains and curled up on the sofa with Sandwich, who launched into one of her dribbly tickle episodes.

Just after half past six, Mum arrived home from work.

'What have you got the curtains all shut up for?' she asked, opening them again. 'It's summer. It's still light out.'

'I . . . er . . . had a headache,' I lied. 'Mum. Can I ask you a question?' I said, getting up from the sofa and dropping Sandwich onto the floor. 'When they found Uncle Jonah . . . in the field . . . did he have his QWERTY on him?'

She turned and looked straight at me. 'Why do you want to know that?'

I looked away. 'I was just wondering where it was. There might be some interesting stuff on it.'

'Well, it's funny you should ask. He wasn't wearing it when I got there. Unusual for Jonah because he loved his QWERTY – always had the latest model.' She put her hemp bag on the table. 'I assumed someone at the hospital must have taken it. Either by accident or deliberately. I was going to report it but . . . well . . . in the end I was too upset to. It doesn't really matter after all, does it? It was just a . . . thing.'

'No.'

I thought back to the letter – the horrible menacing sneer of the words. I thought of the missing QWERTY and the missing QWERTY screen. They'd been taken all right.

Taken to see what information Uncle Jonah had stored on them. Or taken so that nobody else could *find* the information. Whatever the reason, it didn't really matter.

Now I was certain.

Uncle Jonah didn't just die.

Someone got rid of him.

PART FOUR
PINK

14

Boyle

'Brunch. Brunette. Brunt. Bruschetta. Brush. Brushed. Brushstroke. Brushwood. Brushwork. Brusque. Brussels sprout . . .'

'Vivi.'

Vivi looked up from her dictionary. 'Yes?'

'I hope you don't mind me saying this . . .'

'Yes, Paragon?'

Paragon looked like it was shuffling uncomfortably on its deckchair in the middle of the garden.

'But the thing is . . . you see . . . well . . . all this . . . "word" stuff you're doing with me . . .'

'Go on.'

'Well, it's a bit . . . boring.'

'Ha!' I laughed out loud and let myself drop from the branch onto the trampoline below.

'Boring?'

'Yes. Just sort of saying the words out loud like that. It feels a bit . . . tedious. Three days you've been at it now and . . . well . . .' It stabbed a finger at the dictionary. 'We're only on B.'

Vivi looked a bit hurt, but I still couldn't stop myself from laughing as I bounced. It was driving me almost as nuts as it was driving Paragon.

In fact, there were a number of things driving me nuts. You see, I hadn't told anyone my suspicions about Uncle Jonah. Not Mum. Not Vivi. And it was slowly eating away at me, turning me into a nervous mess. At night I lay awake thinking through all the possibilities. Who had wanted rid of him? Could someone have killed him? Over a few nights I had mentally accused everyone from other lecturers at Trinity to Mr Belsey the headmaster. Whenever I went out of the house I always looked around to make sure I wasn't being followed. I had even started to peer under my bed at night to check there was nobody there.

I was worried.

And all the while, at the back of my mind, was the thought of the rainbow machine and the battery that was still missing. The thought of them never went away.

'I mean,' Paragon continued to a horrified Vivi, 'I know all those words anyway. If you asked me to give you a definition for each of them and their etymology . . . well . . . that's something I could easily do.'

'But that's not the point,' Vivi said with a slight croak in her voice. 'I'll bet you knew the word "achromatopsia" before Auden said it the other day.'

'Yes. Yes, I did.'

'But it was the actual word being *said* that made you remember that it was Dr Bloom who built you.'

'True. True. It's just –'

'Just what?'

If Paragon could have sighed, it would have sighed. 'It's just a bit boring.'

Vivi put the book down on her lap. 'But you're a robot. How can you find anything boring?'

'Coming around to my way of thinking now are you, Vivi?' I called over, and she gave me another of her glares. 'You'll be referring to Paragon as "it" next.'

Suddenly Paragon stood up. 'How about a bit of poetry? Lighten the mood.'

'Oh no,' I groaned. But before I could say anything else, it was off.

'*I think that I shall never see*
A billboard lovely as a tree.
Indeed, unless the billboards fall
I'll never see a tree at all.'

Vivi laughed. I laughed.

'Ogden Nash,' Paragon finished.

'I don't mind that sort of poetry,' I said, dropping down onto the ground, feeling slightly cheerier than I had in days. 'Funny poems. I prefer them to all that "aren't daffodils lovely" sort of thing.'

'What about some Edward Lear then?' Paragon asked, its eyes drilling straight into mine.

'Who?'

'Edward Lear. Nonsense poet. Wrote limericks.'

'*Nonsense* poet?!'

'Yep.' Paragon brought its clenched fist up to its mouth and pretended to clear its throat. 'Ahem.

'*There was an Old Person whose habits*
Induced him to feed upon rabbits;
When he'd eaten eighteen,
He turned perfectly green,
Upon which he relinquished those habits.'

Neither Vivi nor I laughed.

'That's just stupid,' I said.

'Well, it *is* a nonsense poem,' Paragon said. 'It's meant to be stupid.'

'Do another one, Paragon,' Vivi asked. 'Please.'

'No. Please don't!' I shouted. 'I don't think I can stand it!'

But Paragon ignored me again.

'*There was an Old Man who supposed*
That the street door was partially closed;
But some very large rats
Ate his coats and his hats
While that futile Old Gentleman dozed.'

Silence.

'They are *reeeeaaally* not funny,' I said.

'Well, they *were* written a long time ago,' Paragon

176

replied. 'I suppose the sense of humour in those days was significantly different to the sense of humour nowadays. Things evolve. Even jokes. Nothing stays the same for long.'

'I can't imagine anyone laughing at that – even back then,' I said, taking the dictionary off Vivi and throwing it to the floor. 'They are just not funny.'

'Hey! What are you doing?'

'Come on. I'm fed up of listening to you reciting the dictionary and Paragon reciting terrible poetry. Let's go and do something fun.'

As we climbed over the broken-down fence, into the field of long-trampled grass, Paragon looked around at the mess.

'Hmm,' it said. 'Sunny Vale. Did you name this place, Auden?'

'No. Why?'

'Well, the quantity of sarcasm needed to come up with a name like that for a place like this would fill an entire desalination unit. Wouldn't you agree?'

I grinned at the stupid machine. 'I would agree, Paragon. Definitely.'

'Are you sure we should bring him here?' Vivi said, a worried look on her face. 'Won't there be people?'

'There might,' I replied. 'But most of the people who come here seem to spend their time down in the office complaining about the place. I don't think they're exactly on the lookout for seven-foot-tall robots dressed in the discarded clothes of an old philosophy professor, do you? Anyway, let's get started. Do you know the rules of hide-and-seek?'

Paragon could barely control the tut that formed somewhere in its amplification unit. 'I understand the rules of thousands of different games. Bridge. Backgammon. Mah-jong. I can calculate the odds for all forms of poker. So of course I know how to play hide-and-seek. What sort of high-functioning creature would I be if I didn't understand the rules of hide-and-seek?'

The word 'creature' made me wince, but I let it go.

'Great. So . . . we have an extra rule when we play around here.'

'What's that?'

Vivi answered. 'We try not to be seen by anyone. Anyone at all.'

Paragon sort of shrugged. Again, if it had eyebrows, it would probably have raised them. 'Are you sure that's not a rule you've only just made up because of the big metal guy you've brought with you today?' I laughed again. Paragon was proving to be very funny. 'You sure it's not because you don't want some randomer or other poking their peepers out at me? Is it?'

Vivi was smiling too. 'No, honestly, we always play like that. You see, we shouldn't really be here.'

'Ah.' Paragon's shoulders swelled like it understood. 'Illegal trespassing. I see.'

'You don't have some program that prevents you from doing anything illegal, do you?' I asked, remembering that this was a robot and that robots should deal in black and white.

Paragon's fingers tapped a rhythm along what would probably have been its lips. It was thinking. 'Hmm. Let me think. Is it just a teeny bit wrong?'

'Oh yes,' I said. 'Really little.'

'On a scale of one to ten, just how wrong do you think trespassing in Sunny Vale Caravan Park is?'

'Ooh, about –'

'Three,' Vivi interrupted.

'Three?' asked Paragon.

'Not even that,' I quickly added. 'I'd say probably about a . . . point five.'

'Point five, eh?' It seriously looked like it was weighing it all up. 'Point five's nothing. Well, practically nothing. Five per cent. One in twenty. Hmm . . .' The fingers tapped out their rhythm. 'OK then.'

'Really?'

'Yep.'

We all edged our way over to where the long-abandoned caravans started.

'Now, you're not allowed to use any of your tricks to try and find us, OK? No heat sensors or movement sensors or anything like that. No lasers. Nothing. Right?'

'O-kay. So I'm going in blind, so to speak?'

'Yes.'

'Should be interesting.' Paragon adjusted the collar on the jacket so that it was sticking up and covering its face. 'Deliberately disabling myself to see just how difficult life must be for you humans. Should give quite an insight.'

'Don't get too excited, bot-brain,' I said. 'It's just a game of hide-and-seek. No big deal. Now, count to a hundred.'

'Do you want me to put my hands over my eyes?' Paragon asked, its fingers spread across its metal face.

'Don't think there's any need, is there? All you need to do is turn off your vision . . . thingy while you count, don't you?'

'Oh no,' Vivi shook her head almost violently. 'I think you should put your hands over your eyes. Makes it all more authentic, doesn't it?'

Honestly. I give up sometimes.

Paragon started counting, and Vivi and I both sprinted away towards the caravans. As we neared the first of the abandoned box-shaped chalets, Vivi peeled away from me and dashed down behind a hefty clump of rubbish. I pushed on past – I knew exactly where I was headed.

Three aisles into the park – way before the potential of bumping into anyone unfortunate enough to actually be staying there – was a caravan under which someone had – optimistically – stuck two water butts side by side. A strip of guttering ran across the roof of the caravan – now complete with a twisted, dislodged aerial – and a grubby plastic pipe slid down into the top of each water butt.

The gap between the two butts was just wide enough for a flexible young man – such as moi! – to fit into. I had used this particular hiding place a number of times before when playing with Vivi, and with a bit of a squeeze and a tight hold of the breath, it was possible to slot myself in and be practically unspottable by the outside world. I shuffled around, let my back slide down the dusty wall of the caravan and crouched out of sight, trying to keep my breathing as under control as possible.

I squatted there quietly and waited. I listened as the breeze gently brushed across the uncut grass and through the straggly hedges.

Suddenly something flashed quickly past the gap – far too quickly to be made out – and I held my breath even tighter. A moment later and –

'Oh!'

It was Vivi's voice, far off.

'Found you!'

Paragon's.

'Now to find Auden.'

Whoosh!

The blur flashed past the gap once again.

I fixed myself to the spot. If that was Paragon, he was moving at an incredible rate. Perhaps that was his purpose. Speed. Perhaps he was some sort of messenger drone – carrying important messages from one place to another. Or a news drone, taking back news stories to the Etherweb composition centres.

Whoooosh!!

I crouched and half squinted up my eyes. The tension was almost unbearable.

Suddenly –

Tap, tap, tap.

Something was tapping on my head. I looked upwards and found myself staring straight into a pair of fake metal eyes. Paragon had climbed up onto the roof of the caravan behind me and was leaning over the edge, knocking me on the top of my head with the tip of one of its multi-jointed fingers.

'Hello, Auden. I appear to have found you. Ha!'

I scrambled out from between the water butts.

'Yes, yes. Very good. Well done.' I dusted the rot and damp from my clothes and tried not to look too impressed with the irritating lump of metal above me. 'Bit of a risk climbing up there though. Might get seen. Might get spotted by someone on the other side of the park. A bit reckless, if you ask me.'

'Oh, nope. I don't think so.' Paragon was now lying, supporting its 'cheek' in the palm of its hand, its 'elbow' digging down into the roof. It looked as if it was resting. 'I disabled my senses with regards to you, but not for everything. I was still aware of what the rest of the world was up to, you know. I even managed to avoid that funny-looking boy.'

'What funny-looking boy?'

'The one with the swollen pink head.'

Suddenly there was a loud shout from somewhere far off. 'I SAID YOU'RE TRESPASSING! WHAT ARE YOU DOING HERE?'

'What's that?' I asked as Paragon shifted position up on the roof of the caravan to try and see.

The shouting continued. 'YOU'RE NOT ALLOWED ON THIS SITE. I COULD GET THE POLICE AND THEY'D CHARGE YOU WITH TRESPASS. THEY COULD LOCK YOU UP FOR IT.'

'It's the boy,' Paragon said, craning its neck. 'He's shouting at Vivi.'

'What?'

Paragon started to climb down.

'No. Wait. You can't be seen. You need to stay there. Keep your head down.'

'But I –'

'No!' I ordered. 'Stay there!'

Paragon gave a sort of tut but did as I said.

I crept my way around a couple of the caravans, towards the area where the noise was coming from. As I came around a corner I could see Vivi up against the side of a rickety-looking shed, her entire body shaking, her cheeks shining with tears. In front of her was a dark-haired boy with his back to me. Even though I couldn't see his face, I could sense that he was knotted up with anger.

'YOU'VE GOT SOME NERVE, COMING ROUND HERE! ESPECIALLY AFTER WHAT YOUR LITTLE FREAKSHOW BOYFRIEND DID TO ME THE OTHER DAY.' He pointed to his forehead, and as he did so he turned a little to reveal a large, dark bruise that had swollen up on the left-hand part of his head.

Boyle!

'BUT HE'S NOT HERE TO HELP YOU NOW, SO I'M GOING TEACH YOU THE LESSON HE SHOULD'VE GOT THE OTHER DAY BUT HE WAS TOO MUCH OF A COWARD TO TAKE.'

'Please, Boyle . . .' Vivi pleaded.

'Fabius! Oh Fa-bi-us!' Suddenly a woman's sing-song voice started calling from somewhere far off .

'WHAT?' Boyle looked confused. 'WHAT IS IT NOW?'

'Fabius! Lunch is ready.'

Boyle sighed.

'Fa-bi-us . . .'

Something softened in Boyle's tone. 'OK. COMING, MOTHER! WON'T BE A MINUTE!' he called back, before quickly turning to face Vivi once again, the snarl in his voice reinstated.

'Tell your freakshow boyfriend that I'm going to make life so hard for you both at school next year that you'll do anything to be expelled.'

184

Without warning, Boyle lurched forward, grabbed Vivi by the shoulders and shoved her into the dirt.

Angry, I stomped forward a step or two, only to be quickly and silently pulled backwards by someone behind me. A cold, metallic hand slipped over my mouth to stop me shouting, and I twisted my head to find myself staring straight into Paragon's unblinking eyes.

'Oh, and . . . er . . . give your boyfriend this little present from me!' Boyle rushed at Vivi and landed a solid kick right in the middle of her stomach.

I wriggled hard in Paragon's grip, desperate to get out and show this bully that he had no right to hurt my friend like that. But Paragon just held on tightly, refusing to let me go.

'Sorry to leave you like this,' Boyle sneered at Vivi, 'but . . . er . . . lunch is ready. Adios, Rookmini.'

He turned and strutted arrogantly away towards the little house on the edge of the site. Paragon kept its arms clasped around me until Boyle had gone inside.

The moment it released me, I raced over to Vivi. She was still crying, her hands clutching her stomach.

'Vivi! Are you OK? Vivi?' I helped her up and tried wiping the muck out of her hair.

'Vivi.' Paragon came alongside her and helped her straighten up. 'Are you hurt?'

'Why didn't you let me go?!' I shouted at Paragon. 'I could have stopped him from hurting her.'

185

Paragon shook its head. 'Not always the best idea. Not when you're angry, Auden. You should never make any decisions when you're angry. You might have made things worse.'

'You don't understand! You're not human! You don't –'

'Please!'

It was Vivi.

'Please! Don't argue. Not now. Not about this. I'm OK. I'll be all right.' She pulled a lump of dried mud out of her trouser pocket. 'I'll live.'

'Boyle? Hmm. Appropriate name', said Paragon.

We were sitting in the back garden of Unicorn Cottage, Vivi dusting herself off with towels.

'His family must own the caravan park,' she said. 'He's not a nice person – as you can see. Doesn't like anything that isn't "normal", in his opinion.'

'The concept of "normal" is, of course, based entirely on the individual's perception,' Paragon started wittering on. 'What one person sees as "normal" is considered completely "abnormal" by others. Thus rendering a generalised concept of "normality" entirely redundant, i.e. there is no such thing as "normal". Or, if you like, on the other hand, everything is "normal".'

'Thank you, Einstein,' I said, before telling them about my encounter with Boyle, Putter and Keane the other day.

'So he said he was going to get me too, did he?' Vivi

looked concerned. 'Thanks, Auden. Thanks a lot. He definitely managed to do that.'

'Now, now, Vivi,' Paragon interrupted. 'Let's leave the sarcasm to Auden. As he's so good at it.'

I gave a sarcastic smirk to confirm Paragon's point.

'Sorry, Vivi. Boyle is such a coward, picking on you like that. If I hadn't kicked him in the head and escaped, he probably wouldn't have been so angry and hurt you. I'm sorry. It's all my fault.'

'No, it's not. He's just a horrible person,' said Vivi.

'Yes,' Paragon added. 'Definitely the sort who needs to be taught a lesson.' It looked straight at me.

Vivi frowned at Paragon. 'What are you saying?'

But Paragon had planted the seed of an idea and my brain was already running away with it, piecing things together and formulating some sort of a plan.

Paragon could be useful.

Vivi shook her head viciously. 'No. I don't think I want to be part of anything nasty. It's not right.'

'He *did* just kick you in the stomach, Vivi.'

'I don't care. I still don't think it's right.'

'It doesn't have to be anything nasty,' Paragon reassured her, but she still shook her head.

'It's OK, Vivi,' I soothed. It was true that she wasn't cut out for revenge. 'You don't have to have anything to do with it. In fact, it's best if you don't even know anything about it.'

15

The Truth

The following evening, rather than hide Paragon away in its underground bunker under the shed, I took it all the way back to Sunny Vale. Always best to be in situ, my dad would say, when you're planning a campaign.

As the light started to dim, we made our way across to one of the long-abandoned caravans with the cracked glass and the mouldy walls. I turned the handle on the door and it opened easily. Stepping inside, I was hit by a fog of stale air and dust that had probably not been disturbed for years.

The furniture had been left to rot, and someone had clearly been in at some point and smashed the place up. Broken-up sticks of wood and snapped and bent plastic were strewn all over the place. Cushions and bedding had been ripped apart, sending fluff and feathers and polystyrene sponge all across the floor. The little gas cooker had been pulled out from its mooring and now lay blocking the passageway to the equally vandalised bedrooms.

'Hmm,' Paragon said. 'This is nice.'

I turned and looked at its face. 'Is that sarcasm?'

'I suppose. Got a good teacher.'

I laughed.

'OK now, I'll be back before sunrise. You wait here and then we'll put our little plan into action. Understand?'

'Yes, boss.'

I tugged the top part of Paragon's coat to one side.

'You know what, Paragon,' I said, my finger hovering over the on/off button.

'What?'

'I think I misjudged you at first. Actually you're OK. You're all right.'

I punched the button and he powered down.

After just a few hours' sleep, I got up, stuffed a quinoa bun down my neck, patted Sandwich on top of her yawning head and softly closed the back door behind me. I didn't want to wake Mum. She would wonder what I was up to. I didn't think she'd look too kindly on me sneaking out to play a trick on a school bully, aided and abetted by a poetry-quoting robot. I somehow didn't think she'd understand.

Twenty minutes later I was pulling open the door to the caravan and powering up Paragon.

'Good morning, Auden,' it said as the lights stuttered to life. It peered down at its chest and gently tapped the one light that still wasn't working. 'Nope. Still nothing.' Paragon looked up at me.

'Never mind that now. It might not be for anything important, or it might just start itself up at some point. I wouldn't worry. We've got a trick to play. Are you ready?'

'Of course.'

It was still dark out, but that was good because I could see so well. Everything was clear to me. Even the smallest detail. As crisp as it was to a 'normal' person in the bright light of day.

We silently worked our way across the park towards Boyle's cottage. There were no lights on in any of the caravans. If there was anyone there, then they were still asleep. Even the birds in the trees hadn't bothered to rouse themselves quite yet, and the early morning breeze was still trying to summon up its own strength.

When we reached the cottage, Paragon slowly paced right the way around it before coming back to me.

'One adult – female – in one bedroom. One young person – male – in the second bedroom. Both sleeping peacefully.'

It looked as if Boyle was an only child. And lived alone with his mother. A bit like me. Only not as nice. Or clever. Or handsome, for that matter.

We went around to the end of the cottage where Boyle slept.

'OK,' Paragon said. 'Now what?'

'Can you climb up to his window?'

'Climb? Ha! I'm the King of Climbsville.'

Paragon leaped onto the wall and scurried up like a spider. Within a second or two it was alongside Boyle's paint-flaky window.

'Wow! Now do your voice,' I whispered.

'Now?'

'Yes. Now.' I moved out of the way and hid behind a large, stinky plastic bin.

Paragon levered the window open, pretended to clear its throat and started to speak.

'FABIUS BOYLE,' it rasped in a – to be honest – pretty scary voice. Sort of hissy and low. It almost made *me* shiver. 'FABIUS BOYLE!!!' it continued. 'WHERE ARE YOU, FABIUS BOYLE?'

A snorting from above. From inside the small house I could hear Boyle waking up. 'What? Eh? What is it?'

'FABIUS BOYLE . . . I AM LOOKING FOR YOU, FABIUS BOYLE.'

Boyle seemed to kind of squeak. 'What do you want?! Who are you?! Mum?!'

'DO NOT CALL FOR YOUR MOTHER, FABIUS BOYLE. SHE CANNOT HELP YOU NOW.' Another squeak. 'YOU MUST FACE ME ALONE.'

'I don't understand! Who are you?! What have I done?!'

'I AM THE PART OF YOUR SOUL THAT FEARS AND HATES.'

I scrambled out from behind the bin, dusting myself off, and ran to about ten metres away from the cottage, where I turned to face Boyle's bedroom window. I could still hear Paragon's and Boyle's voices.

'I AM THE ACCUMULATION OF YEARS OF HATRED AND FEAR. FABIUS BOYLE, YOU HAVE SPENT YOUR CHILDHOOD FILLING OTHERS WITH FEAR. NOW THAT FEAR HAS RETURNED TO WREAK ITS HAVOC UPON *YOU*!'

'But I don't understand!!' Boyle's voice was shaking and tearful and I was filled with a kind of glee.

'TAKE A LOOK OUT OF YOUR WINDOW AND YOU WILL SEE.'

Paragon swiftly crawled up the wall to a position directly above the window. A few seconds passed – Boyle clearly debating with himself whether or not he actually dared look outside – before the curtains twitched and a petrified face appeared. When he saw me standing before him in the darkness, Boyle almost jumped.

'Dare?!'

'INDEED,' confirmed Paragon. 'I HAVE TAKEN THE FORM OF ONE OF YOUR ENEMIES. IT IS TIME TO CONFRONT YOUR FEARS.'

'What's going on?'

I stood still, staring hard and impassively at the window as if I were a ghost.

'STEP OUTSIDE, FABIUS BOYLE . . .'

'No!'

'STEP OUTSIDE AND FACE YOUR FEARS. IT IS TIME.'

'No, it isn't!'

'YES, IT IS.'

'I'm not going out there!'

'BUT YOU *MUST*, FABIUS BOYLE. YOU *MUST*. FOR IF YOU DO NOT, THEN YOU WILL BE DEAD BEFORE THE SUN RISES.'

'Dead?!!!'

'YES. DEAD. D, E, A, D – DEAD!'

I watched as Boyle tried to manage a fit of uncontrollable gulps.

'STEP OUTSIDE, FABIUS BOYLE.'

The face left the window, and at precisely the same moment I saw Paragon clambering to a point above the kitchen door.

The door opened reluctantly. Then slowly – so incredibly slowly – Boyle came out onto the top step, tugging the belt of his dressing gown tightly around him.

'What is this?' His voice quavered. A combination of fear and the cold perhaps. 'What's . . . going on? Is . . . is this some kind of joke? Dare? Are you . . . are you having a little . . . little joke? Eh?'

I stood absolutely still and just stared at Boyle. No reaction on my face. This unsettled him further.

'Am I dreaming? Is that it? Yes . . . I think I must be having . . . a dream.'

He came down from the steps and stood on the patch of gravel in front of them.

'That's all this is . . . a strange lit—'

And then Paragon swooped into action.

Leaning out from the stone wall, it grabbed Boyle on both sides of his head and lifted him clear of the ground.

'Argghhhh!' Boyle screamed, and Paragon quickly repositioned one hand so that a couple of fingers were clamped over Boyle's open mouth. Boyle's legs thrashed wildly and uselessly in the air, and his hands reached up to try and release Paragon's grip. But Paragon was so much stronger and pretty soon the boy found himself tiring and giving himself up to the situation.

I came nearer, to see Boyle's eyes staring pleadingly down at me.

'NOW,' Paragon continued in his scary voice, 'YOU HAVE TORTURED AND FRIGHTENED CHILDREN ALL YOUR LIFE. THE TIME TO STOP HAS ARRIVED. WHEN YOU GO BACK TO YOUR SCHOOL YOU WILL NOT BULLY OR ATTACK A SINGLE PERSON. ALL YOUR TEACHERS AND CLASSMATES WILL NOTICE THE REMARKABLE CHANGE IN YOUR DEMEANOUR. YOU NEVER KNOW – SOME OF THEM MIGHT ACTUALLY LEARN TO *LIKE* YOU AND YOU MIGHT . . . JUST MIGHT . . . ONE DAY FIND YOURSELF WITH A FRIEND – A *REAL* FRIEND – A WHOLE NEW EXPERIENCE FOR YOU, I'M SURE.'

Paragon gave Boyle a little shake to make sure he was listening. 'OF COURSE, IT IS VERY EASY FOR ME TO CHECK THE RECORDS AT YOUR SCHOOL. IT IS A SIMPLE MATTER OF JUST PLUGGING INTO THE SCHOOL'S ETHERWEB AND FINDING WHAT I WANT. AND IF I SEE YOUR NAME CREEPING UP ON REPORTS OF BULLYING AGAIN . . . I SHALL BE PAYING YOU ANOTHER VISIT. DO YOU UNDERSTAND, FABIUS BOYLE?'

Boyle gave a tiny nod within Paragon's large metal hands. The movement was so oddly comical that I couldn't stop myself from grinning. Boyle noticed, and his forehead crumpled into a sort of half-frown.

'I AM NOW GOING TO PUT YOU BACK ON THE GROUND. BUT REMEMBER ALL I HAVE SAID.'

Boyle didn't nod. He just glared at me as Paragon lowered him gently down. As his feet touched the ground, Paragon released him, and Boyle's head swung upwards to see what it was that had just lifted him so easily into the air.

But Paragon had gone.

Boyle straightened himself up and tried to regain his breath.

'What was that?' he murmured, more to himself than to me.

'That was all your years of scaring people rolled into one,' I said, still unable to stop myself smirking. It had been satisfying to see this bully dangling in the air, scared and confused. I know I should have felt guilty for having enjoyed it – but I don't think I did. Boyle had recently hurt my best friend and it was hard to feel any kind of sympathy.

'What . . . what did you just do to me?' He still looked puzzled, but now there was a slight glint of anger in his eyes. 'What just grabbed me? What did you do, Dare? How did you do it?'

'None of that matters,' I answered. 'All that matters is that you never bully anyone again. Because if you do . . . Trust me, you don't want to know.'

Boyle pulled the top of his dressing gown tighter around his neck. 'I don't understand what just happened. And I don't know why you're here like this. Why are you here?'

I sighed. 'I'm here to teach you a lesson. I'm here to stop a bully. After all –' I paused for a second – 'everyone knows that all bullies are cowards.'

'Huh! That's good. Coming from you of all people.'

I took a step closer. 'What do you mean?'

'You know all about cowards, I'm sure.'

It was my turn to look confused now. I shook my head and wrinkled up my face to make it clear that I didn't know what Boyle was talking about. What rubbish was this?

'You know. Don't pretend you don't.'

'I honestly don't know what you're getting at.' I retrieved my smirk and cranked it up to try and make Boyle feel foolish.

'Yes, you do. You know. Lots of people come here to stay. Lots of people from *London*. My mum talks to them all. They tell her things.'

'I've no idea what you're talking about.'

Boyle suddenly looked smug. 'I'm talking about your dad. Everybody knows about him.'

My legs stiffened and I was stuck to the spot. 'What do you mean?' My smirk had vanished, dwindled away into nothing. 'What are you saying?'

'He's a coward. Just like you.'

'What? No, he's not. He's away fighting in Europe. He's been away for months.'

Boyle laughed. 'Yeah. He's been away for months all right. In prison!'

Blood seemed to rush around my ears, and I found myself unable to hear anything but Boyle's grating voice.

'Found guilty of deserting his post. Left some other soldiers to die. So they sent him to prison. He's not abroad fighting at all. Didn't you know? He's in a military prison. Somewhere in this country. For desertion. Cowardice.'

No.

No. That wasn't right.

'You're a liar!'

Boyle laughed again. 'Liar, am I? Well, why don't you ask your mother? I'm sure she'll tell you the truth if you ask her nicely.'

I clenched my fist hard. I wanted to walk the seven or eight paces to Boyle and smash it roughly into the boy's face. Knock him flat on the grass.

But I didn't.

'Fabius! What's going on? What's this noise?' Boyle's mother – bleary-eyed and half dressed – appeared in the doorway behind him. 'What are you doing?'

Boyle ignored her, still spitting his venom out towards me. 'Ask your mother. Go on. Get her to tell you the truth for once. I *dare* you!'

I spun on the spot and sprinted away – the blood still racing around my head.

'That's it! Run away!' Boyle shouted behind me. 'Be just like your dad!'

I kept on running. Over the fields. Along the lanes. My legs pounding, never slowing. For all I knew, the sun might have been starting to come up. My chest might have been screaming out in pain. The wind might have been cold and penetrating. The birds might have been singing to welcome in the new day. But I wasn't listening. I didn't notice any of it. I didn't care.

All I could feel and think about was my dad.

My dad!

Eventually I rounded the corner and came to the lane where Unicorn Cottage sat. Without slowing, I ran onto the drive and into the house.

Mum was in the kitchen. When she heard me come in, she quickly turned around and did her scowl face at me.

'Auden! Where have you been? I've been so worried about you. I just got up and –'

'Mum! Tell me . . .' I was out of breath. 'Tell me . . . about . . . about Dad.'

'What?'

'I want to know.'

'I don't –'

'I want to know the truth!' I shouted 'About Dad. Tell me the truth.'

She didn't even have to say anything. The look on her face told me everything I needed to know.

'No!' I cried.

Mum sat down on one of the wooden chairs, her shoulders bowed. Like a balloon that's lost all its air.

'I'm sorry, Auden. I didn't know how to tell you. I didn't know what to say. I brought us here so we could make a fresh start. Get away from it all. I thought that –'

But I didn't want to hear any more. That was enough.

I ran back out through the door and into the yard. I ran through the small gap in the hedge and into the field with the irrigation pyramids. I ran and I ran across the field, my feet driving hard into the dry crops.

Far off in the distance I could see a shape. It was a man standing with his arms outstretched, like he was waiting for me. I sprinted faster and faster towards him, sweat flicking off my brow. As I got nearer, the arms stretched out even more, opening wide for me, and I pounded towards them.

I thought of my dad, racing me in the park, pushing me on the swings. The games of football. The bedtime stories and the stupid jokes. The tears came flowing down my hot cheeks and I kept on running. I thought of the songs and the rhymes and the bicycle rides. The words of advice and the tellings-off.

My dad.

My dad, the hero.

I ran and I ran towards the open arms until finally I fell into them and they wrapped themselves tightly around me, holding me close and swaying me softly, gently into comfort. I flung my own arms around the cold body and squeezed as hard as I could, never ever wanting to let go. Never wanting to go back and face this terrible truth.

I just wanted this hurt to go away.

I cried. I cried for so long that my tears felt like grit in my eyes and everything became a greyish smear. I cried until my breaths turned to stutters before finally becoming more even once again.

I cried.

And all the time, the arms hushed me. Calmed me. Soothed me. Lulled me into feeling like everything would be all right again. Like everything would be OK.

I looked up at the flickering lights on the chest. The wires along the arms. The metal grille where the mouth should have been.

'Shhh,' Paragon said, his hand resting on my head. 'Shhh, Audendare.'

PART FIVE
PURPLE

16

Stars and Sparrows

'I thought it was a bad idea to try and get your own back.' Vivi squinted through the telescope that pointed out of her bedroom window, over the quad and into the night sky.

'I wasn't trying to get my own back,' I replied a tad annoyed. 'I was trying to teach Boyle a lesson. After all, he did hurt you.'

'Oh, so you did it all for me, did you?'

'Pretty much . . .' I stumbled.

'Quickly, quickly.' She flapped her hands at me and then stood back from the telescope. I bent over and put my eye to the eyepiece. 'See that star? The one in the middle?' I thought I did. 'That's Antares. It's part of the constellation of Scorpius.' The shining dot in the centre of all the blackness seemed to twinkle. 'They call it the Rival of Mars.'

'Why?'

'Because it's a really deep red in colour.'

I turned and gave her a look. 'Well, I couldn't possibly know about that, could I?'

'Oh. No. That's true. Sorry.'

I imagined my mother flicking the little elastic band around her wrist.

It was irritating. No, that's far too mild. Sometimes it was just so *annoying* not being able to see colour. All the time – every single day – I would miss out on some experience or other – or at least have a watered-down version of it – just because I couldn't tell one thing from another. It made me sad and it made me mad.

'Forgiven,' I sighed eventually. I put my eye back to the telescope and watched the dot sparkle a little more, all the while slowly moving across the lens.

'You know, the best way to look at stars with the naked eye,' Vivi rattled on beside me, 'is to look just past them. Try and stare straight at them and you miss a lot of the detail. It's difficult to focus. But look a tiny bit away – take your eyes off them – and you can see them much more clearly.'

'Hmm.'

We swapped places again and Vivi gave the two metal sticks attached to the telescope a couple of little turns.

'So? What are you going to do now? About your dad, I mean.'

I shrugged. 'Not much I *can* do. Mum says we can write letters. He can make a QWERTY call every few months. That's about it.'

I went too quiet too quickly and Vivi picked up on it.

'What? What's wrong?'

'Well . . .' I wasn't entirely sure I could bring myself to even form the words. Even after everything, it still felt vaguely treacherous. 'The problem is that . . . well . . . I don't know if I can.'

'Why not?'

'He left soldiers to die . . . that's what the army says. He ran off and left them to die.' Whenever I thought about it, it made me feel sick. 'I don't know what I'm meant to think. On one hand, he's my dad. And on the other . . .'

The room suddenly became embarrassingly silent.

Vivi broke the silence.

'Well, at least you actually *have* a father. That's one up on me. Even if he *is* in prison.'

I didn't say anything.

'Still, you should have listened to me about getting your revenge on Boyle. It didn't do you any good in the end, did it?'

'Yes, yes, Your Royal Highness.' I put on a fake posh voice. 'I shall certainly be listening to you next time, with your wise and thoughtful words. How foolish I have been not to heed your advice. I bow to your greater knowledge.' I gave a little curtsy.

Vivi stopped what she was doing and looked at me.

'Why are you always so sarcastic, Auden? I don't understand. Why are you always so sarcastic about *everything*?'

The question caught me off guard.

'I, er . . .'

'I'll tell you what I think, shall I? I think you use sarcasm to protect yourself. I think that you think that you can hide behind a sarcastic comment to avoid revealing what you really feel. Am I right?'

I was stunned. She was right. She was absolutely correct. I definitely *did* use sarcasm as a shield. Without a doubt. Even *I* hadn't really realised it before she said it, but now it was obvious.

Of course I wasn't going to tell *her* that.

'Er, no! I don't think so!' I said in a kind of uber-sarcastic way, and Vivi laughed.

'You know, you really are hopeless, Auden.'

I grinned and stared out at the clear starry sky that hung like a poster above Trinity.

We all watched the Sifters below motoring from one large pile of rubbish to another. They picked out individual items with their pincers, inspected them with their visual sensors and pulled the salvageable parts off, stacking them onto a trailer before tossing the useless ends into a large rectangular rubbish bin.

Me and Vivi and Paragon were sitting on top of one of the enormous mountains of discarded trash that dominated the recycling yard. The sun was beating down and I felt so incredibly thirsty, but it was a relief to be out with Vivi and Paragon, not worrying myself witless with thoughts of Uncle Jonah's death and my dad's cowardice.

'We still haven't worked out what *your* job is, Paragon,' I said, my mouth dry and clicking. 'Perhaps you could do that.' I nodded my head towards the Sifters, one of which was now wheeling itself with difficulty over a long sheet of corrugated metal.

Paragon gave a short laugh. 'Nope. I don't believe so. Somehow I don't think that any of those machines down there know anything about the poetry of Christina Rossetti or the paintings of John Constable or the names of all fifty-five of Jason's Argonauts or the Latin name for a three-toed sloth, do you? I mean, why would they?'

'So why do *you* know all this stuff?' I asked. 'Have you been designed to replace a teacher? If so, please replace the one we're having next year. He's vile.'

Paragon laughed again. 'I don't believe I'm a teacher. I don't know why I believe I'm not a teacher . . . It's just a sensation I have. A gut feeling.'

Just days before, comments like that would have made me go purple with rage. A robot, after all, deals in black and white and is not allowed to have 'gut feelings' about things. Is it? It deals in YES/NOs and ON/OFFs. Not in-betweens. Doesn't it?

But now . . . I had come to realise that the world is not always the logical place we like to think it is, and that people are as hard to read as the Bible. Life is not the straightforward, one-after-the-other A, B, C that you imagine when you're young. It's all more complicated than that. More twisted around. Like a ball of string. Or to be more precise, like *lots* of balls of string all tangled together, impossible to pull apart.

So why not accept that a robot might think? Might feel? Might understand what it was I was going through? I remembered the soft metal arms around me . . .

'You're incredibly fast,' I said. 'Is that your main purpose? To be fast? To race? To do something quickly?'

Paragon shrugged. 'I don't know, but –' he picked up a spherical, rubber ball-like thing from the pile of junk underneath us – 'watch this . . .'

He held it between finger and thumb, rolling it slightly as he showed it to us. Suddenly he clamped his entire hand over the ball, hiding it from view.

'Now,' he said, a hint of mischief in his voice, 'what have I got in my hand?'

'A ball,' Vivi replied.

'Aha. But have I?'

Vivi nodded. 'It's a bit like a ball, anyway. Looks like one.'

'Yes. OK. Let's not get too tied up with what the thing actually is – let's assume it's a ball, shall we? It's close enough. What I'm interested in is . . . do I have it in my hand? Do I *reeeeally* have it in my hand?'

The way he said *reeeeaally* reminded me of me.

'Yes. You do.' Vivi nodded again.

'Aha.'

Slowly he peeled his fingers open to show that there was nothing in his hand. Vivi gasped and I just smiled.

'Did you just crush it to dust?' I asked.

'Nope.'

'Where is it then?' Vivi puzzled.

'Aha!' Paragon said for the third time. He brought up his other hand, which was wide open and empty. Steadily he curled his fingers over into a fist before opening them again.

Sitting in the palm of his hand was the ball.

'Whoa!' It was my turn to sound amazed. 'How did you do that? Have you got a secret tunnel running along your arms or something?'

'Prestidigitation,' Paragon said.

'Prestid . . . what?'

He gave his fingers another flourish. 'Magic!'

'You mean it's a trick?' Vivi said. 'Sleight of hand?'

Paragon nodded. 'It's a simple thing to learn. Just a series of moves. That's what prestidigitation is. A combination of skills designed to look impressive. Humans have to practise a long time to make them work. Luckily –' he kind of swaggered where he sat – 'I come pre-loaded with all those skills.' He reached forward and pulled a handkerchief out of my left ear. 'See?'

'I wish you could conjure up some water from somewhere,' I said, the back of my throat burning. 'I'm so thirsty.'

As the afternoon dragged on we made our way slowly back towards Unicorn Cottage. The countryside around Cambridge was largely deserted and we very rarely saw anybody at all. Whenever we did, Paragon would either hide behind a hedge or simply pull up the collar on the raincoat and tug down the wide-brimmed hat, which he had recently started wearing at a rather cheeky sort of angle. Thankfully, today we didn't see anybody. It made things much easier when we didn't.

We took a slight detour from the lanes along which we usually walked and crossed over onto Wandlebury. Thousands of years ago, the Wandlebury Ring was a hill fort. The circular shape meant that the inhabitants could defend themselves easily from attackers coming from any direction. Then at some point it had been turned into a park with a massive stable block dominating one end.

'We were always taught at school that there were two gods, called Gog and Magog, buried somewhere around here,' Vivi said as we climbed towards the ditch that ran around the edge of the park. 'Apparently they used to ride around in a golden chariot pulled by immortal horses.' As we got nearer the top of the small hill, my foot suddenly lost its grip on some rubble and my left leg slid away from beneath me. As I fell to the ground I hit the side of my face on a jagged rock that was sticking out of the earth. Stunned, I just lay there.

'Auden!'

Paragon bounded over and knelt beside me. His hand reached out and seized me by the shoulder.

'Auden. Are you OK? Here, let me help you up.' He grabbed me under the arms and lifted me with ease back onto my feet again, dusting the mess from my shirt. 'There! Oh no, you're hurt.' His fingers dabbed at my face and I could see blood smeared on the tips of them. 'You've cut your head.'

'It's all right,' I said, my own fingers feeling the small gash that had sent blood trickling down my cheek. 'It's nothing.'

'Wait.' Paragon bent over and, gripping the bottom of the trench coat, ripped a strip of material from it. 'Come here.' He wrapped the cloth around my head, covering up the wound, and tied it swiftly and securely, the knot just above my eye. 'There. That'll keep it clean for now. But when you get home you must wash it out. With water. OK? You have to clean it with some of your daily allowance. Yes?'

'I will.' I felt a bit odd with the bottom of a trench coat wrapped about my head. 'It'll be all right though. It's nothing.'

'I know, I know,' Paragon said. 'You'll live.' He patted me on the back. 'You OK to carry on? Or do you want to go home?'

I pointed upwards.

At the top, the ground levelled out. It was flat and dotted with trees. The grass looked mostly dead. The large stable building was grubby and rundown. Nobody had been up here in a long while.

No humans anyway.

Because above us, in the trees, birds sang like it was the first light of morning. Sheltered from the noise of the wind, the birdsong echoed from tree to tree, bouncing like a pinball from one tall pine to another.

The three of us stood there and listened as bullfinches, crossbills, sparrows and siskins (Paragon had spent an entire afternoon teaching us which was which) made their music and sang to each other like a high-up, spread-out choir.

Suddenly Paragon threw his hat and his coat onto the ground and took several strides away from us towards the centre of the circle. He stopped and held his arms heavenward, his head turning left then right as he watched the tops of the trees.

And then he started whistling.

High-pitched.

Like a bird.

I looked at Vivi, who did a sort of don't-ask-me face.

A second or two later something fluttered down from one of the trees and settled on Paragon's right arm. A sparrow. It twitched its head as if trying to make out what sort of strange thing it had just landed on. Paragon watched it as it hopped along his arm towards his face.

A moment passed, and then another sparrow alighted on the top of Paragon's head, quickly followed by another on his right arm, next to the first. Three birds, all of them singing along with Paragon's whistling.

He slowly turned around to face us.

It was usually impossible to tell when Paragon was smiling – his face was probably the most immobile part of him. The grille for a mouth never moved. The lights in the eyes simply glowed. But I knew that at that moment he was smiling like he'd never smiled before.

'This . . .' he said quietly, so as not to disturb the birds, 'this is a special place.' A fourth bird took up its place on Paragon's left arm. 'A very special place. If I were to get all rusted up and left to power down here, I don't think I'd mind. I can think of worse places to be.'

One of the birds on the right arm hopped over Paragon's head to meet the newcomer on the left arm. Paragon laughed and I found myself joining in.

'What do you think, Vivi? Wouldn't make a very good scarecrow, would I?'

'No. You wouldn't.' She grinned. 'One of the worst.'

A smaller sparrow came to join the others. It pecked a little at one of the lights blinking on and off near Paragon's elbow before flying off again.

'*Hope is the thing with feathers,*' Paragon began.

'*That perches in the soul –*
And sings the tune without the words –
And never stops – at all –
And sweetest – in the Gale – is heard –
And sore must be the storm –
That could abash the little Bird
That kept so many warm –'

'Christina Rossetti?' Vivi asked.

'Emily Dickinson,' Paragon replied.

'You're quite keen on her, aren't you?' I said, trying to disguise the fact that for some peculiar reason – right at that very moment, and from out of nowhere – I felt like I wanted to cry. Deep down in my chest, the poem or the sight of Paragon and the birds – something, anyway – was making me want to curl up on the ground and blub. I tried to brave it out. 'You like her poems, don't you? Always quoting her poems, you are.'

Paragon looked hard at me and I knew that he knew. I realised then that he always knew how I was feeling.

'Oh, you know, Auden,' he said, the lights on one of his eyes flickering like a wink, 'she's OK. She's all right. Wouldn't you agree?'

'So when do you think you'll tell your mother all about me?'

Paragon was staring out of my bedroom window, watching the irrigation pyramids spitting over the crops.

'I mean, you can't keep me secret forever. All secrets tend to come out in the end, no matter how hard you try to cover them.'

Sandwich was sitting at the bottom of my bed. She was cuddled up and purring, and every now and then Paragon would stroke her ears gently and make her purr and dribble even more.

'I don't know,' I said, my pencil scratching across the large sketch pad. 'I haven't really given it much thought. I just assumed I'd keep you secret forever and hide you away down under the shed every night.' I was trying to capture the exact shape of Paragon's head, but I was finding it difficult. Each time he moved I could see I was doing it wrong. I'd already worked my way through about a third of a rubber in the time I'd been attempting to draw him. 'I'm not sure how she'll react to a skyscraping robot who's been living under her lawn. I don't think she'll be all that happy.'

'Might be a bit of a shock, I suppose.' Paragon sniffed. 'Although I could be useful. Keep the house tidy. Take care of the garden. Cook dinner. That kind of thing. I might be useful, what with your dad being away.'

I kept on sketching. Badly.

Paragon turned away from the window and looked at me.

'You haven't talked much about it,' he said. 'Not since you found out.'

'Not much to say, is there?' I rubbed one of Paragon's eyes out and blew the crumbs of rubber off the page.

'There's always stuff to say, Auden.'

I sighed and put the pad down on the bed alongside Sandwich.

'I dunno,' I said. 'It's a bit like everything I've ever known has turned out to be wrong. Like finding out the moon's not real or something. Or that there are more than 180 degrees in a triangle. I can't trust any of the things I have always assumed to be true. I'm not sure I can trust what people tell me.'

'Auden –' Paragon leaned back against the wall and folded his arms – 'I may not be a human being, but I know an awful lot about them and the way they behave. It is true that humans are imperfect creatures. They have cracks in their behaviour. But these cracks are – trust me – only tiny. Humans are, in fact, nowhere near as imperfect as they like to believe. Oh yes, there are some that are badly damaged. People who lie and hurt and take pleasure in doing so. A bit like Boyle, I suppose. But for the most part humans are kind and truthful and wise and decent. If you ask someone for help then, chances are they will help you. And that's always been the case. Ever since the first human crawled out of the swamp and stood on two legs. If it wasn't the case then the entire human race would have died out millions of years ago. It is only through support and trust and love that humans have survived.'

'What about wars then?' I asked. 'Why do we have wars? Why are thousands and millions of people off fighting in Europe right now?'

Paragon shook his head. 'I don't know. I honestly don't know. That's the one aspect of human behaviour that I really do not get. Some people say it keeps the world in balance – straightens everything out so that the world can evolve even further. Some say it is mankind acting out behaviour that was necessary at the beginning of time – when they had to fight for food – and that people have never managed to abandon it entirely, despite evolution. But I don't know. It's the one thing that makes no sense to me, war.'

'I wish I could make the war stop,' I hissed. 'I wish this stupid war had never started. If the war had never started then my dad would be home right now and he would never have deserted his post and ended up in prison.' I felt a tear building in the corner of my eye. 'We'd be playing football and making model aeroplanes and things and everything would be OK.'

Paragon rested his hand on my shoulder. 'I know it's not the same, Auden . . . I realise that . . . But I could play football with you and make model aeroplanes. If you wanted.'

I gave him a wobbly smile.

'Like I said, it's not the same thing. I understand. I'm not your dad. But if you wanted me to . . . I think I might be quite good at football.'

'Thanks, Paragon.'

Sandwich got up, arched her back into an enormous stretch, yawned and jumped down from the bed.

'That's OK,' Paragon replied. 'I hope Vivi's feeling better.'

Vivi had QWERTY'd me earlier that morning to say that she wasn't feeling very well and that she wouldn't be going out today. A bad stomach, which meant that she would need to drink more water than normal. That was every parent's nightmare, a child with a bad stomach. They could work their way through their usual weekly allowance of water in just a matter of hours. After that the family would have to scrimp on their usage or – even worse – illegally buy some of the terrible, dirty Cat's Pee on the black market.

'She'll be OK,' I answered, wiping my nose on my sleeve. 'I know that her mum has a small case of water locked away in a cupboard for emergencies. She'll be working her way through that.'

'That's good.'

'You know what I find most incredible about war?' I jumped awkwardly back onto the subject. 'You know the strangest thing about it? It's that they have rules about what to do. What's allowed and what's not allowed on the battlefield. At some point in the past, the leaders of all the countries sat around a big table and decided that, even in wars, certain things were forbidden and other things were OK. You would think that as long as you defeated the other side and killed as many of their soldiers as possible, that that would be all that mattered. But, no. You can only kill people in certain ways.'

Paragon watched me as I let myself chatter on.

'So they came up with a big set of rules about how to fight and kill. Ridiculous! A big set of rules called . . . what is it? It's named after a city in Europe somewhere. What is it? The . . . er . . . that's right . . . the Geneva Convention. They're the set –'

I stopped.

Paragon whirred and straightened up, clanking loudly as he locked himself into the stiff position – arms dangling straight down, head level and staring ahead – like he did on the hilltop a few weeks previously, when he'd heard the word 'achromatopsia' for the first time.

He was doing it again.

Suddenly he spoke, in the same dull, monotonous robotic voice that he'd used on the hilltop.

'Dr . . . Milo . . . Treble . . . The . . . Wellspring . . . Science . . . and . . . Innovation . . . Centre . . . Dartford . . . Road . . . Huntingdon . . . The . . . Fleming . . . Building . . . Third . . . Floor . . . Room . . . F3:18 . . .'

Then he stopped talking and his entire body slumped to the floor, hitting the carpet with a solid thump.

'Paragon!' It was my turn to rush to his aid. 'What's wrong? What happened?'

'Oh . . .' He pushed himself up and steadied himself against the wall. 'I'm OK, Auden. Don't worry about me. Just another of those funny turns. Very peculiar.'

I grabbed his arm.

'What was that you said? You said somebody's name. And an address. Who *is* that?'

Paragon checked himself over. He bent and straightened his limbs and ran his fingers over the lights and switches. Everything appeared to be working as it had done before the episode.

'Milo Treble.'

'Who's Milo Treble?' I asked.

'I don't know. But I believe it's somebody who could help me with this.' Paragon pointed to the dead light on his chest – the one I'd always been so quick to dismiss. 'I think he might be able to help me get this working again.'

'And the rainbow machine!' I jumped up. 'He might be able to get that working too.'

17

The 726

Huntingdon, it turned out, was about twenty miles away. To get there we had three possible options. Firstly, we could tell Mum about Paragon and then – after she'd got over the shock of it (which, let's face it, might be weeks) – ask her to drive us there in the Bot Job. That didn't seem like a sensible plan to me. For a start I wouldn't rely on the Bot Job to get us even to the other side of the city. Since Mum had bought the thing, the exhaust had fallen off at least eight times by my reckoning, and it could only be a matter of time before it fell apart completely. No, it was all too much of a risk.

Secondly, we could walk. Twenty miles was probably nothing to Paragon, who could run so incredibly quickly. But to me and Vivi twenty miles might as well have been a hundred. There was no way we could get there and back in a single day. It was far too far.

In the end we settled on the third possibility. That was to catch the bus. Two buses each way, in fact. One into Cambridge, then another from the bus station to

Huntingdon itself. It would be another massive risk, but with no other way of getting us all there, it was a risk we would have to take.

So far, Vivi and I had always taken Paragon away from the city. Out into the fields and onto the hills where very few people bothered to go. There it was easy to keep him out of the way of inquisitive eyes. But by going into the city with him, we would be exposing him to hundreds and hundreds of people.

He needed a better disguise.

'What –' Paragon held the wig between his finger and thumb and stared at it like it might be a dead rat – 'is *that*?'

'A hairpiece,' Vivi said, smiling.

'Am I right in thinking that you want me to put *that* on the top of my head? So that it looks like I have hair?'

I nodded.

Paragon plonked the thing comically on the very top of his shiny metal skull and looked at us. The hair fell down over his eyes and, as he turned his head, the wig slipped a couple of inches so that it covered his left cheek.

'What do you think? Is it my style? Do I carry it off?'

Vivi and I laughed out loud and Paragon gave the wig a centre parting, which made it look even more ridiculous.

'I think,' Vivi eventually said, 'we might need to glue it on.'

She had brought a large bag of clothes and accessories from her mother's cast-offs sack. She dug about inside and brought out a pair of sunglasses. 'Try these.'

'I think –' Paragon snatched the shades out of Vivi's hand – 'that you are only doing this to have a laugh.' He positioned them on his nose, with the arms behind the small raised bumps on the side of his head where ears would normally be, just under the wig. 'Hey, man!' His voice was deliberately deep and gravelly. 'This is soooo cool. Wanna go and shoot some pool? I hear there's a real rad band playing down at the Golden Nugget.'

Vivi and I struggled to control our laughter again.

Paragon was brilliant at playing the fool. He didn't take himself too seriously. He was happy to sit there and do funny voices and look utterly mad if it meant that we enjoyed it. If we laughed at him.

He reminded me a little of Dad.

'Perhaps you're a sort of acting robot. Designed to act on the stage,' Vivi said.

Paragon stayed in character. 'Me? Some kinda dumb actor? Huh! Are you pulling my string? Are you pushing me under a bus? Whaddya think, like I'm only good for singin' and dancin', huh? Yerra nut. Dat's what yer are.'

By the time we'd fully dressed Paragon, my sides were aching and my cheeks were wet from all the tears. We stood back and admired our handiwork.

Vivi had somehow managed to strap a pair of size-12 shoes around Paragon's feet. She'd had to make a slight cut at the back for them to fit, but somehow they stayed on. Over his legs were pulled a pair of canvas chinos – a belt of string around the waist held them in place. A thick woollen jumper covered the chest and arms, and over that Paragon had put on and buttoned up his rather ragged raincoat. Leather gloves disguised the metallic hands, and the wig, which Vivi had now glued on, covered the sides of his head. The sunglasses hid Paragon's eyes and the wide-brimmed hat – positioned at its usual cheeky angle – threw a shadow over much of his face.

The only things that were not completely covered were the mouth and chin.

'What's the point in keeping the rest of him covered up if everyone can see that he's not got a normal mouth?' I asked. 'They'll spot that straight away.'

'Hold on.' Vivi rummaged about in the bag. 'Here.' She pulled out a stripy scarf. 'Wrap that around the bottom half of your face, Paragon.'

He took it from her and twisted it around and around his mouth.

'Any good?'

'Well . . .' I stood there with my arms folded, shaking my head to myself, 'they're definitely not going to be looking at you because you look like a robot,' I said. 'There's no worry about that. But they *will* be looking at you because you look ridiculously overdressed for such a hot day.'

'That's all right,' Vivi said. 'That doesn't matter. We can just pretend that he's our uncle or someone and that he's not very well.'

'Not very well?' I smiled. 'I don't think I'd feel very well, dressed like that.'

Paragon gave a twirl. 'To be honest, I think I look very dapper. Like a proper human being. I don't think anyone will pay me any attention whatsoever. I think I'll fit right in.'

The bus pulled up and the doors hissed open.

'I'll buy the tickets,' I whispered. 'Paragon, just keep quiet.'

'Okey-dokey.'

We stepped onto the bus and I dug some notes out of my pocket. 'One adult and two children for the city centre, please.'

The driver stared open-mouthed at Paragon.

'I said one adult and two children, please.'

Silence.

'Don't worry. I'm their uncle,' Paragon suddenly blurted out from behind the scarf, 'but I'm not very well.'

The driver's mouth fell even wider.

'Lovely day, isn't it?' Paragon adjusted his scarf and looked nervously around. 'Lovely bus you have here. Very . . . full of seats.'

I slapped some of the notes down on the little ledge. The driver jumped and shook himself back to normality.

'Er . . . eight thousand pounds please,' he said, his eyes leaping back and forth between me and Paragon. He fed the money into his cash machine and three tickets dropped out. I scooped them up and tugged on Paragon's coat.

As we walked up the aisle, the passengers all watched the strange, tall, overdressed man make his way towards the back of the bus. I shoved Paragon onto a window seat and sat down next to him. Vivi took the empty seat in front and twisted around to see us. A second or two later the bus started to move off.

'I thought I told you not to say anything,' I muttered to Paragon.

'Oh, I know you did. But when he looked at me like that I got a bit jumpity. I think this scarf and the sweater are ever so slightly overheating my decision gate boards. Quite frankly, I don't understand why human beings have to wear so many clothes. It can't be good for you, surely.'

'Look, try not to say anything. We don't want to attract too much attention, do we?'

'No. OK.'

As we got nearer the city centre, more people got on the bus. An old lady with a knotty wooden walking stick came and sat across the aisle from us, and out of the corner of my eye I could see her staring.

'Excuse me,' she said.

I tried to ignore her.

'Excuse me.'

'Auden.' Paragon nudged me with his elbow. 'Auden, that old woman wants to talk to you.'

'Shh.'

He nudged me again. 'Don't be rude. She wants to talk to you.'

'Excuse me.'

Sighing, I turned to her. 'Yes?'

'Is your friend all right? He looks a bit hot and bothered to me.'

'No. No. He's fine.' I smiled.

'I'm their uncle,' Paragon pointed to both Vivi and me. 'And I'm not very well. Thank you for asking, madam.'

'Oh.' She sat back on her seat, confused, and looked deliberately out of the window for the rest of the journey.

The bus station was just as stressful. Too many people in too small a space, most of them wondering what the issue was with the tall man in a hat. Why was he wearing sunglasses inside? Why did he have a big scarf wrapped around his face on a sunny summer's day? And why was his hair so lopsided?

'I think the glue's melting,' Vivi said as we scanned the screens to find the correct bus. 'I think he's getting all heated up and the glue's gone and melted.'

'Oh no. Try not to move your head too quickly or your wig'll come off,' I said to Paragon.

'I'll try.'

We made our way to stand 6 and waited for our bus to come in.

'You going to Huntingdon?'

A man with a fluffy beard and a huge head of hair standing just behind us was directing a question at Paragon.

'You waiting for the 726 to Huntingdon?'

'Er . . . Yes. I believe I am,' Paragon replied.

'Dreadful service, the 726,' the man said, seemingly unaware that Paragon was dressed like somebody expecting the worst winter storm in a hundred years. 'Late most of the time. That's if it isn't cancelled. You going to Huntingdon to see family?'

'Er . . . no. No. Er . . . An old friend.'

'Old friend, is it? I have an old friend in Huntingdon. I wonder if it's the same one. Tell me, what's your friend's name?'

Paragon gave a nervous twitch. 'Er . . . Milo Treble.'

'Who?'

'Milo Treble.'

'Never heard of him. No. My friend's name is Rory McDonald. Do you know him?'

'No. I'm afraid not.'

'Nice guy, Rory. You'd like him.'

Vivi and I were trying not to laugh as we listened in on the conversation.

'Used to run a biscuit factory. That wasn't in Huntingdon, mind. That was in Saffron Walden. Doesn't do it any more. Retired, see.'

The man peered at each of us in turn.

'Where is this stupid bus? Tut!'

Suddenly Paragon turned around just a little too quickly and his hat and wig slid to the floor.

'Oh!' The bearded man bent over and grabbed hold of the wig before reaching up and slapping it back onto Paragon's bald, metallic head. 'There you are!' He patted it into place. 'Can't have that coming off now, can we? After all –' he tapped the top of his own head with his finger – 'we toupee wearers must stick together, mustn't we?'

The journey to Huntingdon was quieter than the trip into Cambridge. The three of us sat on the long seat at the back of the bus, Paragon staring out of the window while Vivi and I talked.

'What was the word that started him off again?' Vivi asked softly.

'I said something about the Geneva Convention. Straight after that he began spouting off the name and address.'

'Why "Geneva Convention"? I don't understand.'

I shook my head.

'The Geneva Convention is to do with war, isn't it? Perhaps this Milo Treble man has something to do with

231

the war. Or killing.' She suddenly looked nervous. 'Do you think we can trust him? I mean, we've not even told our own mothers about Paragon. And now, here we are, about to show him to a complete stranger. What if he takes him away from us? What then?'

I didn't want to think about it. It had taken me so long to accept Paragon for what he was that I *reeeaaaally* didn't want to lose him now. I'd only just started to get to know him. It would be like some sort of sick joke. First my dad gets taken away, and then Paragon.

It was too horrible to consider.

Still, I had to trust Paragon. There was nothing else for it.

'Paragon seems to think that he might help him,' I said. 'I'm hoping he might know something about the rainbow machine – might be able to tell us where the battery is. I mean, Treble is obviously a scientist. Perhaps he knew Uncle Jonah well . . .' I decided to spill my guts. 'Vivi.'

'Yes?'

'I've got something important to tell you, but you have to promise not to get all girly and hysterical, what with the big guy over there and us being in a confined space and all.'

'Au-*den*! Just get on with it.'

'Well . . . I don't think Uncle Jonah . . . er . . . died.'

Her eyes went wide as the Grand Canyon. 'You mean he's still alive? Wow –'

'Er, no . . . I mean, I don't think he *just* died.'

Then her brain leaped the Grand Canyon. 'You think he was murdered.'

I gave her a sombre look. 'Uh-huh. Pretty much.'

18

The Wellspring Science and Innovation Centre, Dartford Road, Huntingdon

We hopped off the bus on the very outskirts of Huntingdon and walked the mile and a half to the Wellspring Science and Innovation Centre. The road was long and sweeping, and clearly underused, judging by the hardy weeds that sprang up along the edges of the kerbs. It took us away from town and out into even more sparse countryside. After a while, the view opened up and directly ahead of us we saw the buildings.

It was an enormous complex. Tall, box-like buildings – lots of them – with shiny mirrored windows, sticking out of the ground like the pins on an upturned plug.

'Wow!' I found myself saying. 'Look at this place.'

Around the complex ran a ten-metre-high fence with barbed wire strung across the top. Even from where we were standing, you could hear the strong buzz of electricity running along its length.

As if to hammer home the fact, a signpost nearby warned in a severe font:

KEEP OUT. ELECTRIC FENCE.
RISK OF DEATH.

The road led to a gate, where a bored armed guard was prodding some dried-on old chewing gum from the tarmac with the tip of his boot.

'Not exactly the inviting scene I thought it might be,' I said. 'Do you think they'll even let us in?'

Vivi stepped forward. 'We'll never know unless we try. Come on.'

The three of us strolled as casually as we could possibly manage towards the gate. The guard – having given up on the chewing gum – glared at us as we approached, his rifle at the ready.

'Halt!' he shouted.

We stopped.

'Who goes there? What do you want?'

'We are here to see Dr Milo Treble,' Vivi called back, her voice strong and confident. If she was as scared as I was, it certainly didn't show. 'Dr Milo Treble in the Fleming Building.'

'Do you have an appointment?' the guard asked.

'No. But we are here on a matter of the utmost importance.' Vivi obviously thought that that was a clever thing to say and she gave me a sort of nod to highlight just how clever she thought it was.

The guard, though, wasn't impressed. 'Doesn't make any difference. No appointment means no entry.' He waved the rifle towards us. 'Now run along or I shall have to shoot you for acting in a threatening and terrorist-like way.'

We all stood there for a while, astounded at just how abrupt our visit had been.

'Go on.' The guard waggled the rifle up and down. 'Off you go now.'

'Come on,' Paragon muttered. 'Let's go.'

'But –' I began.

'No buts. Let's go.'

He turned around and slowly started walking back the way we had come, his shoulders slumped.

Vivi and I just stared at each other before racing off to catch up with Paragon.

'You can't just leave it there,' I said as I came alongside him. 'You said Treble could help you. Why didn't you try harder to get in?'

Paragon said nothing. He just kept on walking.

'I'm sure they'll let us in if we explain the situation to them,' Vivi argued as she skipped to keep up. 'Don't you think?'

Paragon marched on, his head bowed.

'I thought you were stronger than that,' I growled.

'I thought you would at least try. For goodness sake, I thought you were brave.'

Paragon stopped dead.

'Don't worry, Auden,' he said. 'I've not given up yet.' He turned and looked back at the guard, who'd gone back to his previous occupation of trying to prise chewing gum off the road with his toe. Suddenly Paragon started walking away from the road and over the clumps of stringy grass. Vivi and I followed. 'You see, if we're not going to get in through the *front* door . . .'

'We'll get in through the *back* door! Of course.' Paragon had not given up after all. He was simply thinking.

'Or a *side* door at least. Come on.'

We trudged over the earth until the guard disappeared from sight, the wire fence buzzing and clicking like a fly trapped in a bathroom. It eventually turned away from itself by pretty much ninety degrees and we continued to follow it. A few hundred metres later, Paragon stopped.

'This is probably good enough,' he said. He slipped off his gloves and handed them to Vivi. 'Now, whatever you do, do not touch me while I'm connected. OK? It could kill you.'

We both nodded and automatically took a step back.

Paragon brought his left hand up next to the fence.

'Paragon!' Vivi squeaked.

Paragon looked towards Vivi and whispered, 'Shh.'

Suddenly Paragon reached out and grabbed the fence with his hand, gripping it with his fingers. Sparks flew from the fence and Paragon gave a small judder, making his hat slide off.

'Paragon?' I asked. 'Paragon? Are you OK?'

He didn't answer. It was like he was miles away, in a trance, the lights for his eyes blinking on and off.

'Is he OK?' Vivi looked worried.

Then he started talking.

'Dr Milo Treble is here today. He electronically signed in at 8.35 this morning. There are three armed guards on duty in the complex. The one at the gate and two patrolling the grounds. One of those guards follows a route that passes the Fleming Building every sixteen minutes or so. The last time he passed it was seven minutes ago, meaning we have nine minutes left in which to enter the building.'

'We could wait until he's passed again,' Vivi said. 'That would give us the full sixteen minutes to get in.'

'Nope,' Paragon replied. 'That guard is about to take his lunch break in the guards' room, which overlooks the entrance to the building. If we wait now, we'll be waiting for well over an hour. During that time, two Scoot drones fly over the area to check the periphery of the site.'

'But you can disable drones from a distance, can't you?' I said.

Paragon shook his head. 'This is open country. If they fly across from the other side of the park then they might well spot us before they are close enough for me to disable them.'

'But how are we going to get in?'

Paragon – still holding onto the fence with his left hand – lifted up his right hand with the index finger extended. Then the weirdest thing happened. The tip of the finger twisted completely back on itself, exposing a tiny pipe. Suddenly a fierce flame started burning. Paragon brought it up to the fence and started cutting away at the wires, melting through them like butter.

'Whoa!'

'Holy guacamole!'

'I'm redirecting the flow of the electricity around the gap I'm making. Nobody'll suspect a thing.'

If you'd told me a few months earlier that I would find myself standing in the middle of the Cambridgeshire countryside with a friend from school and a robot, cutting our way through an electric fence to break into a science park in order to try to talk to a man none of us had ever met before, I'd've called you a loony. But, as it was, it seemed perfectly natural for us all to be there.

In fact, it almost felt like fate.

Paragon worked steadily and, after about four minutes, the last wire was sliced and a wide section of the fence, big enough for us to crawl through, fell to the ground.

'There.' He pulled his left hand away from the fence. 'Let's go.'

Paragon went first, followed by Vivi and then me.

'The Fleming Building is that way. Now walk normally. Don't attract attention.'

I half laughed to myself, remembering the way the driver of the first bus had stared at Paragon. With his height, and dressed the way he was, it was hard for him *not* to attract attention.

Then, from out of nowhere, a small electric van zoomed past.

Quickly Paragon turned us around and pointed up at something as if he was an adult showing us something incredible in the sky and we were two little children, fascinated by whatever it was. The van went on without stopping and disappeared way in the distance.

'Come on.'

We carried on down a long, dull road before turning a corner onto another long, dull road. The whole area seemed deserted. Clearly many of the people who would normally work here were off fighting.

'There it is.' Paragon nodded up ahead.

THE ALEXANDER FLEMING BUILDING, read the flowery sign on the lawn directly in front of it.

We sped up and walked up the steps to the vast glass door. I gave the door a push but it didn't budge.

'Look,' Vivi pointed.

The door was locked and the large touch-sensitive pad on the wall revealed that it could only be unlocked by somebody with a registered handprint.

'We can't get in,' I moaned.

'Paragon. How long have we got?' asked Vivi.

'One minute exactly.'

'What are we going to do?'

'Aha! Stand back.' He stood in front of the touch-sensitive pad and held up his right hand yet again. This time it was the tip of the smallest finger that flipped backwards, revealing a needle-like wire. Paragon felt around the pad before inserting the wire into it. The pad glowed bright and then faded.

'Now, Auden, quick. Put your hand on the pad.'

'But it won't recognise my handprint.'

'No, it won't. But in the millionth of a second it will take to question your print, I am going to register you on the system. Essentially, I am going to race their computer. OK? You ready?'

I positioned myself next to Paragon, my hand flat, ready to hit the pad.

'OK. Go.'

I put my hand on the screen and less than a second later the glass door whooshed open.

'You did it!'

'Phew! It was close though. They've got some efficient software here. I only just got there in time. It required me making several thousand nano-bypasses to be able to do it.'

'That must have been the quickest race ever,' Vivi said, smiling, as we rushed into the hallway of the Fleming Building. Outside, we could see the guard coming down the road, swinging his gun as he headed towards his lunch.

19

Milo Treble

The building was utterly silent. It was almost as if it was due to be demolished and everyone had vacated it, leaving it hollow and echoey. As we made our way up the granite steps, our footsteps bounced around the stairwell like intruders. In silences between you could make out the usually inaudible whirrs and bleeps that came from somewhere within Paragon.

'Where is everybody?' I whispered, though it sounded like a roar in this place.

Paragon shook his head. 'The war? Some might be away in Europe. Others have probably been conscripted into some other government work. Who knows? There are probably only a handful of scientists working in this entire complex now.'

We worked our way up each flight of stairs without seeing a single person. On the third floor we consulted a sign on the wall and tip-tapped down an endless corridor. The lights were all blazing as if the building was still a normal, up-and-running place of work, and a number of the screens on the walls were still flashing up the occasional message.

REMEMBER – WATER IS PRECIOUS.
DON'T WASTE. DON'T SPILL.
CREATIVITY IS THE KEY TO
PEACE AND PROGRESS.
WORK SO THAT YOUR CHILDREN MAY
HAVE A BETTER, BRIGHTER FUTURE.

The messages gave me the creeps. They seemed to have the smell of brainwashing about them. What exactly was this place?

Paragon suddenly stopped.

'What is it?' I asked.

'Drones.'

'Drones? Inside?'

'Yes. They're behind us. Just around the corner. A hundred and twenty-two of them. And they're coming this way.'

'A hundred and –'

'Shhh!' He pushed Vivi and me against the wall of the corridor, next to a metal filing cabinet. What was happening? How could a hundred and twenty-two drones be coming towards us? There was no noise. Surely we would be able to hear them.

I peered around the filing cabinet and something weird

began happening. It was like the air at the end of the corridor was starting to shiver. Quiver. A cloud of what seemed like dust hovered and rippled halfway between the floor and the ceiling. Still there was no noise. Then I noticed the cloud was getting bigger. No. Not getting bigger. It was moving towards us.

'What is it?' Vivi hissed at Paragon, who was standing firmly in the centre of the corridor.

'I . . . can't . . . talk,' he stuttered. 'Not now. Trying . . . to . . . block all one hundred . . . and twenty-two of them. Difficult.' His fists clenched like he was struggling.

'Paragon! Are you all right?'

The cloud got nearer, and then, as it passed into the beam of light streaming in through a window, I could make out what they were.

Butterflies. Tiny, shiny mechanical butterflies.

Butterfly-shaped drones. Each one only a little bigger than an actual butterfly.

'Almost . . . done. Hard to . . . keep them all . . . blocked together.' Paragon looked and sounded tense. 'Now to . . . reprogram them . . . All of them . . . Every . . . single . . . one!'

The fluttering mass of butterfly drones got slowly closer and closer until they were about a couple of metres from Paragon.

'OK . . .' Paragon clenched his fists even tighter. 'Time . . . for you all . . . to . . . go!'

Suddenly one of the butterflies – a largish one with wide wings and spiral antennae – peeled off from the group, flickered upwards, brushed against the ceiling and then flew off back in the direction from which it had come. A few seconds later, two others did exactly the same thing. Then, almost as one, the rest of the cloud seemed to pause before turning back on itself, each of the minuscule robotic butterflies fluttering away from us.

'Wow,' whispered Vivi. 'They're beautiful.'

As the last of the cloud disappeared back around the corner, Paragon seemed to relax his grip.

'Phew! A hundred and twenty-two of them at the same time. That's quite a feat. Really tested my multi-dimensional tasking ability.' He swaggered with pride or wobbled through exhaustion; it was hard to tell which. 'My systems really are getting a bit of a workout today!'

'What sort of drones were they?' I asked. 'I've never seen any like *that* before.'

'Zephyr drones,' Paragon replied. 'Internal surveillance units. Still at the prototype stage.'

'Well,' Vivi announced as we started to make our way along the corridor once again, 'I think that Zephyrs are now my favourite type of drone. They're *soooo* much prettier than the Ariels.'

'Beautiful is not always good, Vivi,' warned Paragon. 'Never judge on appearances . . . Wait!'

'Hmm?'

'Quiet. Can you hear that?'

Vivi and I strained to listen. We strained and then we strained a bit more.

'No. I can't hear anything.'

'Me neither.'

Paragon took a turning off the main corridor. 'It's coming from this direction.'

Vivi and I followed close behind. After about a minute, we could both make out what Paragon must have been hearing.

Music. Classical music.

'What's that?' Vivi asked.

'It's Rachmaninoff's Piano Concerto Number 2 in C Minor, Op. 18. The 1965 recording by Earl Wild.' Paragon tossed out the information like it was nothing to him.

We walked towards the music. It got louder and louder as we got nearer and nearer until –

BANG!

A door flew open and slammed into the wall as a man marched out into the corridor, his head bent over a sheet of paper. He was so absorbed in reading that he didn't even notice us standing in front of him.

'Rubbish!' he muttered to himself. 'Insubstantial lightweight rubbish!' He reached up and opened one of the windows on the corridor before scrunching up the paper and tossing it out.

I looked out of the window and watched it as it fell and landed on a grass verge covered with thousands more little balls of scrunched-up paper.

The man closed the window and turned to go back into the room. That was when he saw us.

'Who are you?' he asked in an annoyed sort of voice. 'What do you want?'

Vivi stepped forward. 'Dr Treble?'

He was a man of about forty with long, curly dark hair and a small, neat beard and moustache. He wasn't fat, but neither was he skinny. He was wearing a T-shirt and jeans that desperately needed a wash. Oh, and his eyes looked very, very tired.

'Yes?' he asked suspiciously.

'We're here to talk to you about Jonah Bloom, sir.' I took a step nearer. 'We'd like to ask a few questions if you don't mind.'

The man barked a laugh. 'I've already answered all the questions I'm ever going to answer about Bloom. Who are you anyway? How did you get in here? This is a secure complex.'

'My name is Auden Dare, sir. I am Jonah Bloom's nephew.'

Treble frowned and looked hard at me. 'You're the boy who can't see colour.'

'Yes.'

Treble didn't say anything. He was obviously weighing things up in his mind. 'Look, I've nothing more to say about Bloom . . . your uncle. I gave a number of statements to the Water Allocation Board. They accepted my version of events. If you've any questions, you'd be better off talking to them.' His hand reached for the handle of the door that led back into the room from which he'd just stomped. 'I'm sorry about your uncle. It's very sad. But, please, I have work to do. Leave the way you came. Goodbye.' He turned the handle.

'Wait,' Paragon called, and Treble released his grip. 'Wait. Dr Treble, I think there's something you should see.'

'Do you now? Well, what exactly is that, might I ask?'

'Me.' In one smooth movement Paragon threw off the hat, glasses and scarf and ripped the coat and jumper from his torso. The light blazing in through the windows reflected brightly off his hard metal body and dazzled Treble momentarily.

Treble stood with his mouth wide open as Paragon approached and stood directly in front of him, towering over the scientist.

Nobody said a thing. Not for ages. Not until Rachmaninoff's Piano Concerto Number 2 in C Minor had finished. And then, eventually, Treble broke the silence with a single word.

'Paragon?' he said.

20

A Revelation

We were in Treble's large and wonderful laboratory. There were huge machines that did things I couldn't understand. There were flames busy bubbling substances that I'd never seen before. There were shelf upon shelf and row upon row of pieces of scientific equipment that I would never know the names of.

It was like a strange new magical world.

Screens and monitors beeped and fizzed, and weird shapes and equations were scribbled all over a scruffy whiteboard.

And the smell!

Rotting eggs, burnt metal, sickly sweet sugar. All mixed together.

Treble stood facing Paragon.

'My, my . . .' he admired as he closely inspected the intricacies of the robot's limbs and head. 'My, my. Magnificent work. Bloom surpassed himself with this. Superb craftsmanship, I must say.'

'How did you know Paragon's name?' Vivi asked.

'Eh?' Treble, slightly annoyed to be distracted, turned to look at her. 'How did I know its name? Oh, because I named it.'

'You named him?'

'Inadvertently, I suppose. Bloom was looking for a name for his next project. He never told me what it was exactly, said it was something that was going to change the world. Something perfect. So I suggested Paragon. A paragon is something which is considered to be perfect, you see.' He went back to his inspection. 'And this is it. Bloom's paragon. My, my.'

'Him,' I said. 'He.'

'Hmm?' Treble half ignored me.

'Paragon is a "him". Not an "it".'

'It's a humanoid robot,' Treble corrected me. 'It's not actually human. Just human *shaped*. It doesn't have internal organs. It's not capable of independent thought. It's an "it".'

'Ahem,' Paragon coughed. 'Should you all be discussing me like I'm not here? Seems like bad manners if you ask me.'

I laughed. Vivi laughed. Treble frowned.

'So you were good friends with Dr Bloom,' Vivi said.

'Well . . . er . . .' Treble hesitated. 'Once upon a time.' He poked at something near Paragon's ear.

'Ouch!' Paragon jumped. 'Do you mind?'

Treble frowned again.

'What does "once upon a time" mean?' I asked.

'It means what it says. It means we were friends once, and then we weren't.'

'Why not?'

Treble sighed. 'It's all very dull, I'm afraid. You wouldn't be interested.'

'Go on. Try me.'

'Stretch out your leg,' Treble ordered Paragon who duly obliged. 'Fascinating. Absolutely fascinating.'

'Dr Treble.'

Treble sighed again. 'We had a professional argument. Over an academic prize. The Geneva Prize for Scientific Advancement, if you must know.'

Geneva? So that was why Paragon was programmed to reveal Treble's name and address. It wasn't the phrase 'Geneva Convention' that had triggered him. Just the word 'Geneva'. I looked at Vivi and she looked at me.

'Anyway,' Treble continued, 'we argued over who was likely to be first to win the Geneva Prize. Silly, I know. But then scientists can be silly over things like that. Vain. We each set ourselves the challenge of being the first to win it, and we went our separate academic ways.' He suddenly sounded sad. 'I didn't speak to him at all for the last year of his life.'

I peered around the laboratory. 'So what are you working on now?'

'A number of things. None of them very successful, I'm afraid.' He patted Paragon on the back. 'Nothing like this.' Treble looked back at us. 'What's its cognitive function like?'

'Cognitive what?'

'How he thinks.' Vivi put me straight.

'Why don't you ask him yourself?' I said. 'He's rather fond of poetry.'

'Poetry?'

'Especially Emily Dickinson,' Vivi added.

Treble looked confused.

'I can quote you some now, Dr Treble. If you'd like.' Paragon cleared his throat and was about to launch into something or other.

'Er, no,' Treble cut him short. 'No. Don't.'

Paragon appeared deflated.

'What about its mobility?'

'He's very fast,' said Vivi, 'and very good at hide-and-seek.'

Treble raised his eyebrows.

'There *is* something though, Dr Treble,' Paragon quietly remarked. 'This light here –' he pointed – 'it's not working. And I've no idea what it's for or how to get it started. I was wondering if you might be able to help me.'

Treble tapped the dead light. 'Might it not just have blown?'

'No,' Paragon answered. 'It's fully functioning. But for some reason it's not reacting to any of my diagnostics.'

Treble thought and as he did so he gently stroked his beard.

'OK.' He walked over to a computer situated towards the rear of the laboratory, clicked a button and a wobbly line suddenly appeared on the screen. 'Does it have a co-axial digital data jack?' He aimed the question at Vivi and me.

Paragon answered by walking up to the computer and flipping back yet another of his fingertips. He proffered the finger to Treble, who grinned and attached a lead to it.

'Bloom really did think of everything. Amazing.'

Treble plugged the other end of the lead into the computer and began to tap at the old-fashioned keyboard.

'Right . . . let's see what the problem is . . .'

A series of shapes started to flit across the monitor. Three-dimensional shapes. Wiry-looking cubes and cuboids. Spheres and cones. Triangular prisms. Twisting all over the screen. And then more complicated things – shapes for which there are probably no names. After that came a number of two-dimensional tessellations, scrolling from left to right then top to bottom. I had no idea what any of it meant, but Treble clearly did.

'Dr Treble?' I ventured as he gazed at the screen. 'I think my uncle was working on a machine to help me see colour.'

'Hmm?'

'Something he called a rainbow machine. We found it at his house but it's missing its battery. I wondered if you knew anything about it? Did my uncle say anything about that?'

'Erm . . .' He was still focusing on the images in front of him. 'No. No. Sorry. Don't know anything about that.' My heart dropped like a stone again. Was I ever going to get this damned rainbow machine to work?

'Did you try passing the secondary load over the central auxiliary system?' Treble asked Paragon.

'Of course.' Paragon sounded a bit put out. 'It was one of the first things I tried. I've attempted all the possible permutations of power to resistance ratio, but nothing seems to work.'

'Inverted the amplitude substructures?'

'Many times.'

'Hmm.' Treble looked stumped. 'Are you sure the bulb hasn't just blown?'

Paragon gave a sort-of sigh. 'It's not that.'

Treble tapped at the keyboard a bit more and the whole screen went zigzaggy.

'What about . . . what about undermining the whole motor system and backtracking the primary load within the pseudo-parameters? Momentarily, of course.'

Paragon tilted his head at a curious angle. 'Why would I try that? I wouldn't want to risk losing all motor function now, would I?'

The whole conversation flew over mine and Vivi's heads like a Scoot drone. Mine anyway.

'No, but . . . if you do it for less than a billionth of a second, there should be no serious comeback. Everything should just work as normal.' He held a finger over one of the keys. 'I can do it for you if you'd like.'

'Er . . . no. I'm not so sure that's a good idea, after –'

'Too late.' Treble hit the button with a loud tap.

'No! . . . Oh.' Paragon looked at his arms and his hands and wiggled his fingers. 'Oh. It's OK. I still have mobility. Ha!'

A second or two passed before and then –

'Look!' Vivi pointed. The light on Paragon's chest had started flashing. Constantly. About once a second.

'Oh! Thank you, Dr Treble,' Paragon rushed up to Treble and held out his hand. 'Thank you so much.'

Treble looked at Paragon's hand like it was something alien before slowly – and perhaps slightly reluctantly – taking it and shaking it.

'That's . . . OK . . . Paragon.'

'So,' I said, the disappointment still showing in my voice, 'now that you've got it going, what does it do?'

Paragon stood perfectly still as if he was giving the matter some serious thought.

'I . . . don't know.'

'What?'

'I've no idea what it is.'

'Hold on,' I huffed. 'You've been worried about the light not working. And now that you've got it working, you don't know what it does?'

Paragon thought again and shrugged. 'Nope. No idea.'

'Unbelievable!'

Treble was still staring at the monitor. 'Wait a minute. There are some other functions that have lain dormant since your initial power-up. I can see something here.'

'What do you mean?' Vivi asked.

Paragon had a puzzled look. 'Other functions? That can't be. Everything in my database is now accounted for. There *is* nothing else.'

'Not according to this, it isn't.' Treble jabbed his finger at the screen.

'But I don't understand.'

'Let me see if I can get it to . . .' The sentence faded away to nothing as Treble focused back on the images flashing on the monitor, his fingers dancing over the keyboard.

'There must be a mistake,' Paragon argued. 'I've fully exhausted every possible operation of my being. There is nothing more that I can do.'

'Yes, there is.' Treble didn't even look up. 'Hold out your arms.'

'I'm sorry?'

'I said hold out your arms. Straight in front of you.'

Vivi and I watched perplexed as Paragon levelled his arms so that they were horizontal.

'Now watch.' Treble jabbed at another key.

At that, something moved on the back of each of Paragon's forearms. Two rectangular plates of metal lifted away from each arm by about a centimetre or two, then separated and curled around both sides of the forearms.

'What's going on?' I wondered out loud.

Slowly, a long, thin, dark metal pipe rose up from inside each arm until it was sitting along the length of the arm. There was a click as the pipes locked into position.

'What are they?' I asked.

Treble swivelled in his chair. 'Machine guns. They're machine guns.'

21

The Utmost Danger

Treble produced some ersatz meat-paste sandwiches from out of his plastic lunchbox and handed them around. 'There were rumours. About Jonah Bloom. You see, the scientific world is actually a rather small, close-knit one. Everyone has a fair idea of what everyone else is doing. So even though he and I hadn't talked for a year, I was still vaguely aware through colleagues and members of various scientific establishments, of what he was up to.

'And the first rumour was that he was doing some work for the Water Allocation Board. No one knew what precisely, but something. Something big. The second rumour said that he had fallen out with them and was refusing to complete the project. On ethical grounds. And not long after that second rumour bounced about the scientific establishment, Bloom was found dead.'

'Yes,' I said quickly, looking at Vivi. 'I think he was murdered.'

Treble's eyebrows arched.

I told him about the way Unicorn Cottage and Uncle Jonah's rooms had been trashed. I told him about the threatening letter we'd found in a file. The clues that both Vivi and I had been left in order to find Paragon. All the tiny little pieces of evidence to suggest that Jonah Bloom had not died a natural death.

Treble put his own sandwich down on the desk. 'It's exactly what I've been thinking ever since he was found. Of course I couldn't prove anything. I doubt anyone can – not even you, Auden. But it seems rather more than a coincidence that Bloom dies soon after walking out on a top-secret scientific project.'

'What about the police?' Vivi leaned across the desk. 'Didn't you tell them that you thought Dr Bloom was murdered? Wouldn't they find out the truth?'

Treble gave an awkward shrug. 'The police investigation found nothing untoward. What could I do? Anyway, the police and the Water Allocation Board are too closely interlinked to be completely fair and unbiased. They are basically in each other's pockets. They're the same thing.'

We sat in silence as we digested the information.

The Water Allocation Board were responsible for killing my uncle.

'Soon after Bloom was found dead,' Treble eventually continued, 'the WAB paid me a visit. The first of several actually. Questioned me – well, interrogated me, to be more accurate. Asked me if I knew anything about Bloom's current work. Had I had any contact with him recently? That sort of thing.' He picked up another small sandwich and shoved it into his mouth whole. After he had swallowed it, he went on. 'They also asked if the word "Paragon" meant anything to me. Obviously I feigned complete ignorance. I think they bought it. And to be honest, apart from giving him his name, I knew nothing whatsoever about Paragon. Until now, that is.'

Vivi put her hand up suddenly like she was in class. 'Does this mean that Paragon . . .' her voice quavered, 'is in danger?'

'It means,' Treble responded, his expression stern, 'anyone associated with Paragon is in danger. Very grave danger. The utmost danger.'

I felt a shiver pass like a draught through the room.

I got up and went over to Paragon. He was sitting some distance away from us, on a stool, and was bent over and staring at the floor. Since the guns had been revealed he seemed to be in a kind of depressed stupor.

'Paragon?'

'Hey, Audendare.' He looked up at me but the glow in his eyes seemed a little dimmer than usual.

I knelt beside him and put my hand on his shoulder. He'd been there for me when I needed him, when I found out my dad wasn't a soldier but a prisoner. He'd supported me and comforted me and told me everything was going to be OK.

Now I was going to do the same for him.

'How are you feeling?' I asked.

'Oh. Not so good.'

I put my arms around him and held him tight.

'You know, I don't understand,' he said, his hand patting my arm. 'All this knowledge I have. All the poetry and language and art and nature. Why do I have it? Why was I given it? It doesn't make sense.'

'I don't know.'

He gave a bitter laugh. 'Weird, isn't it? All these weeks, you and Vivi have been wondering what exactly my role is. We've exhausted most things. Doctor. Teacher. Farmer.' He shook his head. 'And then it turns out I'm nothing more than a killing machine.'

He squeezed my arm, his hand soft and careful. Gentle. It was not the touch of a killing machine.

'I see how you felt now. Finding out about your father,' he said. 'Coming across a truth that hurts. Everything just dropping beneath you. The whole world falling away. Like a big hole that you hadn't noticed was there. A pain you weren't expecting.'

'What does any of it matter?' I said, trying to sound cheery but with tears in my eyes. 'It doesn't make any difference. I mean, my dad's still my dad. And you're still you. Just because you were designed in a particular way, doesn't mean you have to *be* that way. You're better than that. You've risen above it. You're Paragon. You're *my* Paragon. And I love you.'

'D'you think we can trust him?' I asked Vivi after we'd got Paragon safely back to the shed, blinking light and all. 'Treble, I mean.'

'I guess so.' She tucked a blanket around Paragon's legs. 'Why would he warn us of danger otherwise? If he wanted to harm us, surely he'd reassure us we were safe, then make his move.'

'Good thinking, Six Six!'

'That light worries me though. It reminds me of Morse code. What if there are other Paragons in the world and *our* Paragon's signalling to them?'

'Oh no.' I smiled, placing a cushion under his head. 'There's only one of this guy. He's unique. Sleep tight, dude.'

PART SIX
YELLOW

22

The Water
Allocation Board

The loud bang awoke me. Without thinking, I threw the covers off and stood up. *What was that?*

Voices. Growly voices. And footsteps. Heavy boots pounding up the stairs.

Something wasn't right.

I pushed the window open and leaned out of it. Suddenly my bedroom door flew open so I leaped out, grabbing hold of the tree branch and dropping down onto the trampoline before bouncing hard onto the ground, my bare feet scratching on the dry earth.

'He's got out of the window!'

'He's in the garden!'

Loud, angry voices from above me.

I didn't know what to do, so I sprinted towards the hole in the hedge. If I could get through it and away across the field I might be able to hide and assess what was going on.

But Mum!

Suddenly I thought of Mum. I couldn't just leave her in the house. Whatever was going on, I couldn't just desert her. I had to go back.

So I slowed.

That was when one of them tackled me to the ground. They thumped roughly into my shoulders and dragged me down.

'I've got him!' he called to the others. 'I've got the boy.'

My face was buried in the dirt and I couldn't see. The man pulled my arms behind my back and tied something around my wrists so I couldn't move them. Then he picked me up by my pyjamas, stood me on my feet and turned me around.

The man had tough features and cold eyes. His chin was covered in a thin, scratchy-looking layer of stubble. And he wore the dark uniform and protective helmet of the Water Allocation Board. Over his chest, crossing from top right to bottom left, was a belt of bullets, and on his hip, strapped away within a leather case, was a revolver.

'Come on. Move!'

He gave me a harsh shove, forcing me back towards the house.

The house was full of them. Dozens of them. They were kicking things over and pulling pictures from the walls. I could hear a loud ripping noise coming from the sitting room as one of the soldiers sliced a big hole in the sofa.

The man who had tackled me kept jabbing me in the back as we made our way past the men, through the house, to the kitchen. 'Keep moving.'

'Here he is!' It was a smooth, educated, well-spoken voice that greeted me as the soldier gave a final shove and closed the kitchen door behind me.

My mother was sitting at the table, a terrified look on her face. Next to the back door, another of the soldiers was standing to attention, his watchful eyes pinning both me and Mum down.

But it wasn't him I was interested in.

In front of the sink – the window behind him – was a man dressed in the uniform of a Water Allocation Board officer. He was older than the other soldiers. More lined around the eyes. His slick hair looked greyish and a bushy moustache dominated his top lip.

'Good of you to join us, Auden. Please –' he indicated a chair – 'sit.'

I sat on the chair next to my mother and felt her arms pulling me nearer.

'Now,' he turned to the sink. 'I hope you don't mind, but I'm feeling rather thirsty.' He took a glass and turned on the tap, filling it to the very top. He spun back to face us and took a long sip from the tumbler. I noticed that he'd left the tap running behind him.

'That's better.'

'Who are you?' I said. 'What do you want?'

'Now, the second of those questions I believe you already know the answer to. So let me answer the first.' His movements and his speech reminded me of a snake. 'I am General Heracles Woolf of the Second Infantry Division of the WAB. British Aquarian Protection Cross (First Class). Distinction in the Field of Utilities Medal, awarded with Honours.' He gave an almost sarcastic little bow, and I hated him straight away.

'Please.' My mother's voice quivered. 'What do you want from us?'

'Why don't you ask your son that?' Woolf remarked bitterly. 'I'm sure he can tell you. After all, he's been a very busy boy.'

I didn't understand. Why were they here now? Why hadn't they come to get Paragon earlier? What had changed?

And then it dawned on me.

Treble.

Treble had contacted them and told them where Paragon was. He'd probably made a deal with the WAB, asking for some involvement in developing Paragon so that he could try and win the Geneva Prize. His academic vanity had got the better of him and he had betrayed us all. Including my uncle.

At that moment I hated him more than I hated General Woolf.

'Now, Auden –' Woolf took another sip – 'there are a thousand questions that I need to ask you. A thousand questions. And, in due course, I will ask you every single one of them. But, at this moment in time, I only need the answer to one.' He stared straight at me. 'Where is it?'

I tried to look away. 'I don't know what you mean.'

Woolf shook his head. 'Come on, Auden. Credit us with some intelligence. We know it's around here somewhere.'

I looked down at the floor and ignored him.

'Oh,' he said, 'look.' He turned back to the sink, where the tap was still trickling out water. 'Silly me. I left your tap running.' He twisted the tap and the water suddenly started to gush out even faster, making the warning gauge flash. 'Look at me, wasting your allowance like this. How remiss of me. Be a shame if I were to use up your entire weekly allowance by being careless like this, wouldn't it?'

He turned the tap off, folded his arms and looked directly at me again.

'Where is it?'

My mother swivelled her head towards me. 'What is he talking about, Auden? What have you done?'

My chest felt tight. The soldiers were all over the house and garden. It was only a matter of time before they pulled up the floor in the shed and found Paragon's little hiding place, surely.

'Just so you are aware –' Woolf scooped Sandwich up from the floor and started stroking her – 'there is another team of WAB infantry currently tearing apart Miss Rookmini's rooms at Trinity College.' He held Sandwich close to his face and snuggled her close to his chest. 'I do love cats. Such independent creatures. Always on their own. Never trusting of anyone. Perfect.'

I watched Sandwich wriggle in the General's tight grip and I found myself thinking of Vivi and Immaculata. Their warm, cosy rooms being ripped to ribbons like they didn't matter. It didn't seem fair. How could this be happening? Vivi and Immaculata didn't deserve this. They were the nicest, most caring people in the world.

I felt sick. My mind raced over all possible escape routes. But I knew deep down that I had to give Paragon up. He was my responsibility. There was no other way.

'OK,' I said.

'What?'

'You want to know where he is?' I could barely bring myself to look at Woolf. 'Then I'll show you.'

Two of the soldiers ripped the floorboards out of the shed, tossing them into the garden like they didn't care where they landed.

'The boy's right,' one of them called over to General Woolf. 'There's a space beneath the shed.'

'Why didn't you notice that the last time we searched the place – would've saved a hell of a lot of time.'

'Er . . .'

'Well, get down there. And be careful. It might be booby-trapped.'

Woolf was standing next to me and Mum – both of us still handcuffed – on the scrappy lawn in front of the shed. We watched as the agents busied themselves, stripping apart everything they could get their hands on. At one point I saw a particularly dozy-looking soldier clamber beneath the overhanging trees and fiddle about with the rainbow machine that I'd shoved under there all those weeks ago. He obviously didn't think it worth investigating, because he quickly left it where it was to go and find something more interesting to meddle with instead.

'I hope for your sake you've been telling us the truth,' Woolf half growled as we watched the last of the boards being chucked out onto the lawn. 'I'm not exactly known for my patience.'

I didn't say anything. I simply kept staring at the scene that was playing out in front of us.

A minute or so later, a soldier came out from the shed and held up his thumb. 'We've found it. It's here.'

Woolf breathed a heavy sigh of relief. 'Good. Get it out.'

The soldier nodded and went back into the shed.

'Corporal.'

'Yessir.' The soldier who'd been standing to attention in the kitchen stepped up before Woolf, his eyes keen and alert.

'Put these two in the van. Take the boy to the temporary camp.' Woolf nudged his head towards me. 'We'll interrogate him properly there.'

'Yessir.'

The soldier grabbed Mum and me by a shoulder each and marched us around the side of the house to where a military van was sitting. He opened the rear door and we both climbed in before the door slammed shut behind us. The engine started and, just before we started to move off, I peered out of the little window.

Three soldiers were carrying Paragon's body out of the shed. They hadn't switched him on, so he looked limp – like he was dead. The only thing that showed he wasn't was the recently restarted, constantly pulsing light that sat in the middle of his chest.

It flickered and beat just like a heart.

'What's happening, Auden?'

'It's all right, Mum. It'll all be OK in the end.'

'I don't understand what's going on.' She looked lost, like she was trapped in a weird dream and anything could happen.

'Please, Mum. It's all going to be all right.' It was as if I was the adult and she was the child. Our roles were reversed. I was the one who knew all the answers and she was the one asking all the questions. I didn't like that feeling one bit.

'What were they looking for in the shed?'

'Just . . . something . . .'

'Something?'

I took a deep breath. I couldn't put this off any longer.

'Look, Mum. There are some things you need to know . . .'

So I told her. I told her everything. The clues in the Snowflake letters. The key in the attic. The messed-up rooms of Uncle Jonah. Six Six/Vivi. The metal chamber under the shed. The invisible ink. The Pisces constellation. The discovery of Paragon. The note to Uncle Jonah from the WAB. Teaching Fabius Boyle a lesson. Finding out about Dad. The journey to Milo Treble. The machine guns hidden in Paragon's arms. On that ride from Unicorn Cottage to the WAB military camp I gave her all the details and she sucked them up without saying a single word.

And, to be honest, it felt good to tell her. All these weeks I had held onto the secret – well, Vivi and I had held onto the secret – and it was only once I had let it out that I realised just how heavy it had been to carry.

Secrets are like weights. They are chains tied about your legs. If they don't slow you down, they will trip you up.

So at that moment I knew exactly how my mother must have felt, holding onto the secret about my dad. It must have been so difficult and draining for her, trying to keep up the pretence. Protecting me. It must have made her very sad.

I shuffled closer to her along the bench and she kissed me on the forehead.

* * *

The makeshift camp had been erected virtually overnight on a disused field that I knew quite well. Temporary buildings made of slatted wood sat alongside almost circus-sized tents and long metal constructions that looked like adapted freight containers. Some of the site had not yet been completed; a crane was lifting sections of buildings into position and swarms of soldiers were carrying supplies into and around the camp.

The whole place looked busy.

Was this all because of us?

The corporal who'd driven us threw open the door and barked orders to get out. Mum and I stood up awkwardly to go.

'Not you!' He stabbed a finger towards Mum. 'Sit down. Just him.'

'What?'

'You heard.'

'No!' Mum reached over and tried to throw her handcuffed arms around me. 'No! He's only eleven. He needs to stay with me!' Her face was suddenly soaked with tears.

'Mum!' As I pushed myself into her lopsided embrace I realised that my face was wet too.

'No!' The corporal climbed into the van and peeled us apart as easily as the skin from a banana. 'You're going somewhere else.' He shoved her hard back into the van, pulled me out and slammed the door closed.

'Mum!!'

'Get on!' He banged the back of the truck hard, twice, and it revved its engine before slowly moving off.

The man grabbed me by the collar of my pyjamas and marched me over to an open-sided tent where an officer wearing glasses was ticking items off lists. He looked over the rim of his glasses as we approached.

'Dare?' he asked the corporal behind us.

'Yessir.'

'QWERTY, please.'

The corporal yanked my QWERTY off before tossing it onto the table.

'Container B2. Make sure you remove the restraints.' He stared at my pyjamas. 'And give him some clothes.'

'Yessir. Come on, you.'

We walked over the churned-up field, past a kitchen where the smell of porridge was thick as a cloud. We stumbled past men laying out long, thick snaking trails of electrical cable and others with large plastic water coolers strapped to their backs. I wondered if Vivi had been brought here too.

Outside one of the more solid-looking wooden buildings I saw a man dressed differently to everyone else. He wore a long white jacket and the sort of thin hat that you sometimes see doctors wearing. He was smoking a cigarette, and when he'd finished he tossed the end away before going back inside. Instinctively I knew that that was where they were going to take Paragon. The man was a scientist. There would be others too. Was Treble among them? Was he inside that building right now? Was he preparing to cut up Paragon? They would open him up and poke around inside and plug him into machines. They would check to see if he was operating correctly. They would replace the parts that were wearing out.

They would wipe his memory.

Soon Paragon wouldn't recognise or remember me. All the things we'd done together would be gone forever – erased in the blink of an LED eye.

None of this could be happening. Could it? Please let me wake up, I cried silently. Wake up and let all this dissolve into the night.

We arrived at one of the adapted freight containers – a heavy corrugated metal box with a barred window cut into it. The corporal tapped on the number pad, which gave out several different-pitched beeps and the door swung open.

Glancing back over my shoulder, I could see another small truck. Out came Vivi, looking as scared and as dazed as I had been. She too was marched, hands behind her back, towards the officer with the glasses in the open tent.

'Vivi!' I called. She looked over.

'Shut up,' the corporal said, and pushed me into the cell, the door banging shut behind me.

The only light in the cell came through the window – no electric light had been strung into position – so the whole place was dim and dusky. Of course, that wasn't a problem for me. With my condition, I could still see everything as clear as a glass of water.

In the corner was a bed and on top of the bed were some scratchy sheets and blankets and a pillow that looked as though half the stuffing had fallen out. A wobbly table was pushed against the wall, a hard wooden chair rammed under it. The bucket that was tucked into another corner was something that I didn't want to think too much about – the smell that came from it wasn't very pleasant.

I moved the table to just under the window and climbed up. From that position I could just about see what was going on in the camp. Trucks came and went and by my estimation there must have been somewhere between a hundred and two hundred WAB soldiers in the compound.

Not long after I was put in there, another soldier came with a bowl of porridge and some clothes for me to change into. The porridge tasted awful and the clothes were old and stale and at least one size too big for me, but I didn't care – my mind went round in a dull circle: Paragon, Mum, Vivi, Paragon, Mum, Vivi.

Just before lunchtime I was taken to be interrogated.

In one of the wooden buildings, General Heracles Woolf was sitting behind a desk, some sheets of paper spread out across it. I was made to sit in a chair facing him. There was nothing and nobody else in the room.

'Auden.' He didn't even look up from the papers. 'I understand you have difficulty seeing colour.'

'No. I don't have *difficulty* seeing colour,' I responded in a sour tone. 'I can't see colour *at all*.'

'Mmm.' It was as if he didn't pick up on the bitterness in my voice. Either that or he just batted it away like it was nothing but a fly. 'So you see everything in black and white. That's interesting. A little like the way your uncle always saw things in black and white.'

He stood up and strolled slowly around to the front of his desk.

'What do you mean?'

'Auden . . . some people have a very simplified view of the world. There's left and there's right. There's right and there's wrong. There's black and there's white.' He leaned back against the desk. 'The problem is that life is much more complicated than that. It's not so clear cut. In between black and white there are a million different colours.'

I frowned.

'Your uncle couldn't see the true worth in what he was doing for us. He thought there were good guys and there were bad guys and, like I said, life isn't always as simple as that. He got scared. He began to question which side he was on.'

'And what was he doing for you exactly? Designing a machine that could kill hundreds of people?'

Woolf gave a sickly smile under his grey moustache. 'We are living in difficult times. Our coastlines are constantly under threat from our enemies. The desalination units are precious to this country. Without them we are as dry and as dead as many other previously great nations. And I don't know if you've noticed, but most of our fighting-age population are abroad right now, helping countries less fortunate than us.' His fingers came up and stroked his moustache. 'We cannot leave the protection of the desalination units to old men. We need something better than that. That was the purpose of Project Rainbow.'

Project Rainbow. Project Rainbow? I didn't understand. So Project Rainbow wasn't about helping me to see colour at all? It wasn't anything to do with a rainbow machine? It was about having robot soldiers protecting the desalination units? How stupid. How selfish I'd been. Making it all about me.

Woolf continued. 'The Paragon machine that Dr Bloom created was originally designed to protect the coastline. That was his brief from the WAB. The problem was that your uncle – only seeing things in black and white, like you do – didn't exactly take to the idea of a mindless machine that would do whatever it was told. He wanted to create something that could make decisions. Decide for itself. He filled it full of useless information and gave it the ability to think.' He snorted. 'I mean, what is the point of an android – whose primary functions are to defend and to kill – what is the point of its being able to tell you the Latin name of a shrub or some such thing? Pointless.'

Aaron's rod. *Verbascum thapsus*. I don't know why I thought of it, but at that moment it flashed through my head.

'So . . . soon after we'd asked Bloom to revise his approach, he destroyed his blueprints and hid the Paragon machine from us.'

Then another of those funny sort of clicks happened in my mind. The letter from the WAB. The initials at the bottom. A 'H' followed by an 'M' or a 'W'. No, definitely a 'W'. Without a doubt a 'W'.

Heracles Woolf.

'And that was when you killed him.'

Woolf glared at me through half-shut eyes.

'Dr Bloom had a congenital heart condition that not even he knew about. It was just unfortunate that it decided to make itself apparent at that particular time.'

'You killed him!'

Woolf said nothing.

Then he got up from the desk and walked to the window.

'We tried to find the machine. He'd hidden it and we tried to find it.'

'Ha!' I laughed. 'You didn't try very hard, did you? He was buried under the garden all along.'

'According to our experts, Bloom had placed a signal-smothering device of his own design within the code boxes down there. Ingenious. It meant that our sadly outdated equipment could never pick up on the fact that there was an entire room beneath the lawn.' He watched as someone walked past the window. 'Nevertheless, heads will roll for that. Heads will roll. And mine won't be one of them, I can assure you.' Woolf gave a small sigh. 'It's a pity really. Bloom was highly talented. If only he'd understood his position in the whole set-up, he would have proved exceedingly useful to us. Such a shame.'

'Well, at least you've got Milo Treble on your side,' I barked. 'I bet he likes to follow your orders and do as he's told.'

Woolf looked confused. 'Treble?' His eyes honed in on mine. 'What makes you think that Treble is "on our side", as you put it?'

It was my turn to be confused. 'But . . . didn't he inform you? About Paragon? After yesterday?'

Woolf gave one of his acid little laughs. 'Inform? Treble would refuse to even tell us his own shoe size. No, we managed to find the machine because the tracker started to work again.'

The tracker?

'Bloom obviously disabled it and that left us blind. But yesterday, when it began transmitting again, we followed the signal from Treble's office all the way back to your horrible little cottage.'

The light on Paragon's chest! We had fixed the one bit of Paragon that we really shouldn't have fixed. By getting it to work again we'd attracted the attention of the very people that Uncle Jonah was trying to avoid!

I felt sick again. Sick with guilt. Guilt for betraying Paragon. Guilt for doubting Treble. Guilt for putting everyone in danger.

'What are you going to do with Paragon now?' I asked.

'What's it to you?'

'I'm interested.'

'Because your uncle destroyed the blueprints for the Paragon machine, we've no idea how it was constructed. So . . .' Woolf sat back in the chair and crossed his arms, 'in order to be able to build others, we'll need to *de*construct it.'

'You mean kill him?'

He sighed. 'Like I said, we need to take it all apart.'

23

The Brilliant
Vivi Rookmini

As the afternoon wore on, I found myself lying on my bed staring over at the barred window. From that angle I could watch the clouds in the sky and it reminded me of the skyspace in Vivi's bedroom ceiling.

It seemed like a thousand years ago since I first followed the clouds 'scudding' (that was the word she used) across the sky. Hopeless, wispy clouds that carried so very little rain.

Vivi.

I hoped that she was OK. That she wasn't too scared. None of this was her fault. It was only because she knew Uncle Jonah that she had been caught up in all this mess. It had nothing to do with her. Not really. But she was being punished for it all the same.

I worried about Mum too, taken away to a cell of her own, worrying herself half to death about me.

And I thought about my dad. Was this how he felt every day? Stuck in a room with nothing to do except stare at the sky and think. Was this the way he was living his life right now?

After what seemed like days, a soldier brought me my supper – a plateful of warmed-up frozen vegetables with a splodge of reconstituted potato and a tiny – and I mean tiny – sliver of roast beef. I gobbled it up hungrily and sipped gingerly from the cup of what looked like Cat's Pee.

A little after that a loud bell rang in the camp and suddenly there was a huge collective muttering and a clatter of boots outside. Within a couple of minutes, the camp was the quietest it had been all day.

I climbed onto the table and peered out through the bars. Far off, in the distance, everybody was queuing up for dinner outside one of the big tents. I stayed there and watched the line of hungry soldiers shift slowly along.

'Auden!'

There was a whisper from just below the window.

'Auden! You there?'

'Veev?' I stood on tiptoe and looked down in amazement. She was standing flat against the freight container, straining upwards to see if she could see me. 'What are you doing here?'

Vivi smiled. 'I've come to break you out.'

'Holy guacamole! How'd you get out of your cell?'

'By singing!'

'Huh?'

'The lock,' she explained. 'It was activated by the keypad tones.'

I recalled the different-pitched beeps as the soldier punched the code in.

'When the guard brought my supper to me, I listened and tried to remember the notes. Then, after he'd gone, I put my head close to the door and sung them back. Took me some time to get them exactly right – I'm not the greatest singer in the world – but I got there in the end.' She seemed pretty pleased with herself.

'Genius!' I grinned.

She waved a piece of paper triumphantly up at me. 'This is the list of codes. I borrowed it. Go to the door and I'll let you out.'

I climbed down from the table and waited. Outside, Vivi punched the code into the keypad and it beeped accordingly. There was a click and the door unlocked itself. I pushed it open and stepped outside.

'Have I ever told you how brilliant you are, Vivi?'

'Not often enough.'

The camp looked almost deserted. Most of the soldiers and officers and scientists were busy feeding their faces in the canteen, and there were only one or two unlucky soldiers patrolling the compound.

'We have to find Paragon,' I whispered urgently. 'Before it's too late. They're going to rip him apart.'

Vivi gasped.

'You know that light you were worried about? Well, you were right to be. It was a tracking device. That's how they found him.'

'Not Treble?'

'No. Not Treble.'

She looked around. 'Have they brought him here? Do you know?'

'There's a large wooden building. Possibly the biggest building. I saw a scientist outside it when I was brought in. I think that's where they were going to take him.'

We slipped down past a couple of tents towards the wooden structure. And froze. It just so happened that this particular place had a guard on duty right outside. We ducked down and hid back behind one of the tents.

'What are we going to do?' Vivi asked. 'We can't get past him.'

I didn't answer. We had to find a way.

Quietly, I tiptoed around the tent and peered carefully out. One of the large water coolers had been placed against the side of the tent, in direct view of the soldier on the door. I went back and told Vivi.

'So? How does that help us?'

I thought a little more.

'We could use it as a distraction.'

'How can we use a water cooler as a distraction?'

I held the flap of the tent open and waved her inside. We could see the outline of the water cooler against the canvas.

'Let's knock it over,' I said.

'What? Are you mad?'

'Probably. We'd need to do it with one big push. If we have to push it and push it again and again, the guard'll see us and we'll get caught. As long as we can do it in one go, he won't notice us and he'll just think it's some sort of accident.'

She had a look on her face that showed she thought I was mad.

'Then what?'

'Then . . . we'll see.'

She shook her head. 'Not the greatest plan I've ever heard. In fact, hardly a plan at all. But . . . time's running out and we need to do something. You're sure he's in there?'

I nodded. 'Why else keep a guard on the door?'

'True.'

We positioned ourselves near to where the water cooler stood. Neither of us knew exactly how heavy a water cooler was, so the amount of strength required was going to have to be a bit of a guess.

'Just give it everything you've got,' I whispered. 'On the count of three . . . One . . . two . . . three!'

We both ran hard into the side of the tent, knocking the water cooler – which turned out not to be as heavy as either of us had imagined – out of its mooring. It hit the ground with a thud and a slosh.

Vivi and I quickly slipped out of the tent and, peering round the corner again, watched the guard on the door.

He was staring at the cooler, his whole face a big question mark. Then he looked around and saw that there were no other guards nearby to put the cooler back into its position. You could almost see the debate he was having in his mind being played out over his features. Should he leave his post to put it right? Or should he stay where he was, watching precious water leak slowly out of a couple of cracks and seep wastefully into the ground?

The soldier licked his lips.

Then left his post.

He disappeared from our view, and as we heard him lower his gun to the ground to get hold of the cooler, we made our break. Running softly on the most soundless parts of our feet, we covered the twenty metres in seconds – Vivi in front, me just behind.

At the door, Vivi turned the handle without making a noise and pulled the door open just enough for us both to slip in. With the tiniest of clicks, the door locked itself closed behind us.

The room was filled with equipment and, if I'd paid it much attention, I would have thought that it resembled Milo Treble's laboratory. But I didn't pay it much attention. Because strapped to a table in the centre of the room was the only thing that I wanted to focus on.

Paragon.

Wires were attached to his arms and legs and wound their way into monitors and computers. The screens flickered and danced and bleeped and buzzed even though he was lying perfectly still. He was in standby mode and the only part of him that looked alive was the flashing tracker light, fluttering like a heartbeat.

But he was intact.

They hadn't started ripping him apart yet.

'What are they doing to him?' Vivi looked at all the wires.

'This is nothing,' I warned. 'Another day or two and there wouldn't be anything of him left. He'd be gone forever.'

We both stood there for a minute or two, imagining this machine so full of soul, so full of life, being demolished.

'We need to get him away from here,' I said, leaning over and flicking the on switch. 'Quickly.

Paragon whizzed and whirred back to life, his limbs rising slightly from the table, his head twisting left then right.

'Where . . . where am I?'

'Paragon?' A wave of panic washed over me. Had they already cleared his memory? Would he look at me as if he'd never seen me before?

'Hey, Audendare! Vivirookmini! What's going on?' He was fine. The same old Paragon. Then a moment of recognition. 'Oh. That's right. Now I remember.' His head tilted at a sort of concerned angle. 'Are you both OK?'

'You need to keep the noise down,' I hissed. I could hear the guard taking up his position right outside the door again.

'Oh. OK.' Paragon turned to face me. 'Auden. There's something I need to tell you. Something important.'

'Not now,' I replied. 'First we need to get you out of here.'

'What are we going to do about these?' Vivi was holding up one of the wires that fed into Paragon's legs.

'Don't worry too much about those.' Paragon sat up and ripped all of the wires out of himself, tossing them aside. 'They aren't important.'

Then he stood up and made a movement that looked as if he was stretching after a heavy night's sleep. 'That's better. What's the plan?'

We were trapped in a building with one door, directly outside of which stood an armed guard.

'Er . . . I dunno,' I said. 'I was rather hoping you might come up with something.'

Paragon looked around the room. 'O . . . kay.' He was staring at a large window at the rear of the room that looked out onto another temporary wooden structure. 'If we can't use the door at the front, we'll have to make another one.'

Paragon pushed a table of equipment aside to get to the window. He tapped the glass with his knuckles.

'Not especially thick . . . so . . .'

Suddenly his right thumb bent all the way back, exposing something small, sharp and shiny.

Then out of the palm on his left hand sprang a rubber pad. He pressed it onto the window pane and then started scraping the glass with the sharp implement.

'High-grade industrial diamond.' Paragon looked at us over his shoulder. 'Cuts through glass like a chainsaw through a bucket of jelly.'

'Holy moley guacamole!'

Vivi and I watched as Paragon scored a deep groove upwards, then across, then down and then back to where he'd started. Once the ends were joined, he slotted his thumb back into its usual position.

'Now, just a little push . . .'

He pressed with his left hand and . . .

Clink.

. . . the large rectangular piece of glass came easily out of the window.

Paragon carefully pulled it in through the hole he had made and leaned it up against the wall.

'There! That's how we get out. Now, let's go.'

He bent over to pick up Vivi.

'Wait!' I cried, remembering something in a panic.

'What is it?'

'That!' I pointed at the flashing light on Paragon's chest.

'What about it?'

'It's a tracking device. It's how they found you in the first place.'

Paragon looked down at the light. 'A tracking device?' He sounded sad. 'Is that what it is? But I thought –'

'Yes,' I said almost as sadly, 'I know. It's what we all thought when it started beating.'

We stood silently for a few seconds watching the light on Paragon's chest pulsing.

'I thought it was a heart.' Paragon touched the light with the gentlest tips of his fingers. 'Or at least . . . sort of a heart. A representation of a heart.'

Vivi stepped forward and touched him on his arm. 'I'm afraid it's not. It was just a way of keeping track of you and that's why Dr Bloom switched it off. I'm sorry.'

I checked behind me and saw the outline of the soldier on duty through the frosted glass. Time was running out.

'Look. Can you disable it?' I asked.

Paragon shook his head and sighed. 'Nope. It runs on a system that I can't override. Only a human can switch it on or off.'

'But you can't escape with it active. They'll find you in minutes.'

'Let *me* try.' Vivi was holding one of the discarded wires.

'You can't do it!' I said.

'Auden –' Vivi gave a huge sigh – 'some of us actually pay attention to things. When Dr Treble got the light working yesterday. I was watching everything he did. It wasn't that complicated. I'm sure I can turn it off again.'

'You think?' I realised as I said it that it sounded as though I didn't trust her.

Vivi shook her head. 'Honestly, Auden.'

'Vivi,' Paragon interrupted, 'I have perfect faith in you. Absolute one-hundred-per-cent perfect faith. As does Auden.' He took the wire from her and plugged it back onto the tip of his finger. 'So . . . let's do it.'

Vivi stuck the other end into a computer. All the while we were aware that dinner might soon be over and that the scientists would be back to carry on working on Paragon.

We needed to be quick.

Vivi sat on a stool at the computer and tapped away. Lots of strange shapes flashed up and scrolled across the screen. Her fingers danced like lightning – I'd never seen anyone type so fast in my life.

Then she paused.

'Right . . . I think this is the correct thing to do. But there's a faint chance I might be isolating the tracking device, making it impossible to turn it off. It's one or the other.'

'Vivi –' Paragon brought his head down close to hers – 'go for it.'

Her fingers continued to race across the keyboard.

'Ready?'

'Yep.'

'OK . . .'

She hit a button and . . .

The light on Paragon's chest flickered faster for a second or two and then . . .

It stopped.

We nearly cheered but just about managed to prevent ourselves, remembering the guard outside.

Paragon grabbed Vivi's shoulders. 'Have I ever told you how brilliant you are, Vivi?'

She laughed. 'I really do think we ought to get out of here.'

'Yes. You're right.' Paragon went back to the large rectangular hole in the rear window. 'Come on. I'll lift you both through.'

He picked up Vivi and eased her gently through the gap before picking me up and feeding me through. Then he climbed as silently as he could manage out into the early evening light.

'Follow me.' We made our way around a couple of the flapping tents and the wooden buildings, ducking and hiding from the occasional daydreaming guard. We dashed across thirty or forty metres of unoccupied space to the barbed-wire fence, crawling underneath into the field beyond.

Once through, we squatted down to plan our next move.

'So,' I said, 'we're out. Now what?'

'We can't go home,' Vivi pointed out. 'They'd be waiting for us there.'

The evening was a clear one, and already the temperature was beginning to drop. We needed to find somewhere indoors to hide away.

'I know where we can go,' Paragon said.

'Where?'

He ignored the question. 'The thing is, we need to move quite quickly. Any minute now suppertime will be over and people are going to realise we're gone. Then they'll be after us.'

'We need to start running then.'

'Ah yes. The problem is, neither you nor Vivi can run very fast. If we go at *your* speed, we're going to get caught within minutes.'

'But . . .' Vivi was thinking aloud, 'if we go at *your* speed . . .'

Suddenly Paragon scooped us both up, one in each arm, so that we were sitting on his forearms.

'Exactly. Now,' he said, standing up, 'bear in mind that this is something I've never done before. And obviously you've never done it either. It's a new experience for all of us. Hold on as tight as you possibly can. And don't panic.'

Vivi's eyes were wide with fear. Like me, she'd seen how fast Paragon could run.

'Oh my . . .'

'Don't worry, Vivi,' Paragon reassured her. 'I'm not going to let you fall.'

'Yes. Don't worry, Vivi.' I smiled, hardly able to hold in my excitement. 'This'll be fun!'

It *was* fun. After the initial lurch as Paragon set off, that was. He didn't seem to slowly build to his top speed like most runners – he just started incredibly fast and stayed incredibly fast. The air whipped over our faces and flicked our hair backwards.

Vivi had her eyes shut tight and she was clinging around Paragon's neck. I gripped onto his shoulder, but watched as the landscape flashed by. A tree, a telegraph pole, a passer-by rubbing his eyes, his dog a-yap. What had they seen? A trick of the yellowing light perhaps as I, clad in silver metal, strode magnificently by. Was this how it felt to fly?

We were across the first field in a matter of seconds, and as we neared the hedge Paragon showed no sign of slowing. If anything he sped up slightly.

'What are you –' I started to ask but didn't have time to finish, because a few metres away from the hedge, Paragon jumped.

Vivi squeaked. So did I.

We sailed through the air and over the hedge.

Thump.

We landed with a jolt and Paragon carried on running like nothing had happened. Within seconds the hedge on the far side of that field approached.

'Oh no!' Vivi cried, and buried her face into Paragon's neck.

'Oh yes!' I screamed as Paragon soared over that one too, landing just as surefootedly.

A couple of hedges later and even Vivi was half giggling as Paragon jumped them with ease.

We turned onto a long lane that we had all used several times, then took a quick left onto a rougher dirt track. One more skip over a hedge and Paragon came to a standstill.

'Here we are.'

I looked about and recognised the less than salubrious edge of the Sunny Vale Caravan Park. We had only been running for about three minutes, but I estimated that Paragon had covered about six or seven miles in that time. If my maths was any good, that meant he'd been racing along somewhere in the region of one hundred and thirty miles an hour. That was the fastest I'd ever moved in my whole life!

Paragon lowered us both to the ground.

'I do *not* ever want to do that again!' Vivi said, eventually prising her arms from Paragon's neck. 'That was scary.'

'No, it wasn't,' I said staring madly into Paragon's eyes. 'It was great!'

Paragon gave us both a friendly pat on the head and we all walked towards the nearest deserted caravan.

'No place like home, kids,' he joked in an uber-sarcastic Auden Dare sort of way.

24

The Truth About
the Truth

It was the same caravan I'd left Paragon in the night before the Boyle disaster. The mess was still there and Paragon had to help Vivi over the dislodged oven. Clearly no one had been to clean the place since our last visit.

Paragon gave the door to the main bedroom a shove and we went in.

Thankfully the bedroom was in a much better state than the rest of the caravan. There was no bed, admittedly, but the mattress on the floor looked clean and comfortable. Stacked to one side were a couple of limp pillows and some blankets. They were dusty, but a quick shake outside soon sorted that.

'I wonder if they've noticed we're gone yet,' Vivi said, pulling the flowery curtains closed.

'Probably.' Paragon tried slapping some life into one of the flat pillows.

'What will they do?' I asked.

'Well, first they'll check the camp. They won't believe that two children and a robot could get very far, I'm sure. They will underestimate us. Foolishly. The first fifteen or twenty minutes after discovering our disappearance will consist of checking out all the buildings and vehicles around the camp. After that, they will widen the search to the surrounding areas and the routes towards your homes. By the time they've exhausted that, it'll be dark.'

'They'll search for us through the night though, won't they?' I said. 'They won't stop until they find us.'

Paragon nodded. 'Yes. They'll keep searching. Night time makes things difficult though.'

'But if they've got heat-sensing equipment, they might well be able to detect us in here.'

'Don't worry about that,' Paragon said as he hunched down next to the mattress and wrapped his arms around his knees. 'Dr Bloom provided me with a piece of software to take care of such things. I can disguise the heat from your bodies. They'll never pick up on it.'

'That's good.'

I took one of the blankets and pulled it around myself, sitting down on the mattress with a pillow between my back and the flimsy wall of the caravan. Vivi did the same.

'What are we going to do?' Vivi mumbled. 'We can't go home. We can't go anywhere. We've got no food or water. We're stuck.'

I didn't say anything. I was thinking about Mum. Where she was. How they were treating her.

Vivi looked distressed. 'They're going to catch us in the end, aren't they? They're going to catch us and take us away from our mothers. I just want to see her . . .'

Paragon reached over and gave her shoulder a soft pat. 'Shh, Vivirookmini.'

'I don't care what we do,' I said. 'We can't let them get their hands on you, Paragon. They can't rip you apart and turn you into a killer. That's not what you are. We have to keep you away from them. Even if it means we have to keep running for the rest of our lives. I'm not letting them take you away from us.'

We sat in silence for a while, the light through the curtains dimming by the minute.

'There's something I need to tell you, Auden.' Paragon's lights flickered and glowed in the small dusty room. 'Something I found out.'

'What's that?'

Paragon shifted his position slightly. 'When the Water Allocation Board scientists had me strapped to their computers and were busy assessing me, I managed to access the army's military-records database.' He picked a thread of cotton off his metal kneecap and dropped it onto the floor.

'Yes?'

'Once I'd breached the protective software, I . . .' He paused. 'I accessed your father's file.'

I caught my breath. Did I want to hear this?

'As you know, Leo Dare is currently in a military prison for having deserted his post.'

Why was he telling me this? I knew all this. Saying it again wasn't going to help the situation. Wasn't going to pull me back from the shame of my dad's predicament. Nothing was going to be able to make this better.

Paragon continued. 'But do you know *why* he deserted his post?'

I shook my head. Of course I didn't. Why would I? Why would I want to think about it any more than I had to?

'The reason he deserted his post was because, if he hadn't, three children would have died.'

'What?'

Paragon's eyes glowed brighter than I had ever seen them glow before.

'I don't understand. What three children?'

'Sit back,' Paragon ordered, 'and I'll tell you the whole story.'

'Your father's battalion was making its way through a small town just outside of Liberec in the Czech Republic when they came under enemy fire. The trucks they were travelling in were hit hard by anti-tank missiles fired from sniper zones. They tried to escape, but as the trucks zoomed out onto a side street one of them clipped a passing car. The car flipped over onto its roof and burst into flames.

'The captain of the battalion ordered his men to continue their retreat. So truck after truck passed the burning car without stopping.

'But the driver of the last vehicle *didn't* pass by. Against orders he pulled over, and with one of the army-issue fire extinguishers quickly got the blaze under control.

'Inside the car were a thirty-two-year-old mother and her three young children – aged four, seven and ten. The mother was dead. But the children were still alive. Despite still being shot at, the driver managed to drag each of the children away from the car and to a place of safety nearby. They were then taken to a military hospital.

'However, despite having saved three lives, the army court-martialled the soldier for deserting his post. It was claimed that some of the army deaths could have been avoided had he continued on past the burning car.

'The thing is,' Paragon dropped his voice, 'while I was strapped to the computers back there I examined all of the footage that was captured on that day. And what the army court said is nonsense. The evidence shows that the deaths of the soldiers – four of them – happened *before* the trucks had even hit the car.

'So the only conclusion I can come to is that the army wants soldiers that do as they are told. Not soldiers that think for themselves. As far as they're concerned, a soldier that can step out of role even for a second is a dangerous thing. It's something they find difficult to handle. They can't control them. And so, for that, they have to be punished.'

I found my fingers clutching the blanket far too tightly. 'That driver –' I forced myself to loosen my grip – 'that was my dad, wasn't it?'

Paragon nodded.

'So you see, Auden, your father is hardly a criminal. In fact, he is even more of a hero than you thought.'

I felt tears beginning to build in my eyes. 'But I . . . I thought he was a coward. They said he was . . . a . . . coward.' The tears began to roll. I felt like a traitor. 'And I believed them.'

Paragon shuffled in between Vivi and me and put his arms around us. 'I don't think you did believe them really. I think that deep down – somewhere inside your spirit or soul or whatever you might want to call it – deep down, you knew the truth. You knew that the person you called "Dad" was certainly not a coward.'

He stroked my cheek and wiped the tears away.

'There are things we just know. Instinct, I suppose some people call it. Now, instinct may or may not be a real thing. Perhaps it is simply an accumulation of data and a refinement of our judgement. But there are some things that we seem to automatically know.'

Paragon gave a sort of awkward cough. 'I realise I am a robot and that my experience of these things is pretty small, but I'll try to use an analogy that even I feel comfortable with.

'Consider the order of things. We always say, "Left. Right." The "left" comes before the "right". Does anyone ever say, "Right. Left."? I doubt it. Or on a form, you will see the options "Yes/No". Never "No/Yes" Similarly, "up" comes before "down," and "on" before "off." We have come to understand the order of things and it almost feels like instinct. So if you were to see "No/Yes" written somewhere, you would think it strange.

'That's what happened when that terrible Boyle child told you your father was in prison. It struck you as wrong. Everything you had ever known about your father suggested he wouldn't leave his post. He wouldn't run away. It was against all you knew. And that's why you struggled with it so much. Because you knew it couldn't be right.

'So, yes. Deep down I think you realised it couldn't be true. You knew your father wasn't a coward.

'After all, who could know a father better than his own son?'

We fell silent.

Dig deep, Auden. Dig deep.

We all became aware that outside we could hear the distant *woompf woompf woompf* of a helicopter's blades. The noise got louder and louder until it sounded almost overhead, and a strong beam of light flashed left then right over the top of the caravan. Paragon pulled us both closer and after a few seconds the sound slowly faded away and the light disappeared.

We didn't move or say anything for a while.

'Was that them?' Vivi whispered.

Paragon nodded. 'Don't worry. They won't find us. I guarantee it.'

A little later, after Vivi had managed to drift off to sleep, I propped myself up on my elbows and looked at Paragon, who was still sitting watching over us.

'The problem is that *I* know my father's not a coward, and *you* know it, but the army don't care. He's going to be in prison forever. They're never going to let him out.'

'Ah . . .' Paragon began and I could sense that he was about to say something designed to make me feel better. 'Well. After I checked out your father's military record and the footage of the incident, I made a copy of it all.'

'You stole it?'

'That's . . . one way of putting it. I made a copy and sent it to the International Court of Human Rights.'

'What?' I sat up.

'I also posted it to a number of charitable bodies. And, to be on the safe side, I sent it to a few news agencies – some of the bigger ones.' If he could have smiled at me, then I'm sure that at that point he would have done. 'So all the information is out there, and one of those organisations at least will make an issue or a story out of your father's case, I am sure.'

I reached over, took his hand and squeezed it.

'Thank you.'

Paragon squeezed back, and we sat that way until my eyelids began to droop and the comforting fog of sleep eased over me.

25

Everything

When I woke up the next morning, Paragon was gone. I shook Vivi, who was still fast asleep, and she opened her bleary eyes and rubbed her hand across her face, looking about the room.

'Where is he?' She barely formed the words in her exhaustion.

'I don't know.' I was anxious. 'What if he's gone back on his own? To save us! He might think that by –'

Suddenly the door to the bedroom sprang open and Paragon came in carrying something.

'Here!' He tossed a couple of cereal slices and two slightly bruised apples at each of us. 'Breakfast.'

I sighed, relieved. 'Where did you get these from?' I asked, ripping open the packaging with my teeth.

'Don't ask,' he said, and set two bottles of mineral water on the floor in front of us. 'Let's just say that some of the holidaymakers staying here might find themselves having to eat out this morning.'

Feeling guilty, but mainly hungry and thirsty, we tucked

in, Paragon watching us and scooping up any mess we made, putting it into a neat pile in the corner of the room.

After we had eaten, I pulled the curtain back a little and looked up at the sky. The clouds were the thin and wispy type. High up and barely there, like a thin streak across the sky. I thought hard, back to the time Vivi had told me the names of the clouds. It seemed like a hundred years ago now. So much had happened since. *What were they called?* I wondered.

Then I remembered.

'Cirrus,' I muttered.

'What?' Paragon asked, quickly standing up. 'What did you say?'

'Cirrus,' I repeated.

Suddenly Paragon started his stiffening and straightening, his arms locked at his sides, eyes fixed directly ahead.

'It's happening again!' Vivi shouted.

Within a second or two, Paragon's body began to relax. It was then that the idea struck me.

'Cumulus!' I called, and Paragon's body jerked back into position again.

'Stratus!' Vivi joined in, and Paragon seemed to shudder where he stood.

A moment or so later, he collapsed in a heap on the floor.

'Paragon. Paragon!' I came alongside him and pulled at his arms. 'Get up, Paragon.'

Vivi went the other side and we started to lift him.

He was so heavy that even with both of us, we couldn't move him at all.

Suddenly the lights on his eyes flickered and his head twisted one way and then the other.

'I . . .' he began to speak. 'I know *everything* now.'

We were all too aware that we might be spotted. Crossing the fields that led away from Sunny Vale, all it would take would be a passing WAB unit and we'd have been done for. Seized and locked away, Paragon destroyed.

But there was nothing.

Perhaps they were still too busy searching the area just outside of the camp to come this far out. Perhaps they were waiting for backup before starting the search in earnest. Perhaps we'd just got lucky.

'Where are we going?' I asked.

'There.' Paragon pointed to a telegraph pole slap bang in the middle of the next field.

'Why?'

'I need to make a phone call.'

Vivi and I looked at each other again. It was barely eight o'clock in the morning and already it was turning into a strange day.

When we arrived at the base of the pole, Paragon told us to wait there and then began climbing to the top of it.

'What *is* he up to?' I asked as I watched him reach out and grab hold of one of the wires.

'There's no point asking me,' said Vivi. 'I know about as little as you do.'

Up at the top of the telegraph pole, Paragon sounded as if he was talking to himself. A couple of minutes later he jumped down, landing with a thump just in front of us.

'Who were you talking to?'

'Dr Treble. There's something he needs to see.'

'What's that then?'

Paragon tilted his head. 'You'll see for yourself soon enough. Now, we've got a busy morning ahead of us. Vivi?'

'Yes?'

'I told Dr Treble that you would meet him near the Wandlebury Ring.'

'Eh?' Vivi looked nervous.

'It's OK. I'll take you there.' Paragon bent over and picked her up.

'Oh no. Not this again,' Vivi muttered, squeezing her eyes tight shut.

'Hold on.' I took a step forward. 'What about me?'

Paragon turned to face me. 'I'll be back for you in a minute. Well, seven minutes and forty-ish seconds as an estimate.' He positioned Vivi on his arm and she gripped on tight. 'Then you and I are going back home.'

With that they were off, Vivi's shrieks disappearing into the distance along with them.

26

Return to
Unicorn Cottage

Seven minutes and forty-ish seconds later, Paragon pulled up beside me like a sports car.

'What do you mean, "going back home"?' I frowned at him.

He looked a bit puzzled. 'I mean, we're going home.'

'What? To Unicorn Cottage?'

'Yep.'

'Are you mad? There'll be millions of Water Allocation Board soldiers there. They'll be pulling the house to pieces. They'll capture us before we get past the front door.'

'Millions is a bit of an overestimate, don't you think? At the most there will be about forty of them.'

'Forty?!' I cried. 'How are we meant to get into the house if there are about forty soldiers – *armed* soldiers – waiting for us there? Anyway, *why* are we going back?'

'Because there is something there that we need to get.'

'What?'

'Something your uncle built. Perhaps you've seen it. It's about this high –' he held the palm of his hand flat about a metre off the ground – 'this long –' he stretched his hands about two metres apart – 'and this wide –' one metre. 'It's on wheels and has a sort of cover over it.'

I thought. 'Wait. You mean the rainbow machine?'

'The rainbow machine?' He gave a small laugh. 'Yes. I suppose you're right. Do you know where your uncle kept it?'

'It was in the shed. Above you. But we took it out from there. Just before we discovered you.'

'Where is it now?'

'I pushed it against the fence. Under an overhanging tree.' I thought of the previous day when one of the soldiers started to inspect it but quickly got bored and shoved it back. 'I think it's still there.'

'Good.'

'But why are we going back for that? It hasn't got a battery. It doesn't work.'

'Oh, it will,' he said, picking me up and preparing to set off again.

While Paragon was running, I could see military trucks in the distance, no doubt scouring the roads and lanes for any sign of us. At one point, Paragon had to quickly change course when we saw a troop of soldiers, spread out across a field of succulents, slowly picking their way across it, apparently hoping to stumble over some clue as to what direction we had gone.

Not long after, we came out onto the field behind Unicorn Cottage. The pyramid-shaped irrigation towers were spraying their five-minute morning allocation of water over the crops, and as we rushed past them we got beautifully and hilariously soaked. Diving into the small cluster of trees that backed onto the garden, we fell onto the earth and laughed.

'I hope I don't start rusting,' Paragon joked.

After we had recovered ourselves, we peered through a gap in the fence. I couldn't see anything, and then I realised why. The rainbow machine was in the way.

It was literally millimetres away from us. The problem was that it might as well have been a million miles away. The fence was in the way and I could hear a pair of soldiers talking at the other end of the garden. Getting the machine out was going to be impossible.

'How are we going to get to it?' I whispered.

'Aha!' Paragon held up his hand and a fingertip flipped back to reveal the tip of a screwdriver.

'Is there anything you haven't got hidden away in your fingers?' I asked.

'Lots of things,' he said, as he inserted the head into one of the screws in the fence, 'but I won't start listing them now.'

The screwdriver tool was almost silent. It turned anti-clockwise and twisted the screw out with absolute ease. After it came free, Paragon removed another one and another. It reminded me of the time I unscrewed all the floorboards in the shed, not five metres from where we were now squatting. When the last of the screws in that one piece of fencing was out, I took hold of the plank and laid it gently on the ground nearby.

Board after board came away until we had a space big enough through which to pass the rainbow machine. The problem was going to be the beams of wood that ran horizontally along the top and bottom of the fence. We were going to have to somehow lift the rainbow machine between them.

'Don't worry.' Paragon leaned forward and grabbed both side of the machine. 'I can get it myself.' He pulled and lifted and, with enormous strength, deftly brought the thing through the fence and set it down in the field beside us.

Suddenly the overhanging branches of the tree parted and a soldier's face appeared, staring right at us. He opened his mouth to shout something, but Paragon hurriedly clasped his hand over the mouth, climbed through what was left of the fence and disappeared.

Twenty seconds later he returned.

'What have you done with him?' I asked.

'Locked him in my little room under the shed. It's quite cosy, you know. Someone will find him eventually.' He grabbed hold of the handle at one end and turned the machine around. 'Come on. We'd better go before any more of them spot us.'

It was slow going. Paragon could push the rainbow machine much faster than I ever could, but compared to the racing speeds of earlier, it felt sluggish. The problem was that the wheels on the machine were not designed to go over rough ground.

'It's no use,' he finally admitted. 'We're going to have to use the roads.'

'But they'll see us,' I protested.

'If we stick to crossing fields they're going to see us anyway. At least on the roads we might have a chance.'

He wheeled the machine through a gate and onto a small lane.

'Now, jump on,' he ordered.

'What?'

'On that.' He nodded towards the rainbow machine.

I climbed onto the top of the machine and gripped tightly onto the tarpaulin.

'Here goes.'

Paragon started racing again – still slower than normal, but at least it felt as if we were making progress. He steered the thing around bends and over bumps like a Formula 1 driver and I held on for all I was worth.

But then I heard the roar of an engine.

Behind was a large truck. And it was gaining on us.

Paragon sped up but the truck still got closer. I looked back and could see the eyes of the driver glaring down at us.

Suddenly there was a loud bang and a spark flew off the back of Paragon.

They were shooting!

Paragon moved even quicker, the wheels of the rainbow machine spinning uncontrollably beneath me.

Then, without warning, Paragon practically spun on the spot and veered off onto a smaller dirt track to the left. It wound its way up a small hill, and I recognised it as the hill Vivi and I climbed with Paragon the day after we discovered him. The hill where the word 'achromatopsia' had opened up a load of information within his memory bank.

'Grip tightly,' Paragon shouted at me.

I looked behind and saw that the truck was too big for the track. Soldiers were jumping out of the back and running towards us, their rifles at the ready.

'I said, "Grip tightly!"' Paragon half yelled, so I dug my nails even harder into the tarpaulin. A second later I realised why.

Paragon twisted off the track and headed towards the stile over which we had all climbed all those weeks before. Only this time we weren't going to climb over it. Oh no. This time, Paragon was going to smash right through it.

'Hold on!'

I shut my eyes.

The rainbow machine hit the rotting wooden structure with such force that it splintered apart. Unfortunately I couldn't have been holding on tightly enough, because as it hit, I bounced off the top of the rainbow machine and bumped onto the grass before rolling a fair distance down the incline.

'Auden!' I heard Paragon's voice somewhere above me.

Bang! Bang!

Gunshots. Followed by the *ping ping* of bullets hitting metal.

As I sat up, two arms grabbed me and lifted me clear of the ground.

'Come on, let's go.'

Paragon carried me, shielding me from the firing soldiers, and plonked me roughly back on top of the rainbow machine.

'Stay where you are!' a voice ordered. 'Do not move.'

Paragon ignored the voice and began to push the machine along once again.

'I said, "Stay where you are!" Or we'll shoot the boy!'

Paragon stopped and lowered the handle. Then he turned around.

'Paragon? What are you doing?' I asked.

Paragon raised both his arms. The panels on the forearms slid apart and the barrels of the guns came into view. He pointed them at the soldier who had just spoken.

'Paragon! No! Don't!! Don't do it! That's not who you are! Please. Don't shoot them.'

The soldier backed away slightly, lowering his gun.

Paragon took a step towards him.

'No!! Don't!!' I screamed. 'Don't hurt them!'

He stood still, his guns still trained on the man.

'Please.'

Nobody moved or said anything. The only sounds came from the wind and the squeal of traffic miles away.

'Withdraw,' Paragon said to the men after a while. 'Take your guns and let us be. We have important work to attend to.'

The gun barrels retreated inside his arms and Paragon turned his back on the soldiers and continued to push the rainbow machine, me on top of it, slowly along the path that wound its way around the bottom of the hill.

There were no more gunshots. There was just silence. Beautiful, clear silence.

PART SEVEN
WHITE

27

The Power Source

'This whole area is swarming with Water Allocation Board soldiers,' Treble said as we approached him and Vivi. 'I've never seen so many in my life. They must really want to get hold of you, Paragon.'

'Oh, they do, Dr Treble. They do.'

Treble stepped forward. 'They came for me last night. Luckily I managed to escape out the back door without any of them spotting me. I don't think they're the brightest of organisations, you know.'

Paragon laughed. He was still pushing the rainbow machine as I walked alongside. After racing around so much over the last two days, it was a huge relief to just walk.

'Have you had an accident?' Vivi asked, staring at the massive rip in one of my trouser legs. It must have happened when I fell off the top of the machine, only everything was so intense and scary at that point that I hadn't noticed. Now that Vivi had pointed it out to me, I wondered how I could have missed it.

'Yes,' was all I said.

'I hope you've not been waiting too long.' Paragon started to push the rainbow machine along the path that led to the top of Wandlebury.

'Not at all.' Treble sounded surprisingly cheerful, considering there were men with guns trying to hunt us down at that very moment. 'Vivi and I have been having a rather interesting discussion about planetary formation, haven't we?'

'Yes, we have.'

It was weird. They both sounded so similar.

'It seems we have the same ideas about the Big Bang.'

We made our way up towards where the trees started, Paragon pushing the machine, the rest of us close behind.

'Tell me, Paragon,' Treble looked quite excitable, 'is it true? Do you think it will work?'

'Yes.' Paragon answered without hesitation. 'It will work.'

'How do you know?'

'Because Dr Bloom programmed me to know.'

'Oh.' Treble stopped for a second, unsure how to take in that information.

Why were they so keen on the rainbow machine all of a sudden? What was so impressive? What was so important about it that we were all risking our lives?

We entered the wood that ran along the brow of the hill.

'I wish Bloom had told me all about this. I wish he'd told *anybody* about this,' Treble muttered. 'Why didn't he just tell people what he'd done?'

Paragon didn't even turn around to look at Treble. 'Because he didn't get the chance to, I suppose. He left the instruction buried within me because he knew he was at risk. I think he wanted to run it through more tests – to be certain – before going public with it, but he gave me the instructions just in case.'

I suddenly found myself wishing Milo Treble wasn't there. He was chattering on and taking away from the fact that this whole adventure should only have been about Paragon, Vivi and me. No one else. Why was he involving himself now? Or, to be more accurate, why was Paragon involving him?

As if in answer to my question, Paragon spoke. 'I think it's right that you are here to see this, Dr Treble. We need a recognised member of the scientific community to witness what will happen here today.' Treble seemed to swagger. 'Someone with the kudos and the respect of the wider scientific world. Someone they can trust.'

'Well . . . er . . . I . . . I guess . . .' Treble could hardly disguise his slightly swollen-headed pride.

Paragon looked back and gave me one of his little winks.

That made me feel better.

'Wait!' Vivi was staring back down the hill, her arm outstretched, pointing.

Water Allocation Board trucks. Dozens of them. On the roads below.

'They've found us!'

Paragon stopped pushing the rainbow machine and stared down the hill. He then turned and stared back up to where we were headed.

'Too soon. They're here too soon.' He sounded disappointed. 'By my rough calculations, a few minutes later and we would have had enough time to get it done.'

'Get what done?' I asked, but nobody answered me.

'You need a distraction,' Vivi said, 'something to take their attention away from you. Buy you more time.' She took a few steps away from us. 'I'll run out into the open and go down the opposite side of the hill. I'll make sure they spot me.'

'Vivi –' Paragon began to protest.

'No. It's the best way.'

Treble interrupted. 'Paragon, it is *vital* that you do what needs to be done.' He walked towards Vivi and turned back to Paragon. 'I'll go with her. Tell me, you do know *exactly* what to do?'

'Yes, but I'll need someone to stay with me.' Paragon turned to me. 'Auden, will you help me do it?'

'I don't know what it is that –'

'Will you help me?' he asked again. 'I can't do it on my own.'

'Yes.' I came and rested my hand on his arm. 'Of course I will. I'll do anything to help you. You know that.'

Treble pulled his coat tighter around his shoulders. 'Good. Then Vivi and I will distract them. Get yourselves into position and start the thing up.' They started to run off.

'Vivi!' Paragon shouted after her.

Vivi stopped and looked back.

'Thank you,' Paragon said. 'You are without the smallest shadow of a doubt the bravest and cleverest girl that ever lived.'

Vivi smiled before rushing off with Treble out beyond the trees.

An eruption of shouting came from the bottom of the hill. I peered through the trees. Soldiers that had leaped from the trucks had spotted Vivi and Treble running around the side of the hill. One of them squatted, taking aim with his gun.

'Vivi!' I gasped.

'No shooting! Your orders are to take the children alive,' barked another distant voice. I shifted my position and could see General Woolf climbing out of a military car. 'Give chase. And find that robot.'

'Come on, Auden. We need to get going.' Paragon had got ahead of me, but I couldn't take my eyes off the scene down below. Because out of Woolf's car came two more figures. Handcuffed and guarded.

Mum and Immaculata.

'Mum!'

'Auden! We don't have time!' Paragon called to me. 'Please!'

Woolf's voice boomed through a megaphone: 'Auden Dare, this is General Woolf of the Second Infantry Division of the Water Allocation Board. You'll recall we met yesterday. I have somebody with me who wants to talk to you.'

A pause as he handed the megaphone to Mum.

'Auden?' Mum's voice was quaky. 'Auden? If you're out there . . . please . . .'

I stopped where I was. Paragon stopped too and watched me.

'Mum.'

'Auden.' Paragon looked straight at me. His voice was quiet. 'I need you to help me. Without you, I just can't do it.'

I stood still, listening to Mum.

'Auden?' she continued. 'If you can hear me . . . please . . . DO WHATEVER YOU NEED TO DO! DON'T COME BACK UNTIL YOU'VE DONE IT! I LOVE YOU. DO WHATEVER –'

Her voice disappeared as Woolf snatched the megaphone from her.

'Auden Dare, give yourself up *now*! Return the robot to us. It is the property of the Water Allocation Board. Return it to us now and we will dismiss any charges. I repeat, return the robot to us NOW!'

I looked at Paragon, my heart pumping louder and stronger and more determined than ever. My mother wasn't broken by these people, so why should I be?

'Come on, Paragon. I don't know what it is we're doing . . . but let's go and do it.'

Paragon probably smiled.

The top of the Wandlebury Ring was sheltered from the breeze. We came out from the thick edging of trees and into the deserted clearing.

'This will do,' Paragon announced, dumping the rainbow machine a few metres in from the path. He spun around and looked at the whole area. 'You know, I'd almost forgotten what a beautiful place this is.' He stared up and laughed at the birds that were swooping across the wide open sky.

'Paragon,' I said, aware of our lack of time, 'what do we do?'

'First let's take the cover off.'

'OK.'

We knelt down, one on each side, and unclipped the tarpaulin. Paragon lifted it up and threw it roughly onto the ground nearby.

'Now what?'

He walked around the machine until he was standing directly in front of me, and put his hands on my shoulders.

'Audendare,' he said, sort of sighing. 'Auden Dare.'

'What?'

'*I have no life but this,*
To lead it here;

Nor any death, but lest
Dispelled from there;
Nor tie to earths to come,
Nor action new,
Except through this extent,
The realm of you.'

'Don't tell me,' I grinned. 'Emily Dickinson.'

'Yep.' Paragon laughed.

We both said nothing for a few seconds.

'What's happening?' I eventually asked.

Paragon seemed to pull himself together. 'What's happening is that we both have an incredibly important job to do.' He jumped around to one side of the machine and flipped up the compartment where the battery should have been. 'In fact, *you* have the most important job of all.'

'I do?'

'Yes, you do. You see, you have to turn the machine on.'

'Me? Why me?'

Paragon looked at me with his eyes a dim glow. 'Because it takes thirty seconds for the battery to be fully engaged. By that time I will have run down.'

I shook my head. 'What do you mean?'

Suddenly something happened to Paragon that I'd never seen before. The whole of his chest whirred and whizzed and opened up, peeling away from the centre to his sides. Inside I could see a box-like shape, lights flickering and dancing across it.

330

'The power source,' I whispered.

'Yes,' Paragon said softly. 'We have to remove it from me and transfer it to the machine. After that I have residual power for approximately twenty-three seconds – not enough time to switch the machine on.'

'But . . .' I was confused. 'But we can put it back in you again, can't we? Someone can make another battery that we can give to you?'

Paragon said nothing.

'Please, Paragon.' I strode back towards him. 'We can put the battery back in your chest afterwards, can't we?'

'No.'

'What?'

'I said no.'

'I don't understand.'

Paragon reached up and rested his right hand on the side of my cheek.

'Auden. When Dr Bloom designed me, he deliberately created a glitch.'

'What? What sort of glitch?'

'He built me so that, should my battery ever be removed, my entire system would shut down and all initialisation programs would be obliterated.'

'What does that mean?'

'It means I stop working.' He stroked my cheek. 'Forever.'

'No!' I protested. 'That's impossible. Someone must be able to get you started again. Milo Treble, he can –'

'No. It won't work. You see, Dr Bloom knew just how potentially dangerous I was. He knew that in the wrong hands – or even the right ones – I would be far too much of a risk.'

I threw my arms around Paragon's metal body and rested my head against the blinking power source. 'That's just stupid. You're not dangerous.'

He said nothing, just held me tight and we both stood there, swaying slightly in the warming air of late summer.

Below us, hundreds of men with guns were trying to find us. Hunt us down. But for those few moments, neither of us cared. We were oblivious to all the danger around us.

Just a boy and a robot.

The clearing was silent and we held onto each other like we were both falling to earth.

'Anyway,' Paragon whispered into my hair, 'all these weeks we've been wondering about my role. And now, this is it.' I looked up into his eyes. 'This is what I was designed for. To be here – right now – with you, on top of this hill.'

'But . . . rainbows? Why rainbows?'

'Oh, this machine doesn't make rainbows,' he replied. 'It's much more important than that.'

'But I don't want you to go!'

'Aud—'

'I won't do it! I won't let you go. I'm not going to turn the machine on. And if I won't turn the machine on, there's no point you taking the battery out. You'll have to just be you forever.'

'But when the Water Allocation Board get hold of me – which they will – they won't let me be me forever. They'll have me stripped apart and reprogrammed within hours. I won't be Paragon then. I'll be something else. Something that won't even recognise you.'

'Can't you just hide away? We could hide you –'

'It's no good. They'll still find me.' He glanced around. 'Please, Audendare. We don't have time for this.'

'But –'

'You just have to trust me. You *do* trust me, don't you?'

'Of course. I trust you with my life. I've *always* trusted you.'

'Then you must trust me on *this*. More than anything else. Believe me, this is the right thing to do.'

'But –'

'Audendare.' He pulled away from me and looked me directly in the face. I suddenly realised that it was wet and sore with tears. 'You have a hero for a father, and a mother that breaks the world in two to keep you healthy and happy. You have Sandwich to leap on your head and wake you up in the mornings. And you have the greatest friend in the universe in Vivi Rookmini.' He tilted his head. 'You don't need me.'

'Yes, I do! You've been there for me. You took care of me when I was at my lowest. You cared for me.

You made me feel better about everything. I love you, Paragon.'

'You're right, Audendare.' He leaned in closer and hugged me again. 'I *have* cared for you. I *do* care for you. In fact, I will *always* care for you. Just because I am not there doesn't mean that I stop caring for you.'

'Then why do you have to go?'

'Because . . .' he started. 'Because there are greater things than a silly old robot who can do magic tricks. There's hunger and war and disease and pain. There are people and their lives.' He patted my back. 'I may be full of useless old bits of information, but there is one thing that I really and honestly truly know. And that is that if you get a chance to do something good, then you should do it.' His hand rested on the back of my head again.

'I still don't want you to go,' I mumbled.

'Well . . . I'm afraid it's tough!' he joked. 'You're going to have to manage without me.'

'Yeah. Like I can manage without you!'

Paragon nodded. 'Sarcasm, Audendare?'

'No,' I replied truthfully. 'No, it's not.'

Far off in the distance I could hear the shouting of soldiers.

'You know,' Paragon's voice became gentle again, 'you've had a lot to cope with in your life. Your achromatopsia. Your father going off to war. The idea that he might be a coward. Difficult things to live with. But you're still here. You're still going. None of those things have actually stopped you. They might have tripped you up sometimes – like those sticky little moments of sarcasm – but they haven't really stood in your way. The trick to life –' he did another of his cheeky winks – 'is to struggle on and knock all the terrible rubbish aside. Recognise the difficulties for what they are, and press on regardless. It's actually something you do rather well.'

I said nothing. I just held onto this tall, wonderful, brilliant and beautiful creature that had made me view everything from a different angle. It was impossible to imagine that soon he would no longer be here. He felt so alive.

But it also felt right.

Paragon was doing precisely what he had been created to do. I still didn't know what it was exactly, but getting the machine here and turning it on was what he had been – secretly – designed for.

I had to stop being so selfish.

Paragon twitched a little. He cocked his head at a strange angle like he was listening.

'They're getting nearer. We need to get on with it. Now.'

We pulled apart and both stood next to the machine.

'OK, now,' Paragon explained, 'it takes thirty seconds for the power source to fully engage. Once that's done, you need to hit the on button. Don't hit the off button, whatever you do because, like me, Dr Bloom designed it with a glitch. Hit the off button with the battery in place and you'll destroy the machine.'

I looked at the front of the machine where the two large square buttons were located. It said nothing on either of them.

'Which one's on?'

'The green one.'

I smiled and thought of Mum.

'Haven't you forgotten something?'

'What? That you have achromatopsia and can't see colour? No. Not at all.'

'So how am I meant to know which one's green?'

'Oh, you'll know,' Paragon insisted. 'You see, there are some things that you just automatically know.'

What did he mean?

Before I could argue with him, Paragon jumped onto another subject.

'One more thing, Audendare. When I do finally . . . come to a complete standstill, I want to be left here. Don't let them take me away – it won't do them any good anyway. Please. Tell them that I want to be left in this incredible place. It's the only thing I ask.'

I couldn't believe what I was hearing. It was hard to take it all in. Within minutes Paragon was going to be out of my life – out of everybody's life – forever. How was I meant to deal with this? How was I meant to function, knowing that pretty soon the most incredible person – yes, person – I had ever met was going to be . . . well . . . dead?

The truth was that I *didn't* know how to deal with it. Nothing like this had never happened to me before. So I pushed on and tried to remain me.

Auden Dare, aged eleven.

'I promise I'll make them keep you here,' I said trying to keep my voice level. 'I'll make sure they leave you alone, Paragon.'

'Good.' He nodded. 'Thank you.'

The sound of the soldiers got nearer.

'Quick,' I said, taking control.

Paragon stood next to the machine.

'Remember,' he whispered, 'thirty seconds, then hit the on button. The entire process takes about two minutes after that. Whatever you do, do not let any of them turn the machine off for at least those two minutes. Once they see what's happening, I doubt you'll have any more problems from them. They'll be too amazed.'

'Right.'

'OK, Audendare.' Paragon kind of braced himself. 'Let's do it.'

The power source in Paragon's chest cavity slid out automatically. Paragon grasped it on both sides and pulled it out and away from his body. He bent over the machine and gently slotted it into place. A soft push down and –

Click!

– it was in position.

'OK. Thirty seconds, twenty-nine . . . Then hit the button.'

He backed away from the machine.

'Well, this is it. Thank you, Audendare,' he said as he moved slowly back. 'Thank you for everything.'

'Paragon!' I cried. 'Paragon!!' I couldn't move. I stood there and watched him move away from me. 'I'll never forget you, Paragon! I'll . . .' My voice was cracking '. . . I'll always . . . dream about you.'

'Good,' he said. 'Then it'll be my job to make sure you sleep peacefully.'

With that he turned slightly and raised his arms up into the air.

And then he started whistling.

High-pitched.

Like a bird.

Within seconds the first sparrow came and landed on his arm.

Through the fog of my tears I found myself laughing.

'Hello, little one,' Paragon said, and then laughed himself.

He whistled again and two more sparrows came and landed on his arms.

'*Hope is the thing with feathers*,' Paragon began.

'*That perches in the soul.*'

'I love you, Paragon,' I whispered under my breath.

338

His head turned slightly towards me. 'I love you too, Aud—'

And suddenly the light in his eyes died and he was gone.

Over on the other side of the clearing, something moved. I wiped the tears from my own eyes and tried to focus.

It was a soldier. Then another. Then a whole load more.

I had to do it quickly. Soon they would see that Paragon had stopped moving and they would rush to where I was and overcome me.

I squatted down by the buttons and stared at them.

There are some things that you just automatically know. That's what he had said. What did he mean?

The adrenaline pumped through my body. I had no time to grieve for Paragon. I had to finish what he'd started. I owed it to him.

There are some things that you just automatically know.

I thought hard. The line sounded familiar. Paragon had said something like it before. But what? When?

Then it came to me.

It was when he was explaining my sense of disappointment with my father.

Consider the order of things, Paragon had said. *We always say, 'Left. Right.' The 'left' comes before the 'right'. Or on a form, you will see the options 'Yes/No.' Never 'No/Yes.' Similarly, 'up' comes before 'down' and 'on' before 'off.'*

That was it!

ON/OFF. LEFT/RIGHT.

The green button was the one on the left. It wouldn't make any sense for it to be the one on the right.

I punched the button solidly and a sort of fizzing noise started. The noise got louder and louder until I couldn't bear to hide behind the machine any more. I took a couple of steps back and watched as something started to swirl out of the funnel towards the front of the machine. It swirled up and up, getting bigger all the time. It reminded me of something.

A tornado.

I had seen old films of tornados racing across the flatlands of the USA. Huge, destructive and dangerous. Ripping up houses and tossing cars aside like they were nothing but paper.

But this tornado-like thing was more controlled. Less scary. It kept itself centred around the funnel and tiny flecks of sparkles glinted in the sunlight as it spun around.

Up and up it went, widening at the top as it rose.

It grew beyond the tips of the trees and stretched out into the sky.

The birds that had perched on Paragon got scared and flew off. All except one that dived into Paragon's chest for shelter.

Suddenly there was the hurried stamp of boots and I turned to see three soldiers racing towards me.

340

There was no way I was going to let them turn this machine off. Two minutes Paragon had said, and for that entire two minutes I was prepared to fight like a tiger. I put myself between the men and the machine and clenched my fists, determined to defend Paragon's legacy.

It would have looked pretty strange to onlookers. Three massive, heavily muscled, fully grown men armed with guns, hurtling towards an eleven-year-old boy with a tear in his trouser leg, but I didn't care. I would do all I could to make this thing happen.

'No!' a voice from the main cluster of soldiers bellowed. 'Stand down! Everyone . . . stand down.'

I looked beyond the three soldiers and could make out the outline of General Woolf. His eyes were fixed on the swirling shape that was reaching up into the sky.

'I repeat! All men stand down!'

The soldiers stopped.

Everyone was watching the tornado.

It whirled upwards until it virtually filled the sky above the Wandlebury Ring.

And then it started to pull the clouds in.

All the passing scraps of cloud were sucked towards the vast top of the tornado, dragged like a piece of soap towards a plughole. They came together and stuck to each other, forming an even bigger cloud.

Within seconds the cloud that was being created covered the sky above us, and as more and more small clouds were sucked in, it started to turn dark. Thick, powerful and black. I had never seen a cloud like it before.

Tap.

I looked over to Paragon. A droplet of water ran down the side of his forearm and dripped onto the dry ground.

Tap. Tap.

Two more blobs of water appeared on the top of the machine.

Tap. Tap. Tap. Tap. Tap.

Rain!

It was starting to rain!

I ran around to the front of the machine and looked at the chalk marks that Vivi and I had spotted all those weeks ago. A bead of water streaked through the middle of the letters, but I could still clearly see them.

Ra
Machi

It wasn't a rainbow machine at all. It was a *rain* machine. Uncle Jonah had created a rain machine!

Suddenly the cloud struggled to hold onto its weight and the water came down in a torrential downpour. I had never known rain like it. It flattened the pathetic tufts of grass and soaked through my clothes. The whole clearing was a hazy blur of rain.

I turned towards the dozens and dozens of soldiers that had started to make their way towards me. Some of them had thrown their weapons to the ground and were dancing in the cloudburst, their heads tipped back and mouths wide open. Others had got their water canisters out and were holding them up to the sky, refilling them.

In the middle of the soldiers I could see General Woolf, holding his face up to the rain and feeling it running down over his face.

And next to him – each of them handcuffed – stood Mum, then Treble, Immaculata and Vivi. All of them drenched to the skin.

I grinned at Vivi and she gave an awkward handcuffed wave back.

Woolf noticed and barked an order at a soldier who quickly removed the cuffs from all four of them. Woolf turned to me and nodded – a nod of appreciation and of understanding – before turning his face back to the sky.

I held my hands out in front of me, the water collecting in my palms, my fingers cold and white.

Doctor Jonah Bloom – Uncle Jonah – *my* uncle – had made something that was going to change the world. A machine that could make rain.

He had also made something that had changed *me*.

I looked at Paragon, silent and still, his arms in the air like he was feeling the rain for the very first time.

EPILOGUE
THE
RAINBOW

It took another year for the wars to stop. The world seems to work so slowly sometimes. Nothing important is ever rushed. So by the time the rain machine was accepted by the authorities, followed by the months and months of mass production and distribution, it took up to a year and a half after the incidents on the Wandlebury Ring before all of the more remote parts of the world were getting water.

Eventually, though, the machines were everywhere. From the tops of mountains to endless flat plains. From tiny isolated farming villages to the centres of sprawling, bustling cities.

'Phenomenal,' Dr Milo Treble had said after being involved in the initial inspections of the machine. 'Silver oxide particles and an intense negative-ion generator coupled with what I've termed the Cumulative Cumulus Device.' He shuffled. 'As difficult as it is to admit, I have to say that Bloom was an *utter* genius.'

That was confirmed the following year when Uncle Jonah was posthumously awarded the Geneva Prize for Scientific Advancement.

* * *

After it had all happened, Dr Treble started spending an awful lot of time around at Vivi and Immaculata's rooms in Trinity.

'He keeps bringing Mum flowers,' Vivi said, giving her head a little shake. 'The thing is, she's started making dresses for herself. And she washes her hair all the time, now that we've got so much water.' Vivi fiddled with the ponytail in her own dark hair. 'If you ask me, it's weird.'

We made our way up the stone steps and she pushed the big wooden door open.

'Ah, Auden.'

It was Treble.

He was sitting on the sofa alongside Immaculata, Migishoo perched on the mantelpiece.

'Dr Treble. Mrs Rookmini.' I nodded hello.

'Hello, Auden.' Immaculata smiled.

'Am I pleased to see you.' Treble leaped up from the sofa. 'I've got something that I want to show you.'

He dug into the back pocket of his jeans and fished out a little wooden box.

'Here.'

I took it from him.

'What is it?'

'Open it and see.'

I clicked the tiny latch on the box and flicked it open. Inside was a curved piece of plastic a few centimetres long.

'I call it the Optiborg. It's my latest invention and – with a bit of work and luck – will secure me next year's Geneva Prize.'

'What does it do?'

'Clip it behind your right ear and see.'

I took the thing from out of the box and pushed it behind my ear.

'Now. Look at –' he leaned over and picked up an apple from a bowl on Immaculata's sewing table – 'this.'

I looked at the apple. Suddenly a really high-pitched noise screeched into my head.

'Ow!'

'That's a red apple.' He put the apple back onto the table and picked up a pear. 'Now look at this.'

I stared and the Optiborg screeched again, this time with a slightly lower note.

'That's a green pear.' He tossed the pear back into the bowl and picked up another apple. 'Right. You ready, Auden? Tell me what colour *this* apple is.'

I looked at the apple. The thing behind my ear squealed, again with the lower note.

'Green,' I said.

'Correct!' Treble laughed, picking up the first apple again. 'You can tell the difference. Green apple,' he held it up and the sound was low. 'Red apple,' he held *that* one up and the sound was high. 'Green, red, green, red.'

'That's . . . that's . . .' I didn't know what to say.

'*Genius*, I think is the word you are looking for!' Treble cried. 'Try a different colour. Here.' He picked up a piece of fabric from the table. 'This is blue.'

I stared at the fabric and an even lower note sounded.

'And this . . .' Treble was excited by his own invention. 'This is also blue, but . . . tell me . . . is it a lighter blue or a darker blue than the first piece?' He lifted another section of cloth. The Optiborg whined with a slightly higher note.

'Lighter,' I said. 'It's lighter.'

'Ha!' Treble jumped up in delight.

'This is incredible.' I moved around listening to the different pitches of the objects in the room. 'Absolutely incredible.'

'With practice,' Treble chattered on as Immaculata went and prepared some sandwiches in the sectioned-off kitchen, 'anybody with achromatopsia would be able to distinguish the subtleties of colour within a matter of weeks.'

'It's amazing,' I said, pulling the Optiborg from behind my ear. 'You deserve to win the Geneva Prize with it.' I held it out to Treble, who shook his head.

'No, Auden. It's yours.'

'Mine?'

'To keep. Don't worry – I've made a couple of them.'

'Really?' I didn't know what to say. 'Thank you.'

'Don't thank me.' He suddenly looked sad. 'You know, I wasn't the greatest of friends to your uncle in the months before he died. There were so many things I should

350

have done and said, but I didn't because of my stupid professional pride. If I hadn't been so self-absorbed . . . well . . . I might not have been able to prevent Jonah Bloom's death, but I'd certainly feel a lot better about things, knowing that he'd died as a friend.'

And in that moment I could see the months of pain that had burrowed away at him. Months of wondering 'what if' and 'why'. Here was somebody else for whom life had changed due to Uncle Jonah's death.

'I think he would be pleased,' I said, clutching the Optiborg. 'I think it would have made him happy to know that you were trying to help me.' I smiled. 'Thank you, Dr Treble.'

Treble seemed to straighten up and his chest puffed out. 'That's quite all right Auden. My pleasure. Unfortunately, it is absolutely impossible for you to ever *see* colour. But at least now you can *hear* it.'

'It is said that the stars are different colours.'

Vivi was on her bed staring through the skyspace at the clear night sky. I was back on the floor, turning the Optiborg over in my fingers. It was a tiny thing, yet so powerful.

'Hmm? What did you say?'

Vivi sighed. 'Do you ever *listen*, Auden?'

'To you? Only when I'm forced to.'

She threw a pillow down and hit me directly in the face.

'Oy!' I laughed.

'Then listen!' She pretended to be annoyed. 'I said that people think the stars are different colours. That they're not all silvery – they just appear that way. They might actually be blue or green or red.'

I sat up.

'We could find out,' I said.

'How?'

I waggled the Optiborg at her. 'With this.'

Vivi scrambled from her bed and quickly popped the lens cover off the telescope. Her excitement had a similar feel to Treble's when he had showed me the Optiborg for the first time.

'Come on. Let's see.'

I slipped the small device behind my ear and waited for Vivi to point the telescope in the right direction and twiddle with the focusing.

'There!' She stood back and I stooped to look.

What I heard made my breath stop.

It was like an orchestra in my head. Big booming bass notes resounded and fell beneath mid-range melodies that swept up and down like violins. Piccolo-type squeaks and the pulsing notes of flutes rolled in and out of the beautiful, elegant music of the sky.

'Wow!' was all I could say.

I stayed there for what seemed like ages, just staring and listening.

When I did eventually pull myself away from the telescope, Vivi raised her eyebrows at me. 'Well?'

'It's . . . unbelievable.'

'You're crying,' she said.

The rain eased off as the Bot Job shuddered to a stop just outside the prison gates.

'Any chance it'll ever start up again to get us home?' I asked as we both got out of the car.

'This car is held together by nothing more than wishful thinking,' Mum replied. 'So just keep your fingers crossed and perhaps pray a bit.'

We crossed the road and waited directly opposite the gates.

'What's the time?' Mum asked nervously.

I glanced at my QWERTY. 'Couple of minutes to ten.'

'Nearly time,' she told herself, pulling her coat tighter. 'Oh, look.' She pointed to somewhere above the tall, solid stone Victorian walls of the prison. 'A rainbow.'

I looked up. I could see the dull, grey arc in the sky, slightly darker at the bottom than at the top.

It was tempting to reach into my jacket pocket for the Optiborg. But I didn't. Not today. Today there was something I wanted to see so much more than a rainbow.

'He's coming!' Mum grasped my arm.

The smaller door built into the massive arched metal one swung open, and out stepped a blond-haired man carrying a rucksack – a man who had recently been granted a pardon by the government, no less. He reached back and shook the hand of someone inside.

'*Hope is the thing with feathers,*' I sang to myself.

'*That perches in the soul –*
And sings the tune without the words –
And never stops – at all . . .'

'What's that?' Mum asked, never taking her eyes off the man at the door.

'Emily Dickinson,' I answered.

'A new friend of yours?'

I smiled. 'You could say that, yeah.'

The door to the prison closed as my dad – my hero dad – turned to us and sprinted across the road, his strong, warm arms outstretched.

Vivi and I would visit Paragon regularly. We would walk out from the city into the green fields and make our way to Wandlebury, where we would follow the winding path up to the Wandlebury Ring.

When the authorities threatened to take Paragon away, I shouted and screamed and made a magnificent fuss. Dr Treble pulled strings within the scientific community and Mum and Immaculata went to the papers. Even General Woolf himself made the case for Paragon staying where he was, as a monument to the bravery of children. Eventually the Water Allocation Board had relented.

'Hello, Paragon,' I would say when I stepped out into the clearing. Of course he wouldn't answer. He would remain in exactly the same position as ever – arms held out to the sky, his face turned to where I once stood. The grass was now thick and luscious at his feet.

And I couldn't ever touch him. To protect Paragon, the WAB had placed an electric fence around him with razor wire at the top. Which sounds like a bad thing, but it wasn't really. It meant that the family of sparrows that had nested within his chest were safe and free to feel warm and wanted.

Paragon would have been delighted.

Sometimes I would stand where I stood the moment the lights in his eyes died, and it would seem as if he was looking straight at me. Other times Vivi and I would run about, or kick a ball, or sketch the trees, or read some thick tedious book that Vivi found fascinating. And it would be like he was there. Watching over us.

Protecting us.

At night I would sleep deeply, with Sandwich on my bed. Soundly and peacefully like Paragon promised. Safe and warm like the sparrows undoubtedly were. And I know that they say nobody ever dreams in colour, but sometimes – just sometimes – I swear I do.

Acknowledgements

Huge thanks to my fabulous editors Georgia Murray and Liz Szabla; unbelievable agent Julia Churchill and the wonderfully supportive Miriam Altshuler; incomparable Talya Baker; the brilliant and compassionate artist Matt Saunders; PR guru Tina Mories; and last, but never least, my family, friends and other animals!

Zillah Bethell

Zillah Bethell was born in a leprosy hospital in Papua New Guinea, spent her childhood barefoot, playing in the jungle, and didn't own a pair of shoes until she came to the UK when she was eight. She was educated at Oxford University and now lives in Wales with her family. Zillah has written three adult novels for a small Welsh press. THE EXTRAORDINARY COLOURS OF AUDEN DARE is her second children's book, following A WHISPER OF HORSES.

By the same author

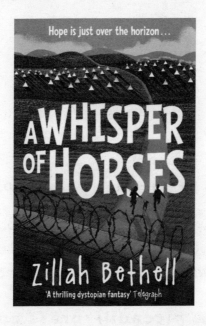

Serendipity loves horses. No one in Lahn Dahn has ever seen one alive, but Serendipity is determined to find one. To do so, she must venture beyond the city walls into the great unknown – but what kind of life will there be for her on the other side?

Thank you for choosing a Piccadilly Press book.

If you would like to know more about our authors, our books or if you'd just like to know what we're up to, you can find us online.

www.piccadillypress.co.uk

And you can also find us on:

We hope to see you soon!